"THERE IS [NO NEED] TO BE ANXIOUS, WIFE," RICHARD WHISPERED.

He took Elissa's hand, but did not kiss it. Instead, he pressed it against his warm, bare chest. "You have nothing to fear from me."

She felt his taut muscles and the beating of his heart. "I am not afraid of you."

"I am glad to hear you say so."

He lifted her hand to his chin so that her fingertips rested against his soft lips, while the stubble of his beard was like sand against the rest of her fingers. It was a simple thing and yet strangely exciting.

Too exciting. She had loved foolishly once; she would not allow herself to believe in love or be swept away by what had to be lust.

"No, do not draw back," he insisted softly.

Then he kissed her as she had always imagined a man in love should kiss the woman he adored, with passion and tenderness in thrilling alliance, as if he were gently persuading her to love him, rather than demanding.

What kind of freedom was he offering?

A Rogue's Embrace

MARGARET MOORE

AVON BOOKS ◆ NEW YORK

AVON BOOKS, INC.
An Imprint of HarperCollins*Publishers*
10 East 53rd Street
New York, New York 10022-5299

Copyright © 2000 by Margaret Moore Wilkins
Inside cover author photo by Towne Portraits
Published by arrangement with the author
Library of Congress Catalog Card Number: 99-95334
ISBN: 0-380-80268-6
www.harpercollins.com

First Avon Books Printing: February 2000

AVON TRADEMARK REG. U.S. PAT. OFF. AND IN OTHER COUNTRIES, MARCA REGISTRADA, HECHO EN U.S.A.

Printed in the U.S.A.

WCD   10   9   8   7   6   5   4   3   2

In loving memory of my grandfather,
Samuel Moore,
who firmly believed in reading
all the fine print before signing.
(I do, Grandpa, I do.)

Chapter 1

London, 1663

Sitting beside his mother, six-year-old William Longbourne grinned at the brawny waterman guiding their vessel along the Thames. "My mama and I are going to see the king!" he declared proudly.

Elissa sighed with exasperation. "Will, please keep silent and sit still," she admonished, wishing she could temper his excitement until they safely reached the shore. As it was, he kept fidgeting and rocking the boat.

And it really wasn't necessary to announce the reason for their journey to everyone they met.

However, she might as well have wished the Seven Seas to dry up as for Will to be less boisterous on this particular occasion. After all, he had no reason to share his mother's apprehension.

"I can see why the king'd want to meet your ma," the waterman observed, licking his lips as he leered at Elissa.

If she had known the insolence she would have to endure from this disgusting knave, she would have taken the Puritan's boat and paid the slightly higher fare.

But she had not, so she tried to ignore the impertinent lout while keeping one eye on Will and studying the massive structures lining the river.

Mighty buildings dominated the north bank, each one seeming to demand homage to its magnificence and to render human beings insignificant. Behind these imposing edifices, a haze of coal smoke rose from the multitude of houses, as well as the industries that lay cheek-by-jowl among them.

She wondered what King Charles, restored to his throne at last, thought of the choking air or the filthy river. Perhaps he was too busy summoning busy widows with estates to manage to notice.

She pondered the hundred things that could be going awry at home during her absence. Then she tried to force such thoughts from her mind, telling herself she would do better to prepare for her meeting with the king, which was to be this very evening.

"You keep your weather eye open when ye're on the river, me lad," the churl said with another disgusting smile that exposed his rotting teeth, "and you might see the king sooner than you think. He's often on the Thames, comin' and goin.' "

"He is?" Will asked, looking around as if he expected to see His Majesty's boat drawing up alongside even as he spoke. "Coming and going where?"

"Ye're too young to know that," the man replied with a chortle before he hawked and spat into the river.

"Will you please keep such remarks to yourself?" Elissa ordered through clenched teeth.

"Oh, look! Look!" Will cried suddenly, rising from his seat and pointing. "There he is! There is the king!"

He started to wave frantically, leaning precariously over the gunwale. "Your Majesty! Your Majesty!"

Flinging the edge of her cloak out of the way, Elissa lunged for Will before he fell over the side of the boat. She caught his jacket and pulled him backward.

"Keep him still or he'll be at the bottom of the river," the waterman muttered angrily as he steadied the small vessel with his pole.

"Not if you do your job," Elissa muttered. Her frown turned into a scowl when she realized the lout was staring at her chest—or, more precisely, at the cleavage exposed by her gaping cloak.

She set Will beside her and wished she had worn her most plain, high-necked gown of dull gray wool instead of this dress of rose-colored brocade. She would change before she went to court.

"Are you sure that's not the king?" Will asked, nodding at a boat that was moving toward them from a short distance away.

In that vessel there was indeed a most magnificently attired man. He was clad in a short jacket and full breeches of brilliant blue trimmed with riotous and colorful embroidery. He also wore a white shirt with a large, lacy jabot and long cuffs, and he sported a hat with the biggest, whitest plume Elissa had ever seen. Beneath the hat was long, curling hair—a wig, no doubt—as well as a round, decidedly average male face unencumbered by a mustache.

Despite his fine and costly attire, if he had no mustache, he could not be the king.

Beside this fashionable vision was another man, dressed all in black like a Puritan, with a plain hat and natural black hair that brushed his broad shoulders. This man sat with astonishing aplomb in the rocking boat, seemingly oblivious to the smells and sights around him, or to whatever his more animated companion was saying.

As they drew closer, Elissa also realized the simply dressed man was one of the most handsome she had ever seen, with a fine nose and strong, clean-shaven chin. Unlike the other fellow, there was shrewd intelligence in his dark, inscrutable eyes and a set to his jaw that told her that it would be risky to trifle with him.

If one of the men in that boat is royalty, she reflected, it is not the extravagantly attired one.

"That's not the king," the waterman informed them scornfully before he shouted a vulgar greeting to the other boat. Its pilot responded in equally earthy terms.

Annoyed that Will had heard such language, Elissa made a sniff of disapproval.

Then the other vessel passed them, and her gaze met that of the arrogant man wearing black.

Elissa's heart began to beat strangely, and her body warmed as if . . . as if this man she had never seen before was touching her. Intimately.

She had not felt this way since William Longbourne had started courting her seven years ago.

No, she silently amended as she swallowed hard, I have *never* felt this way before—and I should not be feeling this way now.

She was a respectable widow, not some . . . some *hussy* to be pleased by the smiles of strangers, no matter how handsome or intriguing they were, or how long it had been since she had been with a man.

Obviously, despite the difference in their clothing and appearance, the man dressed in black was no more of a gentleman than the waterman.

"Will, stop fidgeting," she commanded sternly, wishing he would cease staring with such obvious fascination at those men in the other boat.

Then she feared her own expression had not been much different.

With a bone-jarring bump, the waterman finally brought his vessel beside slick, damp water stairs leading up a wharf. He then put his fingers to his lips and let out a piercing whistle.

"That'll bring somebody to take your baggage, mistress," he explained, nodding at the small, leather-covered, bossed box at Elissa's feet.

The rest of her baggage was being brought to her lawyer's home by one of her farm laborers in a wagon, for Mr. Harding had graciously invited them to stay with him while they were in London.

Mr. Harding had also offered to accompany Elissa to Whitehall, in case the reason for the king's summons was what she feared.

Several ragged men began to crowd the steps, each one begging for the task of carrying Elissa's baggage.

"That will not be necessary. I can manage," Elissa replied even as she noticed another set of stairs several yards away. The boat with the fashionable man and his handsome companion was putting in there.

The waterman ignored her and called to one of the men on the stairs, a tall, thin fellow who looked as if he hadn't washed since birth. "Oy, Mick! Take the fine lady's box here!"

"I said that will not be necessary!" Elissa repeated.

Too late. The waterman lifted the box and shoved it into Mick's outstretched hands. Immediately the dirty, ragged fellow turned and dashed up the steps.

Stifling a cry of alarm, Elissa reached into her purse for some coins and shoved them into the waterman's hand.

"Come, Will," she commanded, helping her son out of the boat, then taking his hand and hurrying up the stairs as fast as the crowd would let her.

As she did, she tried to catch a glimpse of Mick, grateful that she had tied the purse containing most of her traveling money to her petticoat.

"You're hurting me," Will protested.

Elissa loosened her grip slightly as they came to the top of the stairs. Panting, she looked around the unfamiliar, cluttered, and crowded street. Nearby, a fruit seller with a basket of oranges slung over his arm stood with a bevy of haggling women.

Well-dressed, perfumed gentlewomen, servants, and some women whose occupation seemed all too obvious by their slatternly attire mingled on the street, surveying shop windows. A group of well-to-do men discussing the price of candle wax marched past, while a collection of rough-looking seamen argued outside a tavern. Horse-drawn carts jostled for position as they rumbled along the cobbled street. Stray dogs barked and ran about underfoot, and the fishy, filthy smell of the Thames merged with coal smoke, offal, and perfume.

Naturally there wasn't a sign of Mick.

"Madam, do you require some assistance?"

At the sound of the aristocratic male voice, Elissa eagerly turned around—to find not the black-clad man and his overdressed companion, but another fellow, tilting rather oddly to one side and wearing garments of dark green velvet, as well as red-heeled shoes and a feathered, broad-brimmed hat. The explanation for the unusual angle of his stance came to her when she saw the wineskin he was attempting to hide behind his back.

Obviously accompanying him were two other men, similarly well dressed in petticoat breeches, short jackets, plumed hats, and curling wigs, and similarly smiling with every appearance of kind, if somewhat sodden, concern.

Yet when she looked at them closely, she saw the waterman's leer.

"No, we do not require any assistance," she replied, pulling Will closer.

"Oh, you cannot mean that," the first man said, stepping uncomfortably close to her. His wine-soaked breath made her want to gag. "You must allow us to help you. Otherwise, who knows what might happen to such a beauty in this wicked place?"

His friends likewise staggered oppressively closer. Elissa looked around to see if anyone would come to her aid.

Unfortunately, it seemed as if everyone on the crowded thoroughfare suddenly found his own concerns of grave import.

"I thank you, but my son and I do not require any assistance," she repeated defiantly.

The man in green chuckled, and it was a decidedly unpleasant sound. "Gad, every woman requires a man now and then," he slurred, stepping closer.

"Go away!" Will commanded imperiously, but with a tremor in his voice.

This only elicited another chortle from the man and his cronies. They began to move en masse, forcing Elissa and Will back toward an alley.

What can I do? Elissa thought with something close to panic. She could shove her way past them, but they might give chase. How far and how fast could she run with Will? And which way should she go?

"To quote from the play I saw last week,"

the man in green murmured slyly, " 'a flower blooms unexpectedly among the refuse, and who shall pluck it out?' "

"Zounds, Sedley, if you must quote me, have the goodness to get it right," a deep, sardonic, masculine voice declared nearby.

As if in answer to her silent prayer for help, the man wearing black from the other boat shoved his way past the fruit seller and his customers. He sauntered toward them, his sword drawn, yet held loosely in his hand as if he intended to do nothing more serious than clean his nails with it.

His round-faced colleague came bustling along behind him, smiling and nodding as if this were a meeting at a ball or something equally innocuous.

" 'A rose blooms in the rubbish' is the proper line," the stranger from the boat continued, speaking to the man he had addressed as Sedley, "and I never said anything so crude as 'pluck it out.' "

He bowed toward Elissa, then turned toward Sedley's besotted companions. "Good day, Lord Buckhurst."

One of the other men grinned drunkenly and waved his *mouchoir*. The flimsy, perfumed square of linen fluttered about as if he were trying to wave away a pesky insect.

"And good day to you, too, Jermyn," the black-clad man continued. "Is my Lady Castlemaine out of sorts with you again, that you must accost women in the streets?"

"Odd's fish, 'tis the cavalier playwright himself," Jermyn replied with a sneer.

Elissa's eyes widened as she regarded her sardonic savior. Surely he couldn't be . . . ? Of all the men in London!

The cavalier playwright, who had not yet sheathed his sword, ignored the sarcastic remark. He reached out to take Elissa's gloved hand, bending as if he would kiss it.

Instinctively, she snatched it away.

Although the expression in his eyes altered ever so slightly, the man said nothing. However, if he was who she suspected, she didn't care what he thought of her.

"You write plays?" Will asked with all the disappointed scorn a six-year-old could muster. "I thought you were going to fight him."

"There is no need for fighting in the street," Elissa said, desperate to get away from all these men, and most especially the man who had been about to kiss her hand.

The cavalier playwright looked down at Will. "I am sorry to disappoint you, but there must not be a duel." He raised his voice and spoke with apparent gravity. "These fine fellows are friends of the king, you see, and so must be treated with the utmost respect."

Elissa thought it was a good thing these alleged friends of the king could not see the wry mockery in the playwright's eyes.

"Oh," Will mumbled, still disappointed.

The man dropped his voice to a conspiratorial whisper. "They are so drunk, it would hardly be fair."

The playwright's round-faced friend grinned, his expression as delighted as if he, too, were six years old. "I assure you, my boy, this is quite the finest swordsman you're ever likely to meet. Truly, for him to fight them in their present state of inebriation would be most unchivalrous."

Wide-eyed with childish awe, Will nodded, looking at the cavalier, whose lips twisted up into a small—very small—smile.

"Yes, well, we must be on our way," Elissa said, trying to sound firm and decisive even though her heart pounded and her legs felt weak.

Their savior stepped forward, blocking her way, and in his eyes was a commanding look that rooted her to the spot. "The king's friends are leaving."

"Gad, who do you think you are to command me, you . . . you scribbler?" Sedley cried.

"You know who I am," the cavalier replied quietly, and without taking his steadfast gaze from Elissa's face. "Therefore you can surmise that it might be wiser to leave, for I am the king's friend, too."

This seemed to be a cue to the besotted man's cronies to stagger forward and, ignoring his loud protests, half-drag him toward the nearby tavern.

Elissa was very glad to be rid of them. Regrettably, there was still the problem of the man standing before her, who continued to regard her with his dark, inscrutable eyes.

"Has no one ever told you it is impolite to stare?" she demanded at last.

"Has no one ever told you that you are beautiful?"

"I suggest, sir, that you save your flattery for women who will appreciate it."

"Of which there are many," the cavalier agreed evenly.

He swept his hat from his head and bowed elegantly. "You have not permitted me to introduce myself. I am Sir Richard Blythe. Your servant, madam."

His friend likewise pulled his hat from his head and attempted a gallant bow, only to drag his pristine plume through the muck in the street.

"Lord Cheddersby, at your service," he stammered as he straightened. Then he stared at his ruined headwear in dismay, his stunned expression eliciting a giggle from Will.

Elissa gave her son a severe look. "Good day, gentlemen," she said, lifting her petticoat, overskirt, and cloak up out of the dirt, preparing to leave.

"Haven't you heard of Sir Richard Blythe?" Lord Cheddersby demanded incredulously.

"Yes, I have."

Indeed, she knew all about Sir Richard

Blythe. She had heard of his plays, with their sharp-tongued wives and supposedly clever mistresses, and their plots of adultery and deception. She had heard of the immoral verse he wrote.

Nor would it surprise her in the least if, despite his outwardly harmless appearance, Lord Cheddersby was Sir Richard's companion in decadent pastimes. Her late husband had taught her that men were not always what they seemed.

"Good day, gentlemen," she repeated as she resolutely marched away, clutching Will's hand tightly.

Despite her inner turmoil, she noted that the crowd no longer seemed to find their own business so fascinating, for as she pushed her way forward, everyone stared at her with blatant curiosity.

She tried to ignore them all as she desperately scanned the street for a coach to hire. She had heard that the king had tried to limit the number in the city without much success. Why, then, could she not find one now?

She finally spotted a likely-looking conveyance and began to wave her hand, to no avail.

Then, with a start, she realized Sir Richard Blythe had come to stand beside her. Even more astounding, he suddenly put his fingers in his mouth and whistled as loudly as the waterman had.

Will stared at him admiringly when a hackney coach rolled to a stop beside them.

Sir Richard smiled at him. "It's not difficult, you know, with a little practice. I would be happy to teach you."

"I'm sure there's nothing you or your friend could teach my son that he needs to learn," Elissa said, opening the door to the coach without waiting for assistance.

After she and her son had gotten inside, she yanked the door closed as if she were being chased by a band of brigands. Without so much as a glance at the man who had come to her aid, she ordered the coachman to drive to the Inns of Court.

Sheathing his sword, Richard watched the coach rattle out of sight.

A slightly breathless Fozbury Cheddersby came to stand beside him. He sighed rapturously. "Wasn't she beautiful?"

"Beautiful enough to have captured your fancy, I see," Richard replied coolly as he started to walk toward their original destination, Lincoln's Inn Fields Theatre.

The shorter-legged Foz trotted to keep up with him. "Don't you think she's beautiful?"

"I seek something beyond pleasing features to determine whether a woman is truly beautiful."

And if this woman seemed to possess that something composed of spirit and intelligence and determination that made her worthy of his admiration, Richard would never say so to Foz.

Indeed, if he did, the information would likely throw poor old Foz into a spasm of shock.

"She did look as if she were . . . well . . . smelling a bad odor," Foz noted.

If it was only the stench of the city that brought that displeased look to her face and had nothing to do with him, that was a surprisingly welcome observation. "Perhaps she was."

Foz lowered his head slightly and sniffed surreptitiously. "It couldn't have been *me*—or you, either," he hastened to add.

"I never thought it was."

"She didn't tell us her name."

"Nor did she give us any thanks. We would have done better to leave her to fend for herself."

"Richard!"

The playwright deftly sidestepped a particularly malodorous pile of dung. "I didn't mean that, and you know it. Still," he went on thoughtfully, "I think we can assume the fair unknown would have triumphed over Sedley and his friends in the end."

"Do you suppose she's married?"

"Since she has a child with her who resembles her and a ring on the fourth finger of her left hand, we can assume she is."

"How do you know she had a ring?"

"I felt it through her glove."

Indeed, it was almost as if he could still feel her supple fingers in his.

"If she's married, it is no wonder you are not very intrigued by her."

Richard remained silent. This once, however, he was very tempted to break his own rule and ignore the sanctity of the married state, like most noblemen he knew.

"She could be a widow," Foz offered hopefully.

Richard halted. "Foz, if you are fascinated by that ungrateful female, I suggest you refrain from pointing out such possibilities to potential rivals. Fortunately, I have other, more important things with which to occupy my time. My new play is starting in less than an hour, and I have an audience with the king after that."

"Oh, yes, yes, to be sure."

"If you want her, you'll have to find her again, you know," Richard continued in a conciliatory tone as he began to walk again. "If you are truly that desperate, I shall assist you in any way I can."

Foz smiled delightedly. "I shall gladly accept your assistance—whenever you are not otherwise engaged, of course."

Richard bowed and waved his hand regally. "I shall be yours to command, whenever I can spare the time from my important literary pursuits," he said with a subtle self-mockery that was quite lost on Foz.

Foz beamed. "I shall be most appreciative, Richard! The lad was a fine little fellow, wasn't he?"

"Was he?"

"Almost enough to make a man want a son of his own, eh?"

"No."

Richard's tone of finality obviously suggested a change of subject. "Are you worried about what the king wants with you?"

Unfortunately, this subject was not one Richard particularly cared to discuss, either.

"No," Richard lied. "I daresay he merely wishes me to compose an ode praising the latest woman to catch his fancy."

"It could be about your estate."

"If I thought that every time His Majesty summoned me to Whitehall, I would be prostrate with despair by now. He has had plenty of time to restore my property to me, and has not."

"You know why he cannot," Foz said, starting to pant. "It was sold by your uncle—quite legally, at the time. If Charles returns your estate to you as a reward for your faithful service in exile, he will have to compensate the new owner, and then other dispossessed noblemen will demand the same. The king cannot afford it."

"I want only what is rightfully mine. Blythe

Hall and the land around it has been in my family for six hundred years. My uncle was able to sell it only because I was serving the king. Otherwise, I would have been able to prevent him from doing so."

"Perhaps Charles has persuaded the new owners to sell it to you," Foz suggested.

"Charles is not the only one with financial difficulties."

"I know that, and you have but to ask—"

"I cannot afford to pay even a fraction of what it's worth."

"You could if you would let me—"

"No, Foz."

"A mortgage—"

"I don't make that much from my writing."

"There would be the income from the estate."

Richard sniffed. "I imagine it's down to a pittance. The man who bought it died a few years ago, I heard, and left it to his widow. An old woman can't run an estate properly."

"No, no, of course not," Foz agreed. He cocked his head to one side, reminding Richard of an inquisitive chicken. "Are you going to change before you go to Whitehall?"

"Into what? A fashionable courtier?"

In truth, Richard knew where this conversation was heading and was secretly amused.

As he expected, Foz protested immediately. "You cannot wear that to meet with the king!"

"I see nothing wrong with my attire. Black suits me."

"But your breeches—"

"I will not wear those petticoat things," Richard answered, glancing at Foz's own fulsome breeches which were made of enough fabric to drape every window on the street.

They were also slung so low on his hips, they looked in imminent danger of slipping off, and his shirt bloused over the waist so fully he could have hidden an entire loaf of bread in it with no one the wiser.

"I was a soldier," Richard reminded his fashionable friend. "I would feel myself a fool."

"The king—"

"Knew me long ago and will not be offended by my lack of sartorial splendor."

"It looks as if you haven't bought new clothes since you got back from France," Foz muttered.

"This jacket is only a year old!" Richard protested. "And it's the best one I've ever had. Next thing I know, you'll be chastising me for not wearing a feather in my hat."

"Well . . ."

"Foz," Richard warned.

His friend sighed. "Very well. I yield."

"But I do have quite the finest baldric you've ever seen, have I not?"

"You do," Foz agreed with a return to his customary good humor and an admiring glance at the finely worked leather sword belt slung across Richard's broad chest. Indeed, it was a baldric any man would covet, as well as the excellent sword—and the skill with which Sir Richard Blythe wielded it.

For among King Charles's courtiers, Sir Richard Blythe was famous for many things, and writing was but one of them.

Chapter 2

L ater, after a gratifying response to his new play, and seated in a hackney coach, Richard and the faithful Foz passed through the ornate gatehouse of Whitehall Palace. They had been there often enough that they paid no heed to the Palladian beauty of the Banqueting House, even though its design by Inigo Jones ensured that it stood out amid the riot of Tudor buildings that comprised the rest of Whitehall.

Inside the Banqueting House, seven attached columns created small alcoves; above these ran a gallery on the north, east, and west sides. Above all this, and the crowd of courtiers below, was a ceiling painted by Rubens.

One would never know it by the laughter of those gathered there, but it was outside this very building that a platform had been erected, and the present king's father executed.

Trailed by his friend, Richard strode through

the gathering of well-dressed, sophisticated courtiers toward the king's dais. He drew admiring glances from the women and envious looks from the men, for the handsome playwright exuded an arrogant confidence that even the wealthiest among them could not achieve.

Indeed, there was only one man who commanded similar attention, and that was King Charles, seated on the dais at the south end of the room, surrounded by women and playing cribbage.

The fashionably attired women looked like brightly colored birds, clad in silks and satins of lustrous crimson, sapphire blue, and bright greens and yellows instead of feathers.

Or perhaps unclad would be nearer the mark, for despite the wealth of fabric in their skirts, the low, round bodices of their gowns displayed an astonishing amount of bare flesh, and their heavily trimmed overskirts were drawn back by bows and chains to reveal even more elaborate petticoats.

As for Charles himself, he sported a beribboned jacket and full breeches of sky blue embroidered with silver thread that sparkled in the light of the many candles. Beneath the jacket was a fine shirt with frothy lace jabot at the neck and equally lacy cuffs that covered much of the sovereign's hands.

Somewhere up in the gallery, a young man was warbling what Richard assumed was intended to be a love song, accompanied by a small orchestra. Of course, nobody was listening. The courtiers much preferred to talk and flirt with one another, or keep their wary eye on their capricious king.

Charles glanced up from his cards as Richard and Foz approached. The monarch's eyes sparkled with amusement, and the lips below the slender dark mustache curved up in a welcoming smile.

As always, Richard marveled that a man who had led such a difficult life could retain any bonhomie. No doubt it helped that he was at the center of a mostly admiring and amicable court and now resided in luxury, even if the Privy Purse was supposedly constantly empty.

Richard also knew that Charles had a capacity for forgiveness and overlooking the past that he himself did not possess.

Richard removed his hat and bowed low before his sovereign, then smiled at the king's admiring audience.

"Ah, Blythe!" the king cried. "How fortuitous of you to arrive at this moment. We are losing!"

The women muttered in sympathetic protest. Despite their apparent attention to the king's dilemma, however, more than one of them gave Richard a coy smile. He didn't doubt that if the king was not interested in a more intimate relationship, they would not hesitate to let Richard sample their charms, if he were so inclined.

Generally speaking, he was not. The ladies of the court were usually selfish and ambitious creatures. Any relationship with a playwright, even a famous one, would be merely another amorous adventure, an exciting and necessarily brief interlude as they sought out a more advantageous liaison.

To be sure, the actresses he generally sported with had much the same goal. They, however, were less likely to be able to affect his life or his livelihood when the liaison came to an end.

His eyes smiling, Charles glanced again at his cards and sighed mournfully. "It is true, it is true! We are losing most abominably. Someone must take our hand."

Charles looked at the women expectantly, the grin on his face telling Richard that he was considering offering one of them something more intimate than his hand later on.

He finally gestured at a young woman whose name Richard did not know. With an eager and slyly triumphant smile, the woman took the chair vacated by the king, and as Charles handed her the cards, their hands met in a bold caress.

Richard suppressed a sigh and vaguely wondered where the woman's husband was, if she had one, and if he was aware that if he was not already a cuckold, he likely would be soon.

"Come with us, Blythe," the king said in that same friendly manner, yet with an undercurrent of command in his jovial tone.

He glanced at Foz. "Lord Cheddersby may stay and play with the ladies."

Foz flushed bright red, which seemed to amuse the king even more as he led Richard toward his private apartments. "So, Blythe, we hear you have another theatrical success on your hands."

The gossips have been at work already, Richard thought wryly, but in this case, he could not be annoyed. "I have some cause to hope so, Majesty."

"This actress in the main part . . . ?"

"Minette Somerall, Majesty."

"She is a beauty, we hear."

Richard subdued a knowing grin. He was quite sure that the king knew all about Minette. He was also quite sure that Minette would abandon his bed for the king's at the drop of a royal *mouchoir*. And why not? For a girl raised in the streets of London, that was the pinnacle of worldly success.

He owed it to Minette to help, he decided. "She is *very* beautiful, sire."

The king's sidelong glance told Richard that Charles guessed the situation exactly and was pleased.

They reached the doors to the king's lavish

private apartments. A liveried servant opened and closed the door behind them, while another set forth food on a table inside the gilded and richly furnished suite of rooms. In the light of the candles, the gilding glowed a dull bronze, and the tapestries disappeared in shadows.

The king took his place at the table and another servant hurried to pour rich, red wine. "Sit, Blythe, and join us."

Richard did so, then held up his crystal goblet. "Your very good health, Majesty."

Charles nodded in acknowledgment, and together they sipped the delicious wine while Richard waited for Charles to return to the subject of Minette.

Instead, the king reached for a piece of fruit. "Have you ever had a taste of pineapple?"

"No, Majesty," Richard replied, eyeing the bright yellow morsel in the king's fingers. He had heard of pineapple, of course, which came from the New World.

The king placed the bit on a china plate edged with gold, then pushed it toward Richard, who put the surprisingly juicy bit of food into his mouth.

It was delicious, and Richard took the time to enjoy the novelty, pushing the succulent piece of fruit around with his tongue. He swallowed just as the king spoke.

"We have summoned you to discuss the matter of your family estate. It has long dis-

turbed us that we have been unable to help
you regain it."

This was certainly news to Richard. He
thought the king had forgotten his former
companion's predicament, if indeed it did not
suit him to feign ignorance. "I am flattered by
Your Majesty's interest and concern."

Charles smiled graciously. "Our hands have
been tied, Blythe. Well tied. However, we may
have found a way to loosen the bonds."

Richard tried not to sound too eager. "Majesty?"

"The purchaser is dead."

"I had heard that, Majesty."

The king's eyes narrowed ever so slightly,
and Richard thought he might do better to let
the king proceed without comment.

"William Longbourne left a young widow
and son," Charles continued.

The king paused as if waiting for Richard to
speak.

"Yes, Majesty?"

"His will specified that the estate was to go
to his son, with his wife to manage it until the
boy comes of age."

"I know nothing of the particulars of the
man's will, Majesty," Richard answered truthfully.

"Do you know anything of the particulars
of the widow?"

"Majesty?"

"She is but three and twenty, and reputed to be pretty."

"Oh?" Again Richard kept any expression except the most bland interest from his face. However, he could well imagine what a "pretty" widow from the countryside would look like. She would have some of her teeth and hair like dry straw, and she would probably weigh something less than two hundred pounds.

A mischievous gleam appeared in the king's eyes. "We have summoned her here tonight to see if we cannot find some compromise in this difficult situation."

A strange combination of despair, panic, and hope filled Richard, in no small part due to that mischievous gleam.

Before he could say anything, a servant hurried toward another door and ushered in a woman.

Richard's jaw dropped, for he recognized her the moment she walked into the room. The ungrateful woman he had rescued from Sedley and his cronies was the widow of the man who had bought his family's ancestral home? This lovely woman dressed in a gown of plain, demure, and funereal black had control of his estate? And that sturdy, brave little chap owned what was Richard's by ancient right, if not modern commerce?

The widow began to curtsy, then caught

sight of him and halted in confusion, as well she might.

Before the page closed the door to the other room, Richard realized the widow had not come alone. The fellow who had been waiting with her was tall, slender, with broad shoulders, not yet middle-aged—and rather good-looking, in a grim sort of way. A brother, perhaps. Or a friend of the family.

Or a suitor for the widow's hand?

A shocking, unexpected pang of jealousy shot through Richard, which was utterly ridiculous. Had he not calmly discussed Minette with the king? Why, she had been his mistress for over a month, yet he had been prepared to bid her adieu with no more regret than if she had been a puppy who had reached sufficient age to be sold.

The king rose from his chair and went to take the woman's hand, reminding Richard where he was. Charles's motion seemed to have the same effect on the widow, for she finished her curtsy, remaining in the lowest position.

"Come, come, my dear, there is no need to be intimidated," the king said kindly.

Obviously Charles assumed her expression was due to being in the king's presence.

As the king led her to a place at the table hastily set by a servant, the other servant closed the door, shutting out the unknown man.

Richard turned his attention to the woman, forcing himself to regard her objectively, as if considering her a subject for one of his plays.

She could be as young as three and twenty. Her youthful complexion was all cream and pink, and her features exemplary. Her form would make even Minette envious. Her hair, as plainly dressed as her gown, was a rich chestnut color drawn back into a topknot. There were no little ringlets at the sides, the current fashion among ladies of the court, or tiny curls on her forehead. One natural wisp of a curl, however, had escaped and brushed her ear.

Richard suddenly felt the most outrageous urge to tuck it back, a thought that sent a jolt of excitement through his body.

Then he looked at her eyes, her most unique and unusual feature. The color alone was rare, a light hazel. However, it was the expression in their depths that made them, and her, both fascinating and formidable. It was as if she were far older and wiser than her years, and absolutely incapable of surrender.

Another aspect of that type of character occurred to him. She would not give up what she believed to be hers without a fight.

The king cleared his throat. "Mistress Longbourne, allow me to present one of the ornaments of our court and indeed London itself, Sir Richard Blythe. Sir Richard, Mistress Elissa Longbourne."

She smiled blandly as she curtsied. "How do you do, Sir Richard?"

So, she was going to pretend they had never met. Given her rudeness that afternoon, it was not surprising.

But certainly not acceptable, either.

He bowed. "Your servant, ma'am. However, as delightful as this unexpected meeting is, should you not be abed?"

"Sir?"

The king gave Richard an equally puzzled look.

"I fear Mistress Longbourne is ill, Majesty, for it seems she has forgotten that I came to her assistance this afternoon," he explained to the king, who raised an eyebrow as he turned to regard a blushing Mistress Longbourne. "Is this so?"

"Your Majesty, I was so upset by a most distressing situation, I did not take sufficient notice of who came to our aid."

Richard was surprised by her ability to lie with such aplomb, and to the king, too.

Then, to Richard's chagrin, Charles scrutinized *him*. "It would appear, Sir Richard, that you suffer from the same malady, for you did not inform us that you had already met Mistress Longbourne."

"She did not allow me the honor of learning her name."

"Majesty, I thought only of getting away from . . ." The woman wisely hesitated.

Anyone at all familiar with the court would know that it might be better to say nothing of Sedley, Buckhurst, and Jermyn, no matter how rude or drunk they had been.

"From whom?" Charles demanded.

Richard let Mistress Longbourne squirm like a mouse caught by a cat for a moment while he considered whether he should name Sedley and his friends.

He decided against it, for despite their behavior and well-deserved disrepute, they were more powerful at court than he.

"It was merely some scoundrels who spoke out of turn, Majesty," he explained. "A trifling incident."

"A most bothersome incident!" the widow protested, a flash of fire in her eyes.

Then, rather surprisingly, her gaze faltered. "I was in some fear for my son's safety from those ruffians, Sir Richard, but of course, that is no excuse. I must, therefore, beg your pardon."

Before Richard could answer, Charles sat and gestured for the two of them to do the same.

"A most regrettable introduction to London," he said sympathetically. "Nevertheless, we are surprised you do not remember this handsome fellow."

"Our baggage was stolen, too, Majesty."

He had not known that. Zounds, almost any other woman would have been reduced to weeping by that alone without the added trouble of Sedley and his lascivious friends.

At that moment, Richard would quite willingly have forgiven her almost anything—until she cast a sidelong glance at him. Then he saw the shrewdness lurking in her remarkable hazel eyes and cursed himself for a dolt to be so taken in by feigned innocence.

He, so well schooled in hypocrisy, should know better.

"That must also explain why you did not trouble to thank me," he noted dryly.

Elissa's eyes narrowed ever so slightly as she regarded Sir Richard. She was quite sure he saw through her apparently sincere apology, and that was most disconcerting—nearly as disconcerting at sitting at a table with the King of England. "Majesty, I am sure Sir Richard will understand that I did not think it an appropriate time or place for social niceties. Indeed, this is a far more pleasant place to make introductions than the crowded, filthy street."

The king chuckled. "Odd's fish, Richard, that sounds like something from one of your plays."

Sir Richard looked thoughtful. "If I were to write such a scene, Majesty, I believe I would have the female character fall in love with the bold fellow who came to her rescue."

That response made the king laugh all the

more. "Of course! What say you to that, Mistress Longbourne?"

"Since I have not yet had the pleasure of seeing one of Sir Richard's plays, I will have to assume that is a typical occurrence in one of his productions. Therefore, I shall also be forced to assume that he takes no trouble to present anything approximating reality upon the stage."

Sir Richard colored slightly, and Elissa finally felt some of her tension ebb. She would show this impertinent fellow that she was not an ignorant country widow to be threatened by anyone's sardonic manner and supposed sophistication.

Indeed, from what she heard of the king and his court, they were utterly at the mercy of their passions and so, she concluded, not as strong as she, who had conquered hers long ago.

Or had them driven out, her conscience prompted.

She forced herself to think only of the present, and to keep every sense alert until she knew exactly why the king had summoned her here.

"Harsh words, Mistress Longbourne," Charles noted. "This does not bode well for our delightful plan."

What anxiety had abated returned full force as the king looked at her with obvious disappointment, and perhaps even disapproval.

"We have a plan to try to amend this unfortunate business."

"Business?" Elissa demanded warily.

More than a hint of reprimand appeared on the king's face. "Mistress Longbourne?"

"Majesty," she began again, trying not to sound as cowed as she suddenly felt, "I only wonder what unfortunate business you mean."

"For a woman who feels competent enough to criticize my work without seeing it, this incomprehension seems rather odd," Sir Richard mused aloud, apparently to no one in particular. "Surely there is no need to dissemble. She must have guessed the nature of the business to be conducted here when she saw me."

To Elissa's further chagrin, the king's expression assumed a shrewdness she had not suspected he possessed. "We think he has you there, Mistress Longbourne, and he does not even know that you have brought your lawyer."

"Your lawyer?" Sir Richard repeated incredulously.

"Then I gather it *is* of my son's inheritance we speak," Elissa said.

"My family's estate," Sir Richard quickly amended.

"Not after it was *legally* sold," Elissa retorted. "My son is the rightful owner of the Blythe estate. It was fairly purchased and paid for, and bequeathed to him by my late husband. My lawyer has brought all the necessary documents."

"Come, come!" the king cried. His tone was outwardly jovial, but they both heard the undertone of royal displeasure. "We understand the legalities, Mistress Longbourne, and we trust you understand Sir Richard's desire to have what he feels should be his not just by right of birth, but by virtue of the friendship and assistance he offered us during our long exile. Odd's fish, madam, if it were up to us, we would have given him the estate the moment we set foot on English soil.

"Sadly, as you so forcefully observe, the estate was legally sold—"

"My uncle had no right to sell it!"

"You were in Europe, Richard," Charles reminded him, and Elissa marveled as the monarch's tone altered yet again. He now spoke as one old friend to another. "However, we believe we have hit upon a most charming and excellent solution," the king continued pleasantly.

Richard and Elissa regarded him doubtfully.

"You two must be married."

Chapter 3

"To whom, sire?" Richard asked, trying to remain calm.

"Do not play the fool, Richard," the king replied. "To each other, of course."

"That is quite impossible, Your Majesty," Mistress Longbourne declared.

As Charles turned toward her, Richard felt a moment's pity. Charles was inevitably polite and charming to women and often seemed to give way to their desires, especially if to do so meant he could exist in peace.

However, disagreeing with him in such a bold way was not the means to win Charles to one's side.

As if she sensed this, Mistress Longbourne's expression changed suddenly to one of demure modesty that was all too likely to make Charles clay in her slender hands. "Surely, Majesty, this ornament of the court is too far above me," she demurred.

Richard couldn't quite subdue a scowl. She no more meant that than she would if she claimed to be hopelessly in love with him. Zounds, he couldn't have written a more deceitful, clever, scheming heroine if he tried!

The king looked down at the diamond ring he was twisting around his finger, then raised his face, a little smile playing about his lips. "I should think any woman would be delighted to marry this handsome, talented fellow who is a friend of the king."

"Your Majesty, a marriage to me will not change anything regarding the ownership of the estate," Mistress Longbourne observed. "It will still be my son's."

"And not the property of its rightful owner," Richard agreed.

"My son *is* the rightful owner!" Mistress Longbourne protested, her mask of diffident female momentarily slipping.

Richard nearly smiled when he noticed that the king seemed to be growing weary of her insistence in this regard. "Majesty, I fear we must not marry. Mistress Longbourne neither likes nor approves of me and I daresay I would not improve upon acquaintance."

"Nonsense!" the king replied. "We well recall certain recalcitrant women who soon enough clamored to be in your bed, and we cannot remember a one of them complaining afterward."

"Majesty," Richard said in a loud, conspiratorial whisper and with a pointed glance at Mistress Longbourne, "I believe remarking upon my past conquests is not endearing me to my intended."

"We are quite sure you will be able to overcome any reluctance on her part." The king regarded Elissa. "Sir Richard has long desired to return to his home. While he may not be able to regain rights to the estate, as your husband he will be able to live there. Is that not a fine compromise?"

"Live there?"

"With you," the king repeated as if she were quite dim. "As your husband."

Elissa looked at the man the king wanted her to marry, and her imagination conjured certain visions of married life.

Sir Richard Blythe was not William Longbourne, and he surely would have to be a better—

No! she chided her traitorous heart. Sir Richard Blythe was a lascivious, immoral scoundrel, like most of the king's friends, and no matter how handsome he was, or how intriguing his dark eyes, she did not want to see him again, let alone be married to him.

"Perhaps you would care to discuss this matter with your lawyer, since he is so conveniently to hand?" the king suggested with a smile.

Elissa rose and curtsied. "Thank you, Your Majesty, I shall," she said briskly before she hurried out the door through which she had entered.

After she had gone, the king ordered his servants to leave, and then turned toward Richard. "Odd's fish, this must be a most peculiar situation for you, Blythe," he observed.

Richard nodded. "I do not discuss marriage every day, sire."

"At least not your own, eh?" Charles observed with a dry chuckle. "That is not what we meant. That a woman would apparently find you undesirable must be something new in your experience, although how a man of your dark temperament attracts so many is quite a mystery."

Richard made a little smile. "It is a mystery to me, too, sire, unless one subscribes to the theory that most people want what they cannot have. Merely seeming impervious to a woman's beauty or other attributes makes them determined to force me to notice them. Sometimes that determination is quite astonishing. I confess I have been all but attacked on some occasions."

"Such a hardship!" the king mocked jovially.

"One does what one can to endure, Majesty," Richard replied virtuously, and not untruthfully. "However, I must point out that if Your Majesty is nearby, women scarcely acknowledge my existence."

"You flatter us!"

"Majesty, I daresay Mistress Longbourne was upset because she thought you had a more personal interest. It is no wonder to me that she looked horrified at your proposal that she marry me."

"*Horrified* is surely too strong a term. She was surprised."

"As was I, Majesty."

The king chuckled, then grew serious. "We could think of no other recourse to get you home, Richard."

"I thank you again for your concern, sire," Richard said, keeping his tone light and in no way critical. "However, if it is as the lady so adamantly claims and her son has clear title to the estate, even if I marry her, it will never be mine."

"Unfortunately, she is quite right," the king concurred. "We have seen the documents ourselves. Her marriage settlement and the will are indisputable. However, the boy may die, and in that case, the estate reverts to his mother, who shall be your wife."

Richard tried to maintain a nonchalant expression. "Majesty, as much as I want what I believe to be justly mine, a child's death would be too high a price to pay."

Charles smiled. "A noble sentiment. And then, your wife is quite rich in her own right. According to the marriage settlement, she kept control of all her dowry, and when Longbourne died, she was the heir to all his money and moveable goods. The son only got the estate itself, and the mother controls the income. So you see, Richard, when you marry her, you will become quite wealthy. You can purchase another estate."

"It would not be the same."

"It will have to do," the king replied, a slight edge coming to his voice.

"Majesty, I do not favor forced marriages for anyone."

"You write of them often enough," Charles observed, again with a chill in a voice.

Despite the king's displeasure, Richard knew he must be honest, at least to a point. "When I do, Majesty, they are disastrous alliances," he reminded him.

"Come, Richard, it is not as if she is an old hag. To speak the truth, we had no notion she was so beautiful or we would have offered her a place at court. However, you are our good friend, who stood by us in troubled times, and we do not forget. Therefore, you shall have first claim upon her. If, however, you are adamantly opposed to marrying her, we shall have to make other plans. She is far too lovely a woman to waste away in Leicester."

Richard realized he was in the uncomfortable position of deciding Elissa Longbourne's fate. If he continued to protest this marriage, she would have to stay at court, the prey for many lascivious men, including the king.

On the other hand, he was determined to

avoid a repetition of his parents' unhappy marriage.

He must choose between throwing a woman he had only just met to the wolves of King Charles's court and the possibility that he was condemning himself to a life of bitter conflict and lasting regret.

"I shall marry her, Your Majesty."

Elissa sat in a slender chair in the king's anteroom. The opulent furnishings around her seemed to symbolize the court's decadence, and even the scent of perfume and candle wax grew oppressive as she regarded her tall, apparently imperturbable lawyer who stood facing her, his hands behind his back.

"You do not sound surprised," she noted with a disgruntled frown.

"The king enjoys commanding people to marry," Mr. Harding replied evenly. "I had my suspicions that was what he intended when he summoned you here."

"Why did you not warn me?"

"I might have been wrong."

Elissa reminded herself that "Heartless" Harding was said to be the best lawyer in London, despite his relative youth. Unfortunately, he seemed as capable of human feeling as the gilt chair upon which she sat in this sinfully luxurious room.

She would never again hear of the king's financial woes without remembering the heavy, scarlet brocade draperies, the huge wall hangings, the silver and gold dishes, the crystal, the elaborate furnishings, the many candles, and the thick carpets she had seen in Whitehall Palace.

"I don't think Sir Richard expected the king's proposition either," she said, recalling the look of shock that had flitted across the man's features at the king's suggestion.

She suddenly realized that she may have witnessed a moment of vulnerability beneath the playwright's mocking exterior, perhaps— which did not matter in the least.

"That is more surprising, given that they are friends," Mr. Harding replied.

"If they are such good friends, I suppose I should be grateful that the king does not command me to give him the estate," she said sarcastically.

"He dare not. The sale was legal, as were so many other similar transactions during the Interregnum, and if he sets aside one, he will be pressured to do the same for other noblemen, and then the purchasers will, quite justifiably, demand compensation, which the king cannot pay."

"If we are legally in the right, why should I not refuse to marry Sir Richard?"

"I must point out that the person making this proposal is not just any man. He is the king."

"He is not above the law. Was that not the whole point of Magna Carta?"

"One could say it was," Mr. Harding acknowledged. "However, we are not dealing with a document, either. We are dealing with a capricious man who likes to reward his friends, if he can do so with some impunity."

"To the detriment of the entire country," Elissa retorted. "Besides, Sir Richard Blythe is a disgrace!"

"Sir Richard Blythe was years in Europe with the king," Mr. Harding noted. "Even more important, Sir Richard Blythe and his plays amuse the king. When does His Majesty wish the wedding to take place?"

Elissa jumped to her feet. "There must be no wedding!"

She thought she saw a flicker of feeling in Mr. Harding's eyes. "The king wants you to marry Sir Richard, therefore you had best do so."

"But why? The estate will still be my son's, and no marriage of mine will change that."

"Did the king give you no reason?"

"He said that if Sir Richard could not have the estate, as my husband he would at least be able to live there—yet I must have to willingly agree to this, surely. Even the king cannot force me to—"

She fell silent at the sight of Mr. Harding's raised eyebrow. "He can?"

"His Majesty can make his displeasure felt

in many ways, not all of them directly."

"But—"

Mr. Harding rocked slightly on his feet. "But I think you had best obey his wishes in this instance. Why risk royal anger?"

"Because I do not wish to marry again, and especially not a writer of immoral, lascivious plays, even if he is the king's friend."

"Would you rather go to the Tower?"

Elissa stared at the stone-faced lawyer.

"If you do not acquiesce to the king's request, he would not be above sending you there. You have surely heard that he has threatened to send the Duke of Buckingham to the Tower when displeased, and Buckingham has been his closest friend for years. You can make no similar claim."

Elissa reached for the chair and sat again.

"There are worse fates than honorable marriage to a man the king admires. As for the bridegroom himself, I have it on good authority that whatever Sir Richard writes, there is no evidence that he is dishonorable or cruel. The worst thing I have learned about him is that he sometimes has trouble keeping his mistresses from quarreling over him."

Elissa wrung her hands in agitation. "To know that he keeps mistresses hardly predisposes me to think he will be either a good husband, or a fit example to Will. His father . . ."

As she fell silent, she stared down at her hands. Tears filled her eyes, and she willed them away. She had not cried in years, and she would not do so now. "I do not want to marry anybody, whether the king commands it or not. The estate legally belongs to my son."

Mr. Harding leaned forward, his cold, impassive eyes staring into hers. "Mistress Longbourne, the question you must ask yourself is, what are you prepared to do to ensure that he keeps it?"

At last the door to the anteroom opened, and Richard watched Mistress Longbourne glide into the room.

She was beautiful, and shapely, and her hair must fall to her waist when loose. As for her full red lips, he could easily imagine kissing them.

No matter how desirable a bedmate she might be, however, he was still reluctant to be forced into marriage. He knew from bitter experience that desire alone could not ensure that a man and woman could live together in harmony.

Mistress Longbourne curtsied to the king and glanced at Richard with her intelligent hazel eyes. "Your Majesty, Sir Richard, when shall the wedding be?"

It was only as he let out his breath in stunned surprise that Richard realized he had been holding it.

"You offer no further objections, then?" Charles inquired, and Richard, with new awareness, heard the king's slight disappointment.

"I would prefer as soon as possible. I do not wish to be longer from home than absolutely necessary."

"A most conscientious bride, is she not, Richard?" the king asked as he rose. "It shall be as you wish, my dear, and we must insist you wed here at Whitehall."

"Majesty, I am—" Richard began.

"Grateful?" the king interrupted, glancing at him sharply.

"Yes, Majesty," he prudently agreed. "I am grateful."

"Good. We shall leave you two alone while we set the wedding plans in motion. Have some wine and fruit!" Charles commanded with an airy wave of his hand as he departed.

"I suppose we should obey his order and eat and drink," Elissa said, making no effort to sound polite as she sat at the table and poured herself some wine. Indeed, it was taking enough effort to try to remain calm. Unfortunately, her trembling hand threatened to betray her agitation.

"Would you like to have your lawyer join us?" Sir Richard inquired as he took the chair opposite her.

"He has left the palace and gone to prepare the marriage settlement."

"Without the bridegroom?"

"He is drawing up a preliminary agreement.

You can negotiate after you have read it."

Sir Richard's bemused expression did not ease her discomfort. "Indeed I shall. I know what clever fellows these lawyers are, and I would not care to sign away too much."

"So much of the law is against a woman to begin with when it comes to marriage, she requires a good lawyer."

"You seem to have managed very well."

"Precisely because I have a clever lawyer."

"I am not a fool either, Mistress Longbourne."

"I am glad to hear it. It would be terrible to be married to a fool. A playwright is bad enough."

"I write only because I have to, or starve."

"For an honorable man, starvation might be preferable."

He leaned back in his chair and crossed his arms. "You know how it is to starve, then, that you can offer so decided an opinion?"

She flushed. "No, I do not."

"I do, so I think you must defer to my expertise as to what an honorable man will or will not do in order to survive."

"I shall defer to your knowledge of what a *man* will do to survive."

He straightened and regarded her with sudden, menacing intensity. "Since we are to be husband and wife, madam, allow me to offer you a piece of advice. If you wish to live in peace with me, never call my honor into question."

Elissa swallowed hard, sensing this was a moment that could decide the course of their lives together as husband and wife.

Once before she had faced such a moment. Even in her girlish innocence, she had felt in her bones that what she said to William then would set the pattern for their lives together.

Like a simpleton, she had said nothing at all.

Therefore, she likewise leaned forward and glared at Richard with equal intensity. "Sir, I do not know you, and what I have heard of you scarce gives me cause to credit you with honor. If it should be that you are the rogue I think you are, and if you should ever try to steal my son's estate or corrupt him to your lascivious ways, you will regret it."

Sir Richard's eyes widened a little, and then he smiled sardonically. "Why, Mistress Longbourne, you sound very fierce. Perhaps this would be a good time to inquire what happened to your first husband."

"An infection in the lungs." She made a wry little smile all her own. "I had no hand in it."

"I must say I am relieved he did not come to a violent end."

"Where my son is concerned, I will do anything to protect him from anyone who seeks to do him harm."

Sir Richard regarded her steadily. "Rest assured, madam, your son has nothing to fear from me."

Suddenly, he reached across the table and took hold of her hands. Just as before when he had taken her hand, she was surprised by the strength of his grip. Perhaps writing explained that, she thought vaguely, as he lifted her fingers to his lips. Gently, his mouth brushed her fingertips, the simple motion sending the blood throbbing through her body.

When he turned her hand over and pressed a kiss to her palm, she could hardly breathe.

He made a sly, seductive smile. "I fear that I have gotten off to a very poor start," he murmured, pleased that he was now in command, and that he had obviously successfully hidden his extreme anger at her warning. "I confess I was rather peeved when you ran away without telling me your name this afternoon."

She didn't meet his gaze. "And I should have thanked you for helping us."

"You are a very beautiful woman, Mistress Longbourne, and I am very glad I saved you from those drunken fools."

"I am glad you did, too."

He rose and went to her, gently pulling her to her feet.

"Mistress Longbourne . . . Elissa . . . we must try to make the best of this," he whispered, taking her in his arms and feeling a surge of primitive desire when she did not pull away. "Somehow."

Then he kissed her, his lips moving over hers with sure expertise. He had kissed many women, most with some kind of genuine desire, at least at the time, a few simply because he could, and one or two because he was too bored to resist their obvious ploys. Their responses had all been of a rather boring sameness, an almost pitiable passion that said more about their loneliness and boredom than his prowess.

Elissa Longbourne was definitely different, because she responded with . . . nothing. She simply lay limp in his arms as if she had lost consciousness.

Or simply did not care.

A wave of despair washed over him. Despite the king's command, he would never be able to endure the same kind of loveless marriage and shameful truce his parents had devised. No matter what the consequences, he would have to tell the king . . .

Then, suddenly, she was kissing him back, her lips slowly, tentatively moving against his. Her hands tightened on his arms, not pushing him away, but drawing him closer.

With renewed and fierce desire, Richard's kiss deepened. Gently, yet insistently, he teased her with his tongue until she parted her lips. Then, unable to be patient, he thrust his tongue into her mouth while his hands caressed her supple back.

A low moan escaped Elissa's lips as she surrendered to the passionate yearning his kisses enticed into fiery life.

Her husband's kisses had been chaste before they were married, and he had never kissed her after. In their bed, he had taken her swiftly, silently, roughly, so when Richard had taken her in his arms, she had instinctively stayed still, even when he kissed her.

She had not known a kiss could be so . . . so incredible. The sensation of his mouth upon hers, his evident desire, the urge to be taken—

She did not want to be taken, or possessed like an inanimate thing ever again. And she would not be distracted from her responsibility toward her son, not by any man.

"Odd's fish, this bodes well," the king cheerfully declared before she could break the kiss.

As they quickly moved apart, Charles strolled toward them. "We were wise to set the wedding date upon the morrow."

"Tomorrow, sire?" Richard inquired blandly, as if they were discussing nothing more exciting than the price of eggs.

"Yes, tomorrow evening, after the performance of your play." King Charles chuckled. "We trust you can wait that long."

Elissa drew in a deep breath. "Majesty, I fear that will not give Mr. Harding time to draw up the marriage settlement."

The king waved his hand dismissively. "He has all night and all morning. Odd's fish, madam, you certainly looked impatient enough a few moments ago. You will spend your first night here, of course."

"Here?" Elissa whispered incredulously.

The king smiled magnanimously. "It seems the least we could do, given that you are marrying at our command." Then he winked as lasciviously as the waterman. "We are quite certain the groom will make you forget you are in the palace."

"Yes, Your Majesty."

Charles gave Richard a sly, knowing smile. "All seems well in hand. We never doubted you for a moment, Blythe."

"I try to please, Majesty."

The king's raucous laugh filled the chamber. "Well, Mistress Longbourne, can a bride ask for more? Now, off with you both until tomorrow."

Elissa hurried toward the door. She didn't know if Sir Richard followed close behind or not. Dismayed, disturbed, and disgruntled, she wanted to get out of the palace as quickly as she could, and away from Sir Richard Blythe with his dark, distracting eyes and his sinfully seductive lips.

Chapter 4

"**W**omen are usually late," Foz offered the next night as Richard stood beside him in the Great Hall of the palace, awaiting his tardy bride.

They were not alone. Charles was seated on the dais, again surrounded by women and, as always, attended by several fawning courtiers. Courtiers who were not predisposed to fawn nevertheless hovered nearby and kept their eyes and ears open for anything they could use in their own favor.

Queen Catherine was not in attendance, which was not unusual. More unusually, Charles's grand *amour*, Lady Castlemaine, was also absent. Rumor had it she was expecting another child, and there was a possibility it was not the king's, but the product of one of her other liaisons. Likely she deemed it wise to keep some distance between herself and her royal lover.

Richard scanned the bevy of young women who would likely not be adverse to taking Lady Castlemaine's place, even temporarily. At present, the king's current favorite seemed to be a pretty woman who went by the name of Mistress Winters. Apparently, there was no Mister Winters, and Richard doubted there ever had been. Gossip said she had been a maidservant to one of Charles's underlings until the king had taken a fancy to her and provided her with her own house a short distance from the palace. The distance was even shorter if one went by boat, and the king had his own Privy Stairs leading to the Thames.

As Richard watched Mistress Winters allow rather astonishing liberties by the king, he hoped she would keep the king sufficiently occupied that His Majesty wouldn't realize how late the hour was growing, or speculate that Mistress Longbourne had decided she would rather risk the king's wrath than marry.

"My mother was nearly half a day late for her wedding," Foz noted nostalgically.

Richard had met Foz's father before the elderly gentleman had passed away, so he could understand why his mother might have waited until the last possible moment to marry him. It was hardly flattering to think Elissa Longbourne had a similar reaction to *him*.

"How did Minette take the news of your marriage?"

"Rather better than I expected," Richard replied.

Rather better than he had been prepared for, truth be told. He supposed she already had her sights set on another man, and presumably one with more to give.

"I wish you had agreed to borrow my new peruke," Foz whispered as he surveyed Richard with slight disapproval.

"Wigs make my head itch," Richard whispered back. "What would be worse, a bridegroom who displays his own unfashionable hair or one who's constantly scratching?"

The king suddenly laughed, the jovial eruption drawing everyone's attention.

"Perhaps we shall have to send our guards for her, eh?" he called out, looking at Richard. "In the meantime, the ladies are bidding on who shall take Mistress Longbourne's place if she fails to arrive."

Richard bowed in acknowledgment and dutifully smiled as he slowly perused the bevy of painted, overdressed women. Not one of them attracted him at all, but one or two eyed him flirtatiously, making it clear they would consider taking the bride's place, or at least substitute for her in the nuptial bed. "How delightful, Majesty! Who, may I ask, has bid the most?"

"Oh, it would be unchivalrous to say, surely," the king protested. Then he started and straightened, pointing down the hall. "Lo, the bride cometh!"

Richard turned—and then struggled to control the anger washing over him, for his bride came not in wedding finery, but in mourning, from the top of her black-veiled head to the bottom of her stiff, high-necked black gown. Her haughty, aloof expression as she walked slowly toward him was not one to inspire happiness, either. She looked as if *she* were the dear departed, her frozen face a death mask.

Beside her, also dressed in plain black and with an equally dismal mien, was the fellow from the anteroom last night.

Elissa Longbourne's son was nowhere to be seen.

The soft sounds of snickering, both male and female, reached Richard's ears and his jaw clenched.

"She's even beautiful in that horrible gown," Foz breathed beside him. "How embarrassing for her! She must have had nothing else suitable."

"She should have bought something," Richard snarled under his breath.

Foz scrutinized Richard's attire. "*You* didn't."

"That's different!"

"Who's that chap with her? His tailor should be hanged if he can't provide a better fit than that."

"He is her lawyer."

"Ods bodikins, really?"

"Really."

The king rose and majestically strode toward Mistress Longbourne, his usual charming smile on his face. She curtsied and waited until he took her hand to rise, while her lawyer bowed. "Ah, Mistress Longbourne! We were beginning to fear something had happened to prevent you from coming, which would have been most unfortunate."

He glanced back at the women who swarmed around him like bees to honey. "Although some would have been only too happy if you had not."

"I am very sorry, Your Majesty," she said with what sounded like sincere regret. "I was trying to find something appropriate to wear, and failed."

Foz nudged Richard so hard, he had to take a step to keep from falling over.

"You are lovely nonetheless," the king graciously replied as he placed her hand on his arm. "Come and join hands with Sir Richard."

"Majesty, if you please," she said as the king brought her to stand beside him, "Mr. Harding has brought the marriage settlement. Sir Richard should sign it first."

Richard glared and the king frowned. "Marriage settlement?"

"Yes, Majesty," she said with more of a simper than Richard would have believed her capable of.

Mr. Harding stepped forward and held a rolled parchment out to Richard, who snatched it from the man's slender, yet surprisingly strong, fingers. He tore off the ribbon and discovered two long, closely written documents that apparently utilized every legal term imaginable.

"Sir Richard has but to sign the two copies, and then we can be wed," Mistress Longbourne explained as if the proffered legal document were nothing at all important or binding.

"Fetch pen and ink for Sir Richard," Charles genially commanded one of the liveried servants standing nearby.

"Sire, it will take me at least an hour to read it—and more than that to comprehend it, I don't doubt," Richard protested.

"You do not read well?" Mistress Longbourne inquired gravely as she turned to look at him. "That must be a severe handicap for one of your profession, although it may explain some of your work."

"While your Mr. Harding was studying the law, I was with the king in Europe," Richard growled.

"Yes, yes, so you were," Charles said. "Just sign the thing and then we can begin the celebrations. We are in a mood to dance."

"Majesty, I cannot put to my name to a legal document without knowing its contents."

The king's brow lowered ominously and the

gleam of merriment left his eyes. "What can it possibly say that would be important enough to disrupt our plans?"

"My father taught me never to sign a document without reading it first," he replied, not adding that it was the only valuable lesson his father had ever taught him.

Charles smiled placatingly. "That is wise, of course, yet surely there is nothing out of the ordinary here. Come, man, and sign, so that I can proceed to make you Earl of Dovercourt."

Richard stared, while Mistress Longbourne and others in the huge assembly room gasped.

"Indeed, it is true. When you wed Mistress Longbourne, we shall make you Earl of Dovercourt. Sadly, there is no estate to go with the title, but we are certain you will think of a way to amend that."

Mistress Longbourne darted a suspicious look at both the king and her intended husband.

"Majesty, perhaps . . ." she began hesitantly as a servant returned with a quill and pot of ink.

Richard snatched the quill from the servant. "As much as we both might wish for a delay," he whispered harshly to her, "it is rather late for changing your mind." He raised his voice. "Foz, please be so good as to make a back."

His friend obligingly bent over. Richard laid the document on Foz's back and with a theatrical flourish, signed one copy, then the other. He briskly handed one to Mr. Harding and the other to his friend. "Lord Cheddersby, I hope you will be so good as to study this for me at your leisure and tell me what it says in simple English."

While Foz was not particularly clever about most things, or creative in the least, he was well able to read and summarize other men's work, thanks to a most exacting tutor.

"I shall be delighted!" he eagerly agreed. Then he frowned. "Not immediately, I trust?"

"The sooner the better."

"But—"

"After the marriage ceremony will do," Richard amended.

Lord Cheddersby nodded.

"Maybe Sir Richard *should* read it first," Elissa ventured, her misgivings increased by the king's remark regarding an estate for her bridegroom.

How was he to obtain one if the king did not give it to him? By somehow usurping her son's once he was her husband?

"Let us proceed!" the king declared. "Sir Richard Blythe, do you take her? Of course you do. Mistress Longbourne, do you take him? Odd's fish, yes. I therefore pronounce you man and wife. To the happy couple!"

The room erupted into a cacophony of cheers and laughter.

Feeling as if this were another horrid nightmare in a series of bad dreams, Elissa slowly turned toward Sir Richard, who suddenly tugged her into his arms with surprising and unexpected strength.

"Thus, my dear, we are wed," he declared before his mouth possessively took hers.

She twisted, only to find herself clasped to him even tighter, as if he would meld their bodies into one.

As his tongue slipped between her lips, his knee gently pushed between her rapidly weakening legs.

She was going to swoon.

He stopped kissing her. However, he still held her close and although there was fire in his dark eyes, his lips turned up in a roguish little smile. "It is done and there is nothing you or I can do about it. So make the best of it, my lady, as I shall."

Regardless of the people around them, he boldly caressed her body before releasing her. "Believe me, I most certainly shall."

"You despicable—"

He was already gone. Like a conquering hero he sauntered toward the group of women near the king who were dressed in satins and velvets yet painted their faces like whores.

"Now for the wedding feast!" Charles cried, taking Mistress Winters by the hand. "To the Banqueting House!"

The ladies and courtiers curtsied, bowed, and murmured expectantly as Charles began to escort the pretty but garishly attired woman through the crowd and toward the door.

Elissa had no idea where he was going, and her husband was still obviously occupied receiving the congratulations of the women left behind. She was so annoyed, she didn't realize that Lord Cheddersby had come to stand beside her.

"Best wishes, my lady," he offered with a kind and slightly foolish smile.

"Thank you," she replied coldly, wondering when her new husband was going to deign to leave those immodest, impudent women and lead her in to the wedding banquet, wherever it was. "Have you seen Mr. Harding?"

"He's gone."

"Oh."

"Do you want him? I will go after him for you."

"That will not be necessary. Tell me, where is the wedding banquet to be?"

"The Banqueting House."

Elissa flushed with embarrassment. She might have reasoned that out for herself.

"He can't help it, you know."

She looked at Lord Cheddersby quizzically—which was better than looking at Sir Richard and his many admirers. "Who cannot help what?"

"Richard. He cannot help it if women like him. He makes no effort to secure their good opinion."

"Indeed?" As she thought of Sir Richard's

good looks and sardonic, knowing smile, she could see that it might not take much of a personal effort on his part to attract foolish women. And when she recalled his kiss . . . if a woman had experience of *that*, it would take even less.

She told herself it did not matter how many women had enjoyed his passionate embraces. It would not matter to her if they continued to enjoy them.

"Yes. I can't understand it myself, for he can be quite rude."

"That does not surprise me."

"He can be very gallant, too, as you yourself discovered yesterday."

"I prefer not to remember that terrible episode."

"I understand."

Elissa was quite sure Lord Cheddersby understood nothing at all where she was concerned.

"Yes, well, best wishes, my lady. I hope you will be very happy." He smiled weakly, then bowed and walked away.

He had sounded so sincere and kind, Elissa was sorry she had been abrupt with him. After all, it was not Lord Cheddersby's fault she had been forced to marry his friend.

And no matter how she felt about her husband or her marriage, Elissa couldn't help experiencing a guilty twinge of pleasure at the realization she was now a titled lady.

The king halted at the door and glanced back over his shoulder. "Sir Richard," he called out as if vastly amused, "you seem to have forgotten something."

"Sire?"

"Your bride!"

Elissa flushed again as the hall erupted with laughter, then glared at her new husband as he strolled toward her and, with a mocking expression in his dark eyes, bowed. "How remiss of me."

Then his voice dropped to a low, smugly satisfied whisper. "Tit for tat, my sweet," he said, looking at her breasts and smiling even more.

"I do not require your attendance."

"You have it nonetheless," he said, offering her his arm. "The bride and groom must take their proper places upon the stage."

"If we must," she muttered as he placed her hand upon his forearm.

His very muscular forearm.

Perhaps it is so muscular because he is always fighting duels over women, she thought as they made their way through a series of corridors and halls along with the rest of the boisterous, smirking courtiers.

"Ah, here you are!" the king cried when they reached the Banqueting House.

He was already seated at the center of the large head table covered with a pristine white cloth, silver plates and crystal goblets. "Richard, you must sit beside Mistress Winters, and your beautiful bride shall be to our right, so that we can regale her with examples of your many qualities and accomplishments."

With the greatest difficulty, Elissa kept a sneer from her face. She already knew enough about Sir Richard Blythe.

As the servant pulled out her chair, she realized that Mistress Winters was conversing with the king in the most intimate manner and leaning toward him so provocatively, nearly the whole of her breasts were exposed. Elissa would have believed the brazen creature was the latest of the king's conquests, save that Mistress Winters also looked at Sir Richard as if he were a piece of succulent roast beef and she starving.

Perhaps the rumors that Charles had many lovers concurrently and did not care if his women did the same were true.

"Now, my dear, is this not delightful?" the king asked her companionably.

She was about to mutter something innocuous when the king suddenly clapped his hand on her knee.

She nearly jumped out of her chair.

"Majesty?" she said, her voice little more than an alarmed squeak.

"As the wife of an earl, you will have to come to London often."

He started to caress her leg. How was she going to make him stop? How could the King

of England be so disgustingly familiar? "I . . .
I . . . there is much to be managed on the estate, sire."

"But would you not like to come to court?"

Fighting the urge to slap his roving hand
away, she stared down at the table. "The court
is too fashionable a place for me. My husband
may come, if he so desires."

"We cannot believe that any man would
willingly desert your bed, even for our court.
We shall have to command your presence,
perhaps," he said softly, with a very sly smile.

She was so desperate for an end to this impertinent stroking of her leg, she cast a pleading glance at her husband, hoping he wasn't
too enamored of the obvious and earthy
charms of Mistress Winters to see his wife's
distress.

Fortunately, at that precise moment, Richard
looked at his wife, who sat as stiff and upright
as a stone pillar.

He struggled to ignore the sensation of Mistress Winters's heavy breast as she pressed
against his arm. Elissa Longbourne must be
made of ice to sit so when it was obvious that
Charles was exerting himself to be charming
and make her feel important at court. Their
sovereign could be a very delightful companion, and most women would be flattered.

Charles raised his goblet to his lips.

Where the devil was his other hand?

Richard felt as if he had been struck on the

head by a falling limb. The king was fondling his wife's leg! "Charles!"

His Majesty turned to Richard with a shocked expression, as if Richard had suddenly yelled an obscenity.

"Sir Richard?" Charles inquired, by his expression not at all amused at the way Richard had just dared to address him.

Richard tried to contain his temper, especially when he saw both of Charles's hands above the table. "Forgive me, sire. I am rather anxious about my earldom."

"Ah, yes!" Charles sighed, apparently mollified. "Lord Clarendon has the papers at hand, which we shall sign in the morning."

Mistress Winters giggled and leaned against Richard even more. "It will be quite a night, I'm sure," she murmured, her wine-soaked breath hot on his cheek.

Richard ignored her and watched the king's hand slip beneath the table again. He knew the king was not by nature a jealous man, but he could be possessive, especially of a new mistress. So Richard cleared his throat, momentarily catching Charles's attention.

Then, as if he were unaware of that Charles was looking his way, Richard slowly lifted Mistress Winters's hand and kissed it, letting his lips linger on her perfumed skin as long as he could stand it.

The stupid woman giggled again and batted

her eyes, yet she made no effort to take her hand away.

"Perhaps it would be best if the newly wedded couple sat together," the king proposed.

Richard gave him a wide-eyed, innocent look. "Majesty?"

"Here, sit by your wife. You may regale her with tales of your past."

"As you wish, sire."

Obediently, Richard exchanged places with the king.

And then, with a satisfied little grin, he put his hand lightly upon his wife's knee. "Did you miss me, sweet?"

"Take your hand from me," she demanded quietly. "Or should I be grateful you only grabbed my knee and nothing else, even though we are surrounded by a crowd of people?"

"Am I to understand from this reaction that you countenance such liberties only from the king?"

"I did not want him to do it, either, but I knew no way to make him stop."

"You say, 'Stop fondling me, sire.'"

She gave him a sour look. "Thank you for the advice. Stop fondling me, sir."

"This does not bode well for this evening's nuptials," Richard remarked evenly as he obeyed. "I have every right to touch you, since we are husband and wife."

"Do not remind me." She gave him a

pointed, sidelong glance. "Or should I address you as 'my lord'? Perhaps your sudden elevation to the rank of earl is intended to encourage you to bring me back to London, where I will be forced to endure more humiliating experiences at the hands of the king or others at court."

Richard's eyes flashed. "My *sudden elevation* is a reward for loyal service to the king."

Elissa remained silent, and took a drink of wine herself.

"Where is your son?"

"He is at Mr. Harding's."

Richard gave her a coolly measuring look. "How handy. Lawyer and nursery maid all in one. 'Tis enough to make a man wonder what other services such an accommodating fellow would provide."

"You are disgusting!" Elissa retorted between clenched teeth. "But you are quite right. He is much more than a lawyer to me."

Elissa was too angry and upset to note the expression that came to Richard's eyes.

"He is my friend," she continued, "and a good, kind gentleman who treats me with the utmost courtesy and respect, which is something you and these other *ornaments* of the court could not possibly comprehend."

"I am shocked, then, you have not married him."

"I do not want to be married to anyone."

Richard ran his impertinent gaze over her.

"That would be a pity and a waste."

"How is it that *you* are not already married? It appears many ladies here would be only too anxious to be your bride."

"I could not afford a wife."

"I cannot afford a husband."

His eyes gleamed in the candlelight. "I shall have to earn my keep, then?"

"If you can."

"Oh, I can, my dear, and I will."

She flushed and tried to ignore any implication in his deep, seductive voice or dark, passionate eyes. "How? By writing?"

"When we journey into Leicester, I shall not write anymore," he replied, rather abruptly businesslike.

Momentarily confused by the change, she nevertheless regarded him skeptically. "Indeed? You will give up your fame?"

"I will gladly give up what I did out of necessity, since it will no longer be necessary."

"And how will you find Leicester after London, I wonder? We shall all be too dull for you, I'm sure."

She did not doubt he would find the countryside boring—and her, too, probably, after his fame in London and life among the courtiers, which was perfectly fine. She had no desire to live the kind of supposedly exciting, indulgent existence he did.

"The country life will be a pleasant change, if nothing else," he replied, regarding her with a cool smile which unaccountably seemed to raise her temperature.

Or perhaps it was the close confines of the Banqueting House and the multitude of people in it that were responsible for making her perspire as if she were under a midsummer's sun.

"Richard, Mistress Winters confides she is confused by your new play, charming though it is," the king said loudly enough for all to hear. "Will you have the goodness to explain it to her?"

"Delighted, Majesty," Richard replied.

In spite of his ready agreement, as he shoved back his chair, he muttered under his breath, "It would take that woman an eternity to understand anything except lovemaking."

"Like most of the court, I imagine," Elissa added in a mutter of her own.

To her surprise, her husband's lips twisted into a wry smile.

"I'faith, madam," he whispered, bending toward her so that only she could hear, "I would keep such opinions to yourself, lest you find yourself in the Tower. Again, a most disastrous way to spend a wedding night and not at all what I desire."

Chapter 5

If these silly, giggling, drunken women didn't leave this bedchamber soon, Elissa thought, she would scream. She had put up with their unwelcome escort from the Banqueting House to the bridal chamber, and they were supposed to assist her in her preparations for retiring. Instead, they talked and joked about the activities to come and made disgustingly rude speculations about Richard Blythe's physical attributes.

The ladies of the court also seemed far more intent on talking about the various other noblemen who had been in attendance, and their looks and their habits and who had noticed whom, and what they had said to each other than on helping her.

The exception was Mistress Winters. She didn't do anything except stare in rapt fascination at the large brocade-curtained bed in

the gaudily decorated room near the king's
apartments.

Elissa felt as if she were in a brothel, not a
palace.

Not that she had ever been in a brothel.
However, she could easily imagine that the
atmosphere would be similar, if not the furnishings.

"Thank you. Now you all may leave," she
declared.

Astonishingly, she was impertinently
hushed by a young woman in a grotesque
gown of the most brilliant and bilious green
Elissa had ever seen. Another young woman
whose name Elissa couldn't recall staggered to
the door and opened it a crack. She was so
drunk, Elissa expected her to collapse if she let
go of the latch.

"I will tell you when they're coming," she
slurred in a lascivious whisper.

Mistress Winters finally roused herself from
her blissful contemplation of the palatial bed.

"Let me help you with your lacings," she
said, moving behind Elissa.

"I think I can—"

Mistress Winters ignored Elissa's protest.
"Odd's fish, madam, you must be very hot in
this gown."

She took hold of the knot at the back of
Elissa's dress and almost yanked Elissa off her
feet. "Not so hot as you'll be in a little while,
of course, but very hot indeed!"

The women laughed uproariously while Elissa maintained a dignified silence.

"Such an unusual choice of color for a bridal gown."

"I am a widow."

"Not anymore!" Mistress Winters declared gaily, eliciting more giggles. "And with such a husband, your previous one will soon be forgotten."

"I shall never be able to forget Mr. Longbourne," Elissa muttered truthfully.

The young woman at the door started to slip, until Mistress Winters's next pronouncement made her straighten as abruptly as if she were a marionette being pulled from above.

"Minette Sommerall refused to perform tonight, I hear. In Sir Richard's play, that is. Claimed she was ill—but we know better, don't we?" She poked Elissa in the back. "She'll find another man soon enough, I should think. She won't pretend to kill herself like his other mistress did."

Elissa stiffened.

"Oh, have I said something wrong?" Mistress Winters asked innocently.

The other women exchanged amused glances.

A rather plump woman whose rounded bodice displayed more of her breasts than good taste would permit anywhere except the court stumbled toward Elissa, then tugged at her veil like a fishwife spotting a bargain on a tinker's cart.

"You'll tear it," Elissa admonished, reaching up to take it off herself.

"Ladies, I will undress alone," she commanded in a tone of finality that was always effective with her servants.

Mistress Winters grinned and shook her head, making her cosmetic powder crack like aged porcelain. "Oh, no, my lady," she said with a throaty chortle. "We must wait until the groom comes. To do otherwise would be unseemly."

"Very unseemly," the woman at the door echoed.

Elissa sighed. If they would not leave, she would simply pretend they were not there. With that in mind, she began to remove her dress herself.

"Here, let me take . . ." Mistress Winters offered, grabbing the skirt.

"I shall do it," Elissa snapped.

She stepped out of her dress and laid it on a nearby chair. Clad in her chemise and petticoat, she quickly removed her shoes. Despite the warmth of the room, the polished floor was cool on her stockinged feet as she wiggled out of her petticoat.

"Your chemise is only linen," Mistress Winters noted with obvious disappointment as she took the petticoat.

Elissa didn't care that her garment wasn't

silk or satin. She'd had such a garment once, and she had burned it a week after her wedding.

Paying the women no heed, she yanked the combs from her hair so that it fell loose about her shoulders and tumbled in a mass of waves to her waist.

She heard some of the women suck in their breath and permitted herself one small moment of vanity, for she was proud of her thick hair.

The young woman at the door suddenly staggered backward, nearly colliding with Mistress Winters. "They're coming! I hear them!"

At nearly the same moment, the door flew open and a half-naked, bootless Sir Richard careered into the room, sliding to a halt on the polished floor.

Behind him lurched a group of equally drunken courtiers like some kind of debauched band of merry men, led by the king himself. She also spotted servants bearing what looked like trays of food and carafes of wine.

Elissa stared at the man who was now her husband. The skin of his muscular upper body seemed to glow in the candlelight. His black hair was wildly disheveled as if he were some kind of savage, and his face flushed. She did not think it was shame or embarrassment that accounted for that; more likely, it was wine.

She was likewise flushed, and she knew why the hot blood coursed through her body. If he was not ashamed by such a display of naked flesh before all these women, she was embarrassed for him.

And then she remembered she was only wearing her chemise and stockings.

"What ho!" Charles cried. "The bride is not abed?"

Elissa scrambled under the covers. She nearly fell right out again, for the sheets were of unfamiliar and very slippery satin.

She managed to sit and pulled the heavy coverings up to her chin, noting that Mistress Winters stood with the king, while Sir Richard . . .

The groom was at the foot of the bed, regarding her with an annoyingly inscrutable expression.

"Come, man, do your duty!" the king cried, making everyone else in the room laugh. "To the bed!"

Richard glanced over his shoulder at the gang of men behind him, then smiled and bowed to the ladies. "As I am a loyal subject of His Majesty, naturally I shall obey his command."

"And right thankful for it you should be, too!" Charles declared.

"I am, Your Majesty, although just how thankful I shall be still remains to be seen."

Elissa crossed her arms. Then she swallowed hard as Sir Richard slowly—very slowly, like a prowling cat—began to crawl toward her.

"Gad, man, we haven't got all night!" one of the courtiers complained.

"All night?" Elissa whispered, staring at her husband.

He ignored her question and twisted to look over his shoulder. "Is the Duke of Buckingham trying to rush me?" he demanded.

"We all of us would rather be about our own business," the same man retorted, his response drawing a smattering of cheers and vocal agreement from the rest.

"Your Majesty, lords and ladies, gentlemen of the court, I intend to obey the royal command at my own pace, if you please."

Although his features revealed nothing, Sir Richard sounded a little annoyed.

"Come, come, Blythe, you know Villiers has a loose tongue," the king chided.

His Majesty gestured at one of the servants, who stepped forward and began to close the heavy bed curtains. "We envy you, Blythe, and we shall await the stocking."

"What does he mean?" Elissa whispered as her husband sat beside her, his back against the elaborate headboard and his long legs stretched out before him. "What about my stocking?"

As the curtains were pulled to a close by the somber servant, Elissa swallowed hard and tried not to feel entombed. Outside the confines of their bed, she could hear the courtiers and the king laughing and talking. It was as if they were being haunted by lascivious demons.

Then her husband turned to look at her, his features barely visible in the dark. "It is the custom."

"What custom? Why do they not leave us? They are not intending to stay here while . . ." She couldn't bring herself to finish.

"Yes, they are. Nobody will leave this chamber until I throw your stocking to signify that we have consummated the marriage."

"They can't stay!"

"They can and they will. Charles is the king, after all, and what is our humiliation when it amuses the king?"

"It is too . . . too medieval!" she protested.

"Although I agree with you, I cannot command Charles to leave our bedchamber, and while I am not in favor of obligatory marriages myself, we are wed at the king's command. Therefore, I intend to make the best of this somewhat awkward situation."

He shifted closer and his voice dropped to a sultry whisper. "They will be quieter when they have had more wine."

What kind of man would make love with a crowd in the room? To be sure, the bed curtains provided some privacy, but not nearly enough.

Her mind swiftly envisioned all that was to come. He would thrust himself inside her regardless of her pain and discomfort, roughly caressing her body as if she felt nothing. He would say no word, only breathe heavily on her face until he grunted with release. Afterward, he would roll over and snore.

She tried to steel herself to endure the assault—but she had been free of that torture for too long to simply submit. "Are you then a trained dog that can perform upon its master's command?"

He moved back a little. "You find me repulsive?"

"No! Yes! That is, I don't want to make love to you."

"We are merely pawns in the king's game, so there is nothing to be done except obey his orders," Sir Richard murmured as he began to squirm.

"What are you doing?"

"I am removing my breeches."

"Why?"

"In order to make love with my wife. Come, madam, given that you have had a son, there is no need to act the unwilling, ignorant virgin."

"Perhaps you have been around actresses so much, you can no longer tell when a reaction is feigned or genuine. I assure you, Sir Richard, I am not *acting* anything."

"Would you rather disobey the king and risk his displeasure?"

"I would rather have other choices."

Ignoring her remark, her husband sat up and bundled his breeches into a large ball. He listened to the now-thankfully-hushed voices beyond the bed curtains. Then, leaning over her, he opened the curtains and threw his breeches across the room.

Charles's rich laugh boomed. "A most excellent toss, Blythe!" he cried. "You hit Villiers right in the head."

"A thousand pardons, Buckingham. My wife was toying with me at the time."

Elissa gasped and flushed hotly as the courtiers snickered.

"We are glad to hear you are making progress," the king remarked. "Now, who has brought the cards? Shall we play cribbage?"

Ignoring his beautiful wife, who apparently wanted nothing at all to do with him, Richard moved back to his side of the bed and contemplated the horrible irony of his situation. Minette and his other former mistresses might consider it just, perhaps, that he should wed a woman who apparently found him utterly unappealing, while he burned with passionate desire.

As Elissa had stood before him clad only in her thin chemise, her bounteous hair flowing to her waist just as he had imagined, he had thought her the most beautiful, desirable woman he had ever seen.

There had also been a virginal vulnerability about her distinctly at odds with her surroundings and company. Given her subsequent behavior, however, he feared her vulnerability might have been completely imaginary.

And since she had a child, she was most certainly no virgin.

Well, that was something to be thankful for, he thought, his sardonic sense of humor coming to his aid. And there were many worse commands the king could make. Had he not, after all, pledged his sword to the king's service? Of course, he had had a metal blade in mind at the time.

He would simply have to begin at the beginning.

He reached out and ran his hand up her slender arm. He could feel her tension, and his caress did not lessen it. "You do not have to be so stiff, madam. I should be, but not you."

"Tell me, Sir Richard," she said, his attempt at humor obviously completely missing the mark, "do you like to have an audience for everything?"

"I agree that having company in such close proximity is not conducive to intimacy, yet they cannot see us and if we are quiet, will hear little, unless my prowess—"

"I will be quiet. Just do what you must and be done with it!"

"Your current attitude is hardly encouraging."

"Since when has a husband required encouragement? Or a man of your ilk?"

"My ilk?"

"Your experience, then, or your many conquests."

"If one's alleged opponent surrenders eagerly, can it be called a conquest?"

"Are you always so talkative, sir?" Elissa demanded with exasperation. "Or is this what a playwright considers a necessary prologue, like that before the play begins in earnest? If so, given that I am not an ignorant virgin, you may dispense with it."

"My sweet," he whispered, inching closer, "there is no such thing as an unnecessary prologue when I am the writer. Allow me to demonstrate how necessary—and pleasurable—a prologue can be."

Elissa realized he was getting under the covers. In another moment, his naked body would be beside hers.

In another moment, it was.

"There is no need to be so anxious, wife," he whispered. He took her hand, but did not kiss it. Instead, he pressed it against his warm, bare chest. She felt his taut muscles and the beating of his heart. "You have nothing to fear from me."

"I am not afraid of you."

"I am glad to hear you say so."

He lifted her hand to his chin so that her fingertips rested against his soft lips, while the stubble of his beard was like sand against the rest of her fingers.

It was a simple thing and yet strangely exciting.

Too exciting. She had loved foolishly once; she would not allow herself to believe herself in love or be swept away by what had to be lust.

"No, do not draw back," he insisted softly, gently grabbing her wrist so that his lips were still against her fingertips. "You smell of lavender."

"We store our clothing with lavender," she replied matter-of-factly.

"Ah." He shifted closer. "Yes, the delightful scent is stronger on your undergarment."

She broke away, trying to see him in the dark. "What are you doing?"

"The prologue."

He ran his fingers along the neckline of her chemise, grazing her skin ever so lightly. Her skin seemed to burn where he touched her.

"No silk or satin or lace?" he whispered, as if he were truly interested. "Not even at the hem?"

She tried to subdue a gasp when she felt his other hand on her leg. He slowly moved it upward.

"I put no store in such frippery," she said weakly.

"A very utilitarian philosophy," he observed as he took his hand away from her limb.

Of course she was relieved.

She started when she felt his breath warm on her cheek, his lips obviously a mere fraction of an inch away. "Unfortunately, that garment is a hindrance at present—unless you would prefer to leave it on, if you find that more exciting."

Before she could answer—if indeed, she could have found the words to express her surprise that he would want her naked, something William Longbourne had never suggested the whole of their unhappily married life—he pulled her to him and kissed her.

He kissed as she had always imagined a man in love should kiss the woman he adored, with passion and tenderness in thrilling alliance as if he were gently persuading her to love him, rather than demanding.

As if he would ask rather than commandeer, share rather than horde. As if he wanted her to experience all the excitement he did, or maybe even more.

What kind of equality was this? What kind of freedom was he offering?

She broke the kiss, wanting to think—needing to think, or else she would succumb to the powerful spell of his kisses and caresses.

"What is the matter?"

She decided he was, perhaps, deserving of an explanation. "My husband never kissed me when he loved me."

"Did you not love him?"

Elissa's defenses came to the fore. "I meant when he made love to me."

"And I meant, did you not make love with him?"

"Of course I did. I bore him a child."

"No, madam, you misunderstand," he said very gently, and with a new understanding in his voice. "I should ask, did you enjoy making love with him?"

"It is a wife's duty to submit to her husband."

"And so, since I am now your husband, if I were to throw myself upon you and take my pleasure of you as if you were a cheap whore, you would not complain?"

A cheap whore.

Although she had never put the feeling into words, that was exactly how William Longbourne had made her feel.

"Yet, as you say, you bore him a child. Everyone knows that for a child to be conceived, the woman has to be passionately aroused," he said.

"Every *man* believes it, and it is a very convenient way to contradict a charge of rape if the woman subsequently bears a child, but surely I am not the only woman who knows

otherwise. I assure you, sir, I derive no pleasure from the act of love."

"Yet," Richard murmured, silently cursing
the late William Longbourne for a disgusting,
selfish lout.

But he was also thankful that he now knew
how to proceed with her: with patience, with
every subtle method he could recall to arouse
a woman, and with even more self-control
than he usually practiced. He would ensure
that she enjoyed the act of love as she never
had before.

But first, he would get rid of the king and
his courtiers and their ladies.

"Give me your stocking."

"We have not—"

"Let me throw it to them so they will go
away."

Inadvertently giving him a breathtaking
glimpse of her naked leg, she eagerly took off
her stocking, balled it in her hand and gave it
to him.

"Your Majesty," he declared as if lacking
breath, a state not totally feigned, "I am most
extremely grateful."

With that, he leaned over her again, opened
the bed curtains a little and threw the stocking
toward the part of the room where most of the
noise originated.

As Richard shifted back to his side of the
bed, she realized he was not nearly so heavy
as William Longbourne had been. The pres-

sure of his thighs was not unbearable and she realized that whatever the women had thought concerning his virility, they had apparently been somewhat conservative.

Suddenly, and most unexpectedly, the king thrust his head between the bed curtains.

"Odd's fish, Blythe!" he growled, a look of such displeasure on his face, Elissa could scarce believe this was the same Merry Monarch. "Do you take us for a fool? Are we deaf? You have been whispering in here like a pair of spies exchanging information. Now go to it, and don't throw this stocking again until you have made this beautiful lady your wife. Or God help us, we shall take back your new title and throw you both in the Tower until we are pleased to release you! We shall have no one seeking an annulment on the grounds of nuptial rights denied."

Chapter 6

The king vanished as abruptly as he had appeared.

Richard and Elissa sat in stunned silence for a moment before Richard grimly said, "Was that your clever plan, madam?"

"No!" She took a deep breath that did nothing to calm her dismay. "I confess such a scheme never occurred to me—although I rather wish it had. *You* are supposed to be the clever one."

"Alas, I must have been distracted by the beauty of the bride, for I did not think of anything at all save to obey my sovereign."

"Oh, yes, that is all you thought about," she remarked sarcastically. "Not a title or any other reward."

He moved closer still.

"You have caught me in a lie, my dear," he confessed softly. "I have been thinking of

other things that perhaps may also be classi-
fied as a reward."

"Such as?"

With a low chuckle, he put his arms around
her and gently pulled her to him for a long
and lingering, tender and promising kiss.

He half-expected her to pull away and slap
his face—yet she did not.

Amazingly, after a moment's unresponsive-
ness, she yielded.

Her simpleton of a husband had indeed
been a fool not to kiss her. Why, she had the
most perfect lips, both firm and yet softly pli-
ant.

Then, as suddenly as the king had interrupted them, he realized she was doing more
than simply yielding to the inevitable. She
clutched his shoulders and leaned into him,
her desire as obvious as his own.

With mild insistence, craving more, almost
dreading that this was some sort of trick intended to arouse him before she rejected him,
he insinuated his tongue into her mouth.

No trick. No sudden pulling away as their
tongues entwined, doing the old, old dance.

And best of all, no sense that he was merely
being used because he was handsome, or famous, or dangerously exciting, a thing to be
discussed in the same tone as a fine horse or
clever dog or expensive objet d'art.

With his left arm still about her, he ran his

hand through her glorious, luxurious hair. It was as soft as a rabbit's fur and smelled of wildflowers.

A low moan filled the air between them, and Richard realized it was his.

With less patience, his hand left her hair. He must and would taste her satin-soft skin that stretched so enticingly over her collar bone.

His hand encountered her chemise. He pushed it lower, then slipped his hand beneath.

"I will not hurt you," he murmured as he caressed her breast, lightly brushing his thumb across her nipple as she drew in a sharp breath.

He felt her relax again and at the same time, he was aware of his own growing passionate need.

In spite of that, he must be patient. She must enjoy this, and she must be ready when he took her. He would not have any kind of pain associated with their intimacy.

Then he nearly gasped himself when she began to stroke his shoulders and move her hands down his back. Her touch was light, almost tentative, as if she wasn't sure he would like what she was doing.

"Yes, my sweet," he encouraged, kissing her cheek, her jaw and neck. "Do not stop."

He tugged her chemise lower, then laid her on her back before capturing her nipple with his mouth, his tongue lightly flicking.

She began to pant, and he continued to taste
and tease, using his lips and delicate touches
until she arched and squirmed with desire.

It was not yet time.

He stroked her bare leg, and then the one
that was still encased in a stocking, moving
slowly upward toward her honor.

Suddenly, she sat up. Dismay and disappointment flooded through him—until she
writhed out of her chemise and tossed it toward the foot of the bed.

He recognized that this was no vain gesture
intended to show off her splendid body, no
planned move in a game of seduction.

It was the most exciting moment of his life,
until she reached for him and pulled him into
her willing arms, robbing him of all self-
restraint.

He had to take this incredible woman now.

There was no need for him to wait, for Elissa
had never been so passionately excited in her
life. Despite her futile attempt to feel nothing
when he touched her, she had never known a
caress so arousing, a kiss so tender and yet so
inflaming.

Were all these things what a husband was
supposed to do? How much she had missed!
How much more she wanted to discover!

Hot need coursed through her body, engen-
dered by his words, his kisses, and his touch.
Burning, she had to discard her garment. She
had to be naked. She brazenly wanted him to

touch and stroke and caress her everywhere and anywhere.

With zealous passion, she ran her hands over Richard's young and muscular body from his broad shoulders, down his back to his taut buttocks and slender hips. William Longbourne had been old and going to fat, something he had hidden well with his finely tailored clothing.

There was no need for disguise with this man.

Boldly, she moved her hand another place. He groaned softly as she discovered, with no true surprise, that Sir Richard Blythe was a very virile man.

With no prompting from him, she parted her legs and pulled him on top of her. She couldn't wait anymore.

"Oh, sweet heaven, yes!" he moaned as he thrust inside her warm, moist honor.

No more coherent thoughts came to her as she wrapped her legs around his slender waist. With strong, powerful thrusts he took her, and made her his wife in the eyes of God and man.

Excitement and tension took control of her. She writhed beneath him in an ecstasy of tension, until, with a cry that was both shocked and triumphant, the tension burst.

With a low growl rising in his throat and resounding in her ear, Richard pushed hard once more. Then, sweat-slicked, he collapsed against her.

She felt him still throbbing inside her before the rhythmic pulse slowly subsided.

She kissed the top of his head and ran her hand over his dark, curling hair.

"Odd's fish, I do believe a stocking should come sailing forth at any moment."

Elissa gasped at the sound of the king's voice.

"Zounds, I had forgotten," Richard muttered as he slowly pulled away and sat up.

"So did I," she confessed, pulling the sheet over herself, for she would not put it past the king to shove his head between the curtains again.

"You did?" he asked, genuine, almost boyish pleasure in his voice.

"I did."

He chuckled softly. He had a very nice chuckle. "Your limb, if you please, madam."

She sat back, lifted her leg slightly and put her foot in his lap.

"Have a care, my sweet, or tonight's bout may be our last."

"I'm sorry," she replied with a hint of laughter in her voice.

"So you should be," he muttered merrily. "I have guarded those particular valuables well, and I will not lose them now, no matter how charming and beautiful their destroyer."

She bit her lip as he slowly removed her

stocking. He made even this incredibly exciting.

"You have exceptionally lovely limbs, wife."

"Do I?"

"You do, and I am a connoisseur of such things."

Of course he was.

And of course he was an expert at lovemaking, given the number of mistresses he had had. Still had.

Perhaps they all learned of his "prologues," and became like warm clay in his hands, soft and pliable and willing to do whatever he wanted. Willing to pay any price to have him in their bed again.

Perhaps he was counting on those very skills to pry away what was rightfully hers, and to steal what was her son's.

She sat up, grabbed her stocking from him and threw it through the curtains. A boisterous cheer sounded on the other side.

"Come, ladies and gentlemen, let us retire," the king said. "We shall not let Sir Richard and his bride have all the sport tonight!"

"I thought I was the impatient one," Richard noted dryly as the courtiers noisily departed.

Still clutching the sheets over her breasts, she searched for her chemise in the bundle of coverings at the foot of the bed.

Richard gently took hold of her arm. "Come back to me, my sweet. Now we are alone."

"I want my chemise."

She felt him shift and, with a glance over her shoulder, saw that he was sitting up against the headboard again.

She went back to searching.

"I don't know why you need it. I shall keep you warm."

"I don't want to lose it."

"Ah." He remained silent, then she realized the sheet was slowly being tugged away from her.

She yanked it back and held it over her breasts. "What are you . . . ?"

He leaned forward and pulled open the bed curtain. A shaft of moonlight illuminated his handsome, smiling face, his boyishly disheveled hair and his most unboyish body. "I want to see you."

"You have," she muttered as she resumed her search.

"You sound very peevish all of a sudden, my sweet."

She finally found her chemise and quickly drew it over her head. Then, still covered by the sheet, she pulled it down over her body.

"I'm tired," she said, moving back to her place and trying to ignore his puzzled frown.

She lay down as far away from him as she could get. Otherwise, he might be tempted to make love with her again, and she might be tempted to let him.

Her strategy didn't work, for he nestled beside her. Despite her chemise, she could feel the length of him just as well as if she had been naked.

She would need a chemise of iron to prevent that, she decided grimly as she willed herself not to pay any attention.

"I am exhausted, too," he murmured as he lifted a lock of her hair and rubbed it between his fingers, "but most agreeably so. Tell me, my sweet wife, when do you wish to leave for Leicester?"

"At once."

"I do not think the middle of night would be convenient for anybody."

"I meant tomorrow, if possible."

Richard thought of his play, which had just begun its run. The players didn't need his supervision anymore, surely, and Minette would recover from her "ailment" as soon as another man, preferably a rich one, asked her to a late supper.

He thought of the people he would leave behind, including the loyal Foz, who could always come to visit Leicester. Indeed, the man had no other calls upon his time.

New excitement filled him as he thought of leaving London for his family home with his bride.

"I shall have to get my few pitiful goods and chattels together. Will after the noon suit you? We could get a fair bit out of the city before dark."

"That will suit me perfectly."

"Sleep well, then, my sweet," he whispered contentedly as he rolled onto his side.

In another few moments, he was sound asleep.

While Elissa stared unseeing at the bed curtains.

Hurrying to his cramped lodgings above the cheese shop, Richard took the stairs two at a time. As he did so, he rejoiced that this was the last time he would have to endure the stench of cheese as he tried to sleep, or listen to the incessant cries of the street-sellers, or have to endure the coal smoke, offal, and other detritus of life in London.

He also thought of his wife, still sleeping peacefully in Whitehall Palace.

How pretty and charming she looked as she slumbered, the pale light of dawn illuminating her face. Her luscious lips had been parted ever so slightly and it had taken a very great effort not to kiss her. He had not because he had not wanted to wake her when they had a long journey ahead.

So instead, he had contented himself with watching her as he dressed as quietly as if he were a housebreaker with the occupants all at home.

He would have to write to the king to express his thanks for bestowing such a woman upon him. Never had he enjoyed such passionate lovemaking, although enjoyed seemed

far too pale a word for the excitement and fulfillment he had experienced with Elissa.

He opened his door and halted in some confusion as Foz, attired in the most vibrant violet
jacket and breeches Richard had ever seen,
turned to face him. His friend yanked his
abundantly plumed hat from his head and
made a little bow of greeting.

"Dear, faithful Foz!" Richard cried, his eyes
growing somewhat better accustomed to the
sartorial splendor before him. "I might have
known you would come to bid me farewell."
His brow furrowed. "You look very distressed.
What has happened?"

Staring at the floor and shifting like a
naughty boy, Foz ran the large white plume
of his hat through his gloved fingers.

"Come, what is it?" Richard demanded. "I
am in some haste."

Foz shrugged. "I simply wish," he began in
a low mutter, "that is, I am sorry that . . ."

He suddenly raised his face and forcefully
declared, "Ods bodikins, I hate marriages!
What's a fellow to do when all his friends get
married and leave him?"

Richard subdued a grin as he went to pull
his battered wooden chest, which had stood
him in good stead all the years in Europe,
from beneath the ropes of his bed. "I would
say, my friend, that he had better get married
himself."

"That's easy advice for a man like you to offer," Foz mumbled.

With a petulant frown on his round face, he went to the narrow window and leaned against the sill.

"A man like me who was ordered into marriage by the king?"

"No. A handsome man like you who has more women flocking around him than bees around a honeycomb. You could have been married ten—no, a hundred times!—by now, if you wanted to."

Richard opened the lid of the chest, then straightened. "You could have been married many times by now yourself."

Foz made a derisive grunt.

"You could have. After all, you're rich, you're titled, you possess the finest garments and wigs of any man at court, and you are quite the nicest fellow there, too."

Still Foz did not look mollified.

"What have I said that is not true?" Richard demanded.

Foz shrugged again. "I thank you for your compliments—but I also know this: You have lost estate and fortune, you wear nothing except plain, dull black, you do not even sport a wig, you can be shockingly rude, and yet women love you. You are handsome, Richard, and I am not, and all the nicety in the world cannot change that. Indeed, I would give up my entire wardrobe to have even a portion of your looks."

Richard sat on his bed and regarded his friend. "Foz, there are many women who could care deeply for a man like you, and I am not talking about your money and your clothes." Richard thought of Elissa. "You cannot judge all women by those we encounter at court or the theater."

"Well, where else is a fellow to meet women?"

Richard rose. "I have it. Give me some time to get settled at Blythe Hall—say, a fortnight or two—and then come visit us. I am sure there must be some society there into which we can introduce you."

He smiled conspiratorially. "And i'faith, my dear friend, I have been seriously wrong about country women. We in the city are the ignorant ones if we assume them all to be homely bumpkins."

"Is that so?" Foz asked, a smile finally lighting his face. "Then you are not displeased with this woman forced upon you?"

Richard began to gather up his paper, quill, and ink to put into the chest. "No, Foz, I am not."

"I am very glad to hear it."

Whistling a jaunty air, Richard continued to pack his few belongings. He paused as he checked the stopper on one of the clay vessels holding ink. "Have you read the marriage settlement? Did you bring it with you? Just relay the pertinent points."

Foz placed his hat on the small, scarred table where Richard had done his writing, sat in the equally scarred chair beside it, and sighed deeply. "Oh, yes, that."

Richard stopped whistling and regarded his friend with puzzlement, for Foz sounded uncharacteristically wary. "What is it?"

"You, um, perhaps you should have read it before signing."

Richard felt the cold finger of dread slide along his spine and settle in the pit of his stomach as he reached for the document Foz now produced. "You were there. You saw that I was not given the chance to do so. What does it say?"

"It says, I'm afraid . . . that is, the way it is written—and very well written, too, I must say—"

"Spit it out, man!" Richard cried, the legal words making no sense at all to him in his agitation.

"You have no rights to anything except to offer advice concerning the management of your stepson's estate."

"*What?* That cannot be!"

"Unless I've read it completely incorrectly, and you and I both know that is hardly likely given my years with that slave-driver Muttlechop, you have no legal rights at all except to give advice when it is requested of you."

Richard sat heavily on the bed and stared at his friend in disbelief. "I know I cannot have the estate back, yet I thought . . . I assumed that I would have control over my wife's money. That is what the king promised."

"That is what the king may have assumed, too, given that is the usual way of things."

"How can they circumvent the bestowing of my wife's goods upon me?" Richard demanded. "She has become my chattel, has she not?"

"She has, but this document states that all her money and moveable goods remain her property, and when she dies, they are to be equally distributed among her children."

Richard fought the anger surging within him at the knavish trickery of his bride and her despicable lawyer. "Children, or child?"

Foz pointed at a line on the parchment. " 'All legitimate issue,' " he quoted.

"Thank God for small mercies," Richard growled. "At least she will not deny an inheritance to whatever children I beget on her."

"I am sorry to be the bearer of such bad tidings, especially when you seemed so happy before," Foz said mournfully.

"By God, I wish I had not set eyes upon that woman and that the king had married her to anyone but me."

"Oh, you cannot mean that," Foz protested. "Why, if he did, you would not be preparing to go home now."

Richard blinked, then looked at Foz. "You have a point, my friend. As you say, I am going home at last. And only a fool would ever trust any woman, especially his wife."

Chapter 7

~~~◦◦~~~

Elissa had not quite finished putting the last few items into the bossed box when she heard the knocking on Mr. Harding's door, followed by the familiar sound of Richard Blythe's deep voice.

"Who is that, Mama?" Will asked, his question muffled from beneath the bed where he was seeking his lost shoe buckle.

"That is Sir Richard Blythe."

"It is?" Will scooted out from the under the bed, his suit dusty and his gaze full of avid excitement as he scrambled to his feet. "The man we met before?"

"Yes."

"Does he have business with Mr. Harding, too?"

"No," she replied, sitting on the bed and patting a place beside her. "Will, come here and listen to me."

She had convinced herself she had enough

time to tell Will that she was married before
they had to leave, and to reveal the identity of
the man the king had commanded her to wed.
She had postponed the moment as long as she
could but couldn't put it off any longer.

"I want to see Sir Richard! Do you suppose
he has his sword with him?"

"I think that very likely. Now, before we go
downstairs, come here."

With a curious expression on his young face,
Will obeyed.

She put her arm around him as he settled
himself on the bed beside her. "I have some
important things to tell you."

"About Sir Richard?"

"Yes, about him." She thought a moment,
wondering how to begin. "When I went to
Whitehall the day we arrived in London—"

"And saw the king?" Will asked, his impatient glance at the door telling her he wanted
to finish this conversation quickly.

"Yes, and saw the king, His Majesty gave
me a royal command."

That got her son's undivided attention. "He
did?"

Elissa nodded. "Yes, he did. He commanded
me to marry."

"To marry?" It was quite clear Will thought
this sort of command beneath a king—and she
could not fault his reaction. "Why would he
do that?"

"Because he can. And the person he ordered

me to marry had something in common with me, so that is also why."

"Who? Who are you to marry?"

Elissa wished she had not left this so late! "Yesterday I became the wife of Richard Blythe. That is why I was not here last night."

Will jumped to his feet and stared at her. "He is my new papa?" he demanded incredulously.

"He is your stepfather, Will, and I do not intend that he shall replace—"

Before she could finish, Will ran out of the room. As she hurried to follow him, she heard his feet pounding down the stairs.

She lifted her skirts and hurried down the steps and into the withdrawing room located behind Mr. Harding's offices. It was not a large room, and the small mullioned window overlooking an even smaller yard did not let in much light. The oak wainscoting was dark with age, the plaster yellowed, and the draperies ancient. The furnishings were likewise old and unlovely, but then, Mr. Harding was not the kind of man to care much about such things.

Elissa skittered to a halt and saw Will gazing at Richard with undisguised admiration. His hands clasped behind his thin back, Mr. Mollipont, Mr. Harding's middle-aged and deferential clerk, seemed equally fascinated by the cavalier playwright as he stood by the smoke-stained hearth.

What was there not for them to admire about Richard's tall, muscular frame? Or the small smile of cool composure on his darkly handsome face? His black hair curled against his powerful and broad shoulders, and he stood with the easy, natural grace of a large cat, his expression nearly as inscrutable.

As he continued to regard her with his dark eyes, she suddenly had the uncomfortable sensation that he had learned all her secrets in one night.

"Ah, here you are," he remarked. "When I returned to Whitehall with my baggage, you were not there."

She would not permit him to act the wounded party over this particular point. "When I awakened, you were gone without leaving any information as to your whereabouts," she replied just as calmly, "so I told the servants where *you* could find *me*, and here I am."

She turned to Mr. Mollipont. "Where is Mr. Harding?"

"Indeed, yes, where is Mr. Harding?" Richard seconded. "There are some matters about the marriage settlement I wish to have clarified."

Elissa looked at him with barely disguised alarm, for despite the evenness of his remarks, there was intimidation in his tone and, she now realized, barely disguised anger in his eyes.

"Mr. Harding has gone to court, my lord," Mr. Mollipont offered. "He'll be there all day."

"How convenient," Richard replied. "I suppose I shall have to ask my wife my questions."

Elissa was no coward, yet she would have preferred to have Mr. Harding answer all questions concerning the marriage settlement, even if he had ensured that she knew and understood the terms completely.

"I have not yet finished packing for the journey home," she replied with a hint of defiance. "Since I was compelled to sign the settlement before reading it, and thus render it binding, I daresay my questions can wait until we are in our coach."

"Our coach?"

"Yes, a coach and four are our wedding gift from the king."

To be sure, their own coach would make traveling more comfortable and they would likely be home all the faster—but to be cooped up with Richard and grilled on the terms of the marriage settlement without hope of escape . . .

"Mama says you are my new papa," Will declared.

Richard answered before she could correct him. "I am your mama's new husband, and so merely your stepfather, unfortunately."

Elissa came forward and put her arm around her son. "That is what I told him."

"But you will come home with us? You are going to live with us? Will you teach me to fight with a sword?"

"Will!" Elissa cried, part of her relieved that he wasn't angry and upset, the other part perturbed that he was so obviously delighted.

"Yes, I am going home with you to where I spent my boyhood. Yes, I shall live with you since I am your mama's husband." He glanced at Elissa and that simple glance seemed to set the blood dancing in her veins.

Mercifully, he stopped looking at her and turned his attention back to Will. "And I will teach you to fight with a sword as a gentleman should—when your mama agrees it is time."

Richard settled himself on a plain wooden chair. "The coach is in the mews even now. I told the driver I wanted to leave at once, so he is undoubtedly cursing us with every coarse expression at his disposal for taking so long. Therefore, I suggest you make haste, wife."

Elissa knew she was being dismissed, and while his patronizing tone bothered her greatly, she thought it wiser to do as he said. "Come, Will."

"I don't want to go!" her son protested, shrugging off her maternal arm. "I want to stay with him!"

"I'm sure Sir Richard doesn't want to be troubled with you."

Richard slowly got to his feet and if Elissa thought he had seemed intimidating before, she knew now she had seen a pale shadow of the ire of which he was capable. "He will be no trouble at all to me, and indeed, I welcome an opportunity to get to know this fine young man, as I would hope he would have the opportunity to get to know me without being prejudiced against me."

Elissa flushed hotly beneath her husband's gaze. Nevertheless, considering what she knew of Richard Blythe, her mind rebelled against leaving Will alone with him. It was not that she feared any harm from one meeting; it was rather that she would guard her child's mind from an infatuation that might prove harmful in later years. "I need Will's help."

"Mr. Mollipont will surely do," Richard replied.

Elissa looked at her son and saw his suddenly fearful and uncertain glances from his mother to his stepfather.

"I promise not to teach him fencing while you are gone from the room," Richard said, his tone genially bemused.

As Will visibly relaxed, it occurred to her that the change in his tone was meant to reassure her son. She could not do less.

"Very well, he may stay," she agreed.

After all, she told herself as she joined Mr. Mollipont at the door and exited, it would be merely a few moments.

"Tell me about the battles you've been in!"

Will demanded excitedly after his mother had departed.

Richard turned his attention to the sturdy, inquisitive, obviously bright lad before him. "Battles?"

"Yes! Weren't you in battles?"

Richard shook his head. "No. I was too young to fight in the Civil War."

"But you were with the king."

"I joined the king in exile, when the battles were long over."

Except the battles for money, which this lad would not want to hear about. There had been domestic battles before that, of course, but he preferred to forget those.

Apparently Will was not about to give up. "Then tell me about your duels."

"They are not very exciting."

"You *have* dueled?" Will inquired dubiously, his brow furrowing with suspicion.

Even though the person questioning him was only a child, Richard's pride was pricked by any doubt of his willingness to defend his honor. "Yes, I have."

"Well, then, tell me about them," Will said, good humor restored.

"Very well," Richard replied, "I shall tell you all about them on our journey."

That would be as good a time as any to instill in this young man-child that duels were no more great and glorious than two stags locking horns over a doe, even when honor was at stake.

And if it would also take his mind from his distractingly lovely, wily wife while they shared such close quarters, so much the better.

His disgruntled thoughts took quite a different turn, for Will gave his stepfather an admiring and happy smile.

Suddenly, a pang of paternal longing struck Richard harder than any blow he had ever received. He would give almost anything to have a son as fine as this boy.

As he regarded the trusting, upturned face, he vowed he would protect and nurture this child and ensure that Will's life and his memories were untarnished and untainted.

Unlike his own.

Elissa hurried to complete the packing. She did not want to leave Will too long alone with Richard Blythe, with his aura of exotic danger and surprisingly changeable manner.

She hoped Will's presence would dissuade Richard from discussing the settlement on their journey. Unfortunately, as she thought of the look in Richard's eyes, she didn't think this likely.

"There, that's the last one," Mr. Mollipont said, huffing as he pushed down the lid of the large, wooden, leather-covered chest which was all that remained of her baggage. "Now you can have a bit of a rest. You look as overheated as a horse at the Newmarket races, my lady."

He lifted the chest, staggering a bit, and she hurried to help him, but his expression warned her off. "I can manage, my lady," he declared.

"Thank you for your help, Mr. Mollipont."

The older man nodded and departed, leaving Elissa alone to put on her cloak and hood.

Well, she mused, as she looked out the small window, I will be very glad to be out of London and on my way home, at least.

Home. William Longbourne's home. Her home. Will's home. Before that, Richard Blythe's home.

She recalled the day she had noticed the initials carved into the facade of the ornate fireplace in the large hall. It had been done very crudely, as if by a child, and the letters were *R* and *B*—for Richard Blythe, perhaps?

She vividly remembered her husband's cold response to her observation: "If you will find fault with my house, you are welcome to leave it—just as soon as you give me a son."

With pursed lips, Elissa tied the cloak strings about her neck and reminded herself that she had endured many things over the course of the last seven years. If she had survived marriage to William Longbourne and widowhood, surely she could tolerate marriage to Richard Blythe, too.

She went downstairs to join her party in the

withdrawing room, only to find that chamber empty. Reasoning that they must have gone to the mews in preparation for departing, she went out the back entrance and through the gate.

Immediately she spotted Richard standing near a coach, with his arm around Will's shoulder as if they were the best of friends. He was audibly describing the attributes of a very fine, very new, very shiny black vehicle. Nearby, an old man with the gnarled fingers of a driver, clad in a long coat of Lincoln green and muddy boots, leaned against a wall, his arms crossed.

She had not thought about a driver for the king's wedding gift. Now she would have another servant to house, feed, and clothe.

Far more disturbing was the realization that it looked as if her son were now Richard's possession.

Regardless of the dung and muck on the cobblestones beneath her booted feet, she strode toward both them and the magnificent coach. "I trust we are prepared to depart?"

Richard's arm slipped from Will's shoulder as he turned toward her. "If that was the last of the baggage, we are."

"Good."

The coachman pushed himself off the wall while she took hold of Will's hand and helped him inside the coach. She was about to follow him when she felt a hand on her arm.

She immediately recognized the sensation of the length and strength of those specific masculine fingers.

"Are you not going to scrape your feet first? Otherwise, I fear the journey will be most unpleasant."

"Oh."

She did as Richard suggested, dragging the sole of her boots against the stones with more energy than strictly necessary. She would not allow him to befuddle her, she silently vowed.

In another moment she was in the coach, seated beside Will and opposite Richard, who rapped smartly on the roof. The driver called to the horses and with a lurch, the coach began to move. Because of the closeness of the mews, and then the crowded streets, they went at a walk.

Elissa looked out the windows, whose leather coverings were rolled up and tied, and saw Mr. Mollipont waving a farewell. With a forced smile, she also waved good-bye.

"I am hopeful we can make thirty miles today," Richard remarked, crossing his arms leisurely.

"But it is nearly noon," Elissa replied. "Surely that is too far to cover in less than a full day."

"The horses are good, they are fresh, and the day fair. We shall try for thirty, and if we are unsuccessful . . ." He shrugged.

Elissa decided she would not argue the

point, or think about his lackadaisical manner. Obviously he was used to considering only himself. However, traveling with a child allowed no such luxurious selfishness. A hungry, thirsty child was a cranky child.

Elissa turned her attention to her son, whose rapt gaze seemed to find everything outside the coach fascinating. Richard leaned toward the same side of the coach and pointed out the window.

"Do you see that man with the bald head driving the other coach?" he asked. "Dukes have their drivers go without hats, so everybody knows a person of great importance sits inside."

"But what if it starts to rain?"

"What is that to the duke or duchess, as long as everybody knows they are Important Personages?" Richard replied evenly.

"That doesn't seem right."

"I applaud your benevolence, young Master Longbourne. I hardly think it practical, either. The poor man is likely to take a chill or worse, and good drivers in London are hard to find. Why, even the king's coach has had mishaps."

"It has?"

"Yes, and the driver was most fortunate that the king is a forgiving man."

Richard took note of his wife's disgruntled expression at his mention of the king and chose to ignore it. He was trying to keep his mind on a subject other than his spouse while her son was with them. Unfortunately, the jostling of the coach brought his knees in contact with her, or at least her skirts and petticoats. It was a strange sort of half-intimate sensation, and he had to struggle not to imagine how he might proceed if Will were not there.

"Now, do you see that gentleman hurrying inside that shop?" Richard asked. "He is going for a drink of chocolate, which comes from the New World."

"Have you had chocolate?" Will asked eagerly.

"I have, and a more disgusting, bitter drink I have never had the misfortune to taste. They should have left it in the New World, as far as I'm concerned."

With that, and several other observations, Richard amused his wife's son as they left the great city. Finally, however, Will leaned his head against his mother's shoulder and nodded off to sleep.

When Richard was quite sure the boy was sound asleep, he quietly said, "I must commend your lawyer."

Elissa turned a wary eye his way.

"That is an incredible marriage settlement. Tell me, was it his idea or yours to present it under those particular circumstances so that I could not read it beforehand?"

She bristled, yet he didn't care. "For the suddenness of its presentation, you may blame the king," she replied tartly, "since he chose the date and time of our nuptials, not I."

"You might have sent it to my lodgings before I left for Whitehall."

"I did not know where your lodgings were, nor did Mr. Harding," she replied pertly, again turning to look out the window, as if that dismissed the matter.

He leaned forward. "I am sure you could have found out, or come earlier to Whitehall, or sent the document to the theater."

"Mr. Harding had barely finished writing it when it was time to go to Whitehall ourselves."

"He wrote it? Not his clerk?"

"Yes."

"He seems to take a rather personal interest in your affairs."

She regarded him scornfully. "It is clear to me that you cannot comprehend that a man could treat a woman as a respectable client and nothing more. He wrote it himself to save time, if you must know. Mr. Mollipont writes slowly."

"Then the wonderful Heartless Harding should find another clerk."

"Will you stop talking about Mr. Harding in this insolent manner? He has no special interest in me, I assure you, nor I in him. He was a friend of my father's, and if he had not written my other marriage agreement, who can say what might have happened to me when . . ."

Her face flushed as she paused and looked away, her breasts rising and falling with passionate indignation.

He kept his gaze on her irate features. "It doesn't matter what you feel for him, my sweet, or what he feels for you," he lied as he tried to ignore a sudden vision of her in that other man's arms. "What is important is that you understand that I know full well I have been duped, and that I intend to ensure that it never happens again."

He leaned across the coach to put his knuckle beneath her chin, making her look up at him. "That agreement virtually emasculates me."

"I don't think anything could emasculate you."

His lips twisted into a wry, sardonic grin. "I daresay I should be flattered. However, to find one is reduced to a role something less than a steward when one has just been made an earl is another situation entirely."

"I understood all that was required is that you live on your family estate, and so you shall."

"What I wanted was to be master of my family's estate, as I should be. That has been denied me. I shall be nothing more than—"

His wife's eyes suddenly gleamed with what looked suspiciously like mockery. "Chattel?" she suggested.

"You are *my* chattel, my lady," he growled,

"even if I am not to command the estate."

As annoyed as he was, he realized he would have done better not to show it, for the hint of amused mockery disappeared, replaced by cold sternness. "I know what the law says about a wife's place, and how keen men are to keep us there."

"I am not William Longbourne."

"I also know that," she snapped. "But except for your reputation, I know almost nothing else about you, save what I learned . . ." Her voice trailed off to an embarrassed silence.

"Save what you learned last night?" he asked softly, pressing his knee closer to her leg.

"Yes."

All thoughts of her marriage settlement fled Elissa's mind as his expression changed and a slow smile lifted the corners of his lips. "Elissa, have you ever had chocolate?"

Puzzled, she cast a glance at him, then away. "No," she whispered as he took her free hand in his.

He toyed with her gloved fingers, then stroked her palm when she didn't protest. Her chest rose and fell so rapidly that it looked as if her son were nodding in his sleep. "The taste takes some getting used to, but it has other properties that more than make up for its flavor." He placed her hand on his thigh, and his right hand moved slowly up her arm. "It is said to be an aphrodisiac."

Elissa gulped. She could scarcely move, what with Will leaning against her. And she should be angry. Or at least on her guard. She would be, except for Richard's disarming actions.

She could feel the muscle of his thigh straining against the fabric of his breeches. The sensation of his hand on her arm was nearly as overwhelming.

As if these things were not confusing in themselves, she had no idea why he had suddenly decided to talk about chocolate. "A ... a what?"

"An aphrodisiac. It is believed to enflame desire."

At that moment, Elissa knew she didn't need any assistance to have her desire enflamed. Why, if Will were not there, who could say what this man might not be able to do? Or compel her to do.

Suddenly, the coach went over a bump.

"Are we there yet?" Will asked sleepily.

"No, dear, it was just a bump," Elissa said, telling herself she was glad of the distraction.

"We should be at Hatfield soon," Richard noted calmly, "where we shall spend the night."

Chapter 8

As the moonlight shone through the small upper windows of the room at the inn in Hatfield, Elissa tried not to move. The straw in the mattress poked through in several places and if she so much as inched her foot forward, it felt as if tiny daggers were being shoved into her naked skin.

As she lay on her side, staring at the bare, whitewashed wattle-and-daub wall beside her, Will slumbered peacefully in a trundle bed, his mattress having no similar holes. She knew because she had checked the bedding herself for fleas.

She had seen the holes in the large mattress and had thought them insignificant. Perhaps they might be, if she could only fall asleep. Unfortunately, every unfamiliar sound, of which there were many, kept her in a state of constant anxiety.

That, and waiting for her husband.

After they had eaten their meal in the Goose and Gander, he had gone to see that the coachman and horses were bedded down properly, while she took Will to their room.

It had not taken long to get her tired son out of his clothes and into the bed, nor for her to do the same.

She sighed and, forgetting the mattress, rolled onto her back, only to grit her teeth and curse the thinness of the fabric of her chemise.

At least Richard had had no more to say on the subject of the marriage agreement, and for that, she was grateful.

She was also very glad that he treated her son as he did. She had known situations where a stepfather and stepson hated each other on sight and squabbled constantly. This did not look likely; indeed, Will seemed to hold Richard in outright awe.

Still, there was a danger in Will's idolizing Sir Richard Blythe, who obviously represented romance in all its glory to her son. If even a portion of what she had heard regarding Richard were true, the man might lead Will down the same disgusting path William Longbourne had trod.

Elissa closed her eyes and rubbed them hard, trying to rid her mind of those immoral images from the large book she had burned after she had found it in her husband's study—lewd, disgusting images of naked men and women engaging in explicit couplings.

They came to her now like a bad dream remembered, except that the faces of the men shifted and changed, becoming that of Sir Richard Blythe, with his dark, intense eyes and sensual lips.

"Asleep, my sweet?"

Her eyes flew open to see a man hovering above her. "Richard?" she demanded in a whisper.

"Were you expecting someone else?" he replied softly, his tone wry as he peeled off his jacket. He sat on the bed, unknowingly sending more daggers of straw into her.

He pulled off his boots, his shoulders hunched and the fabric tight across his muscular shoulders. Then he rose and took off his shirt.

Closing her eyes tight, she heard him moving about in the room, putting his clothes on the chest in the corner and . . . and taking off his breeches?

The covers lifted and the mattress moved with his weight.

"What instrument of torture is this?" he cried.

She thought of the sensation of those straw spears on his naked flesh and didn't know whether to laugh or offer him her sympathies. "Shh! You'll wake Will."

"This mattress is an outrage," he muttered.

"At least it doesn't have fleas."

"No doubt they could not take the discomfort."

He got out of the bed. In the moonlight, naked, his arms akimbo, he looked like an outraged god of war before he headed for the door.

"Where are you going?"

"To complain to the landlord," he whispered fiercely.

"Without any clothes?"

He paused, then slowly turned back. She tried to keep her gaze on his face.

"I daresay that would not be as effective," he said, and his voice held a hint of amusement.

"He's probably sound asleep."

"And men of his girth are often very sound sleepers. There is probably little chance of waking him tonight short of screaming 'fire!' As tempting as that may be, I daresay the other people sleeping here would not be appreciative."

"Are you *trying* to wake Will up?"

"Not at all." He put on his breeches and his shirt and came back to the bed, once again joining her beneath the generally clean coverings. "There. That is a bit better, I suppose. Nevertheless, I will speak to the landlord in the morning."

Elissa didn't doubt it. "Good night," she said softly, turning onto her side again.

She tensed as he inched closer. "Can you not

feel those thousand slivers through your chemise?" he whispered in her ear.

"Not if I keep still."

His hand came to rest on the curve of her hip. "I do not want you to keep still. Lady wife, you and your clever lawyer have reduced me to almost nothing rather than lord and master. However, a husband does have certain rights and I would like to claim the one you have left me."

It would be so easy to give in to his seductive advances! She had never felt such excitement and pleasure as she had known in his arms last night. In spite of that, and the sensations his touch was arousing, she feared that if she were not strong, he would soon be able to bend her to his will.

Like a weak fool she had believed herself in love and allowed William Longbourne to do what he would. Now, she must be strong, for her son's sake.

"I am tired and very sleepy," she lied, for she had never felt more awake in her life. She rolled over onto her back. "And my son is too closeby."

A wry grin curled his full lips. "Can you not be quiet?"

"Yes. Can you?"

How cold and stern she sounded, and a fierce frown crossed her features before she turned her back to him.

After that moment of intimacy in the coach, Richard had hoped for a more welcoming reaction than that.

He forced himself to think rationally and ignore his disappointment.

She believed him to be a lascivious, immoral libertine. If he persisted now, likely she would take his selfishness for confirmation of his lustful nature. She was also right in that her young son was very nearby.

Better on all counts, then, to leave her alone. If he could.

Of course he could. He was not a slave to lust. He could control his appetite.

To prove that to himself, and to show the lady that he would not simply obey her commands, he pressed his body along hers. He again ran his hand over her slender hip and this time, continued upward, caressing her soft, supple breast and gently teasing her nipple with his fingers.

Her breathing quickened.

He brushed back her thick hair, which smelled of country flowers, and pressed a kiss to the smooth skin of her neck. Putting his arm around her, he pulled her back against him. The softness of her buttocks surrounded his rising manhood and, with a low moan, he buried his face in her hair.

"Do what you must, but please try not to wake my son."

*   *   *

As the coach rolled along the muddy road, Elissa wondered if Richard were going to talk to her at all, or only converse with Will for the rest of the journey.

He was obviously angry with her and had been ever since her warning not to wake Will last night. After that, he had abruptly rolled over and presumably gone to sleep.

She had tried to subdue a sense of disappointment as well as a nagging twinge of guilt. As he had said, he was not William Longbourne, yet to be honest, she was not giving him much of a chance to prove it.

It was for that reason, she supposed, that she had not voiced an objection to his request to have Will sit beside him as they continued their journey, or to let Will hold his baldric and sword.

Tonight, they would be nearly to Owston in Leicester, which was close to Blythe Hall. It would have taken them a mere three days, compared to the seven to get to London when she had answered the king's summons. There was no denying that this coach was a more comfortable mode of transportation, too.

"Tell me about a duel," Will asked, and not for the first time that day, as he tugged on Richard's sleeve. "You promised you would."

"I never promised," Richard replied, ceasing to watch the slowly passing countryside and smiling at her son.

"But you said you would!"

Richard fixed his inscrutable, dark-eyed gaze upon Elissa. "My lady, have you any objections?"

It was a simple question, surely intended to refer to Will's request alone and to have nothing to do with what had happened the previous night, yet she blushed as if he had demanded that they take up where they had left off, Will or no Will.

Her son regarded her with no such inscrutability. He wanted to hear about a duel so much, one might think his very existence depended upon it. "Very well, as long as it was an honorable duel."

"Madam, I assure you I indulge in no other kind," Richard replied as he turned toward Will. "There was a Frenchman who made the mistake of insulting the king's sister, whom he adores. Fortunately for the Frenchman, the king himself did not hear the remark. Unfortunately for the Frenchman, I did.

"Now, whatever one may think of our monarch, his sister is indeed a delightful, charming, and honorable lady."

Elissa told herself she would not be jealous of the king's sister, no matter how her husband spoke of her.

"Naturally, since this is so, I could not let the insult pass."

"What did the Frenchman say?" Will demanded.

"I would not sully my lips by repeating it.

At any rate, I challenged him, and we agreed upon a time and place. It was to be at dawn in a farmer's field outside of Paris, where we could fight our battle in private."

"Did Charles know of this?" Elissa asked.

Richard frowned. "Of course not. How could he be told without repeating the insult?"

"He did not know you were risking your life in defense of his sister's honor?"

At that question, Richard smiled ruefully. "I must confess I did not think myself in any serious danger. Pierre was no expert with a sword."

"And you are!" Will cried triumphantly.

"I was certainly better than Pierre. However, it had rained in the night, and the grass was slippery, so I suggested a postponement." Richard's tone hardened. "Regrettably, Pierre would not agree."

Elissa suspected the Frenchman had made the mistake of implying that Richard's reason for suggesting a delay had nothing to do with the weather, and it did not take much imagination to believe that Richard Blythe would not take kindly to any implication of cowardice.

"So there we were, in the dim light of dawn, both tired, because it's difficult to sleep before a duel. Pierre had been attempting to find his courage at the bottom of a bottle—"

"At the bottom of a bottle?" Will asked, puzzled.

"He was drunk," Richard said simply. "Drunk and tired and young and afraid."

"You weren't afraid," Will said with conviction.

"No, because he was drunk, tired, young, and afraid," Richard replied. "Now, as I said, it had rained heavily, so the trees dripped all around us. The ground beneath our feet was as slippery as ice, and over in the field beside us was one of the nastiest-looking bulls I have ever encountered. Still, we were to fight, so his second gave the signal to begin."

"Who was your second?" Will demanded.

"I did not have one."

"You didn't have one?" Elissa repeated incredulously.

"As I have already said, I didn't want the king to hear about it, so the fewer people involved, the better.

"We drew our swords and began to circle one another," Richard continued. "Pierre was somewhat anxious and impatient, I fear, and after a few moments of this, he lunged at me.

"Sadly, he had forgotten the wet grass, and that his arms were shorter than mine. The poor fellow fell flat on his face, his sword out before him as if he were offering it to the gods if they would only spare his life. I would have ended it there, except that Pierre got to his feet and came at me again. I could see the only thing that would stop him would be to wound him, so I fought him until I did so."

"Did you kill him?" Will whispered, awed.

"No, I cut his cheek. He should have a scar to remind him how he should speak of a lady, I thought."

"You didn't kill him?"

"No, but he died all the same."

"He did?" Elissa and Will gasped simultaneously.

"Yes. He caught a chill from the wet grass and never recovered. Not a very glorpious result, wouldn't you agree, Will?"

"You upheld the honor of the king's sister."

"The man was an idiot, but he didn't deserve to die because of it. I have wounded many men in duels, yet never killed one. And," he finished, "other men have wounded me."

"I saw no scars," Elissa cried impetuously, aghast to think he had been ever hurt dueling—a useless, stupid pastime, as this story aptly demonstrated.

"You have not seen my body in a good light," her husband replied evenly.

Elissa, however, felt anything but calm. Impressed, admiring, embarrassed, even lustful at the memory of his naked body—but most definitely not calm.

"The Barmaid's Arms!" the driver called out as the coach rolled into the yard of an inn.

Richard looked out the window, glad to be distracted from the memory of the pathetic

Pierre. "The Barmaid's Arms. Still here after all this time."

"Why is it called that?" Will asked.

"I have no idea," Richard replied.

He was fast realizing his stepson was curious about everything and everybody. He did not fault him for that, for it was evidence of a lively intelligence. Spare him the child with no spark of curiosity or mischief!

Spare him the wife who could utterly unman him with a few words, and yet enflame his desire simply by looking at him as he told a story!

The coach rocked slightly as Richard disembarked and surveyed the half-timbered building before him. It seemed as if nothing at all had changed since the last time he had been here, when he was fifteen years old and going to France. The structures had aged, of course, so the timbers were somewhat darker, but the number of buildings had not increased or diminished. The same oak tree stood in the yard surrounded by a stone wall, except for the portion across the back, where the river ran. Here willows bent over the water like maidens looking at their reflection.

Over there by the stables, he had bid farewell to his father for what had been the last time.

He put away that unpleasant memory and glanced back at his pretty wife, a wry smile on his face. "If I can feel this pleased about returning to an inn, I hope I do not disgrace myself with an emotional outburst when I first see Blythe Hall."

Elissa thought of the Blythe Hall she had left, and the Blythe Hall he was expecting to see. She would do well to prepare for an outburst of a rather different sort than he was anticipating.

"Ah, Mistress Longbourne, ye're back!" a woman's throaty voice called from somewhere closeby.

Richard spun on his heel to see Mistress Hutchley, the landlady, who also looked as if she had not changed in these many years, standing in the door of the kitchen, her large hands on her broad hips, and a wide smile on her friendly face.

Will ran eagerly toward the woman. "I've been to London and Mama saw the king and I've got a new papa and have you made any more cake?" he cried, the words a happy jumble as he came to a skidding halt before the landlady.

"A new papa?" she declared as she embraced the boy. Her surprised gaze passed from Elissa to Richard and back again. "A new papa?"

As she repeated her shocked ejaculation, a very pretty, plump young woman appeared behind her at the door to the main room of the inn. It is Martha, Mistress Hutchley's daughter, Richard thought, remembering a little girl with that same rosy complexion, bright blue eyes and merry smile.

Martha was a little girl no longer. She was a very well-developed woman who regarded him as if he were a particularly toothsome morsel.

"It's true," Elissa said evenly. "I have been married to Richard Blythe, now the Earl of Dovercourt."

"Richard Blythe, the one who writes the plays and grew up near Owston?" Mistress Hutchley demanded, gazing at him incredulously. Then her lip curled with disgust. "By God, yes! I should have known those black eyes anywhere! Ye're the image of your father.

"Inside, Martha," she ordered sternly. "Get some food for our guests and cake for the young man here, eh? Be quick about it!"

The young woman hurried away, while Mistress Hutchley took Will's hand and led him inside as if she thought he must be protected from contagion.

Richard had indeed been wounded many times, but every cut and gash was as the prick of a pin compared to the pain of the realization that he had been a fool to hope that the old rumors would have died out by now.

Wondering at the woman's scornful reaction, Elissa turned to look at Richard. He merely smiled his sardonic smile and calmly noted, "I see my family is still remembered, and apparently my literary fame has penetrated even this remote corner of England."

"Are you not ashamed to be so notorious?" she asked incredulously.

Not wishing to explain, Richard started walking toward the inn. "I cannot help that my success has made me notorious."

"Mistress Longbourne!"

At the shout of greeting, Richard turned to see a slender, fair-haired man rush from the stable, his not-ugly face wreathed with smiles and open admiration. The fellow must be a person of some wealth, for while his clothes were nothing fancy, they were well tailored and made of obviously fine wool. His bucket boots were plain, and made of expensive and highly polished leather.

There was something vaguely familiar about the man, yet Richard couldn't place him. Perhaps he had been a childhood acquaintance.

The stranger's identity became rather less important than his relationship with Elissa as he all but ran toward Richard's wife like a long-lost lover and took her hands in his. "What a pleasant surprise! How did you come to be here so soon? Where is Will?"

Elissa smiled pleasantly. "I didn't expect to see you here either, Mr. Sedgemore. We have just arrived and Will has gone inside already."

Richard sauntered closer. He did not recognize the fellow's name, but he recognized the greedy, anxious yearning in the man's manner.

"Was that *your* coach?" the decidedly too familiar Mr. Sedgemore cried. "I knew your estate was prospering, but I had no idea you were doing so well. However, I know you shall not put on London airs," he finished softly.

"The coach and four were a gift from the king," Richard announced.

Their heads swiveled toward him.

"A wedding gift."

"A what?" Sedgemore gasped, looking from Elissa to Richard with undisguised shock.

And something else. Was that despair or only surprise in the fellow's brown eyes?

In truth, and despite his momentary jealousy of Heartless Harding, it had not yet occurred to Richard that his wife might have been courted by another man at home. It should have, though. She was, after all, a young, beautiful, vivacious woman.

But he would not reveal the weakness of jealousy. "Yes, we are married, and I will thank you to let go of Lady Dovercourt's hands."

Fortunately for Sedgemore, he did as Richard commanded.

"Lady Dovercourt?" he repeated stupidly, again looking uneasily from one to the other.

"As her husband is the Earl of Dovercourt, that should not be surprising."

"It is quite true," Elissa replied, and Richard couldn't tell if that confirmation held sorrow or not. "Lord Dovercourt, this is Alfred Sedgemore, who owns the property to the north of ours. He has been a very good friend to me."

Richard didn't doubt it; however, he kept his contemptuous suspicions from his face. "Your servant, sir," he acknowledged with a bow.

"Mr. Sedgemore, this is my husband, the Earl of Dovercourt, formerly Sir Richard Blythe."

"Elissa!" the man cried, aghast. "Mistress Longbourne—can this be true?"

"I assure you, Mr. Sedgemore, it is happily true," Richard said in his best imitation of the Duke of Buckingham's sophisticated drawl. "Sadly, I do not recall your name from former days. You must have purchased your property recently."

"Your servant, my lord," Sedgemore murmured, also bowing. He was not ungraceful, damn him, although even Foz made a better bow. "I bought my estate about the same time Mistress Longbourne's—forgive me, Lady Dovercourt's—late husband purchased his."

"You must have been a very young and prosperous fellow."

"I was young, yes, and somewhat prosperous, thanks to my father, who left me some money. I was very glad to find such a delightful property for sale."

"And with such a delightful neighbor, too."

Alfred Sedgemore had done nothing to merit Richard's scorn, Elissa thought, and yet there was no other word to describe her husband's reaction to their neighbor.

To be sure, there was something about Alfred Sedgemore that did seem to invite a certain . . . distaste. Elissa had often felt less than completely comfortable in his presence. He was an avidly curious fellow, and for a long time she had lived in fear of what he might find out about her husband. Men always said women were terrible gossips, yet Elissa had never met anyone who so dearly loved to relate gossip as Alfred Sedgemore.

After William's death, she still dreaded his visits, especially when his attentions altered enough that she started to consider how she would refuse his offer of marriage, if he made one.

Fortunately, he had not yet spoken of such matters, so she had begun to think her suspicions were ill-founded, and that he was merely being a kind and sympathetic neighbor.

"Has the king given back your estate?" Mr. Sedgemore asked.

"No, he has not," Richard replied, his mocking smile growing as he approached them and put a proprietary arm around Elissa. "As you may have concluded, he has given me the former Mistress Longbourne instead."

Chapter 9

Much later that evening, Richard sat alone on the settle in the large room of the inn and slowly surveyed his surroundings. Its timbered ceiling was dark with age and smoke, and the plaster definitely in need of a new coat of whitewash. Sawdust covered the floor, its woody scent battling with the odor of smoke and ale. The moonlight streaming in through the window and a lone rushlight provided the only illumination. All the other guests, including his wife, had retired long ago.

The last time he had been here, his handsome father had stood near that particularly large stain on the wall beside the stone hearth, the blot like an odd sort of shadow.

In the other corner there had been a group of farm laborers seated around that same scarred wooden table. Their conversation had ceased the moment he had entered with his father.

Mistress Hutchley had bustled about just as she had tonight, but he had been too young then to see the scorn beneath her grim expression. Martha had stood near the kitchen door, looking at them shyly and moving her toe in slow circles in the sawdust on the floor.

Whatever their reactions, his father had ignored them all, swaggering about with jovial arrogance as if they were fleas or flies.

It was no wonder, Richard mused, that he was able to perform that attitude so well, even if he did not have the same reason to do so. Indeed, he had performed the role of haughty aristocrat to perfection during dinner.

Elissa had invited Sedgemore to share their meal, which proved to be a very quiet affair. Will was clearly tired, despite another nap in the coach, and Elissa barely spoke. Neither did Sedgemore, because he was too busy staring at her the entire time, when he was not eyeing the new Earl of Dovercourt with obvious disgust.

Because of his reputation as a playwright and friend of the king? Or was there more to it than that?

As he sat alone in the dark, two things gave Richard comfort. The first and most important was the conclusion that Elissa had not heard about his parents. If she had, he realized, she would have cast their alleged behavior up to him before this.

Elissa must never learn the truth, if he could help it. He wanted to retain a shred of respect in her beautiful eyes and shuddered to think that his dead parents could rob him of this chance for happiness as surely as their selfish natures had robbed him of his childhood.

Zounds, he must be turning simple. Happiness? Since when did marriage equal happiness, even if the woman was a beauty? He chuckled mirthlessly at his own stupidity. His mother had been a beauty and she had been the most selfish creature in England, with the possible exception of her husband.

The second thing that gave Richard comfort was that Sedgemore had stupidly tried to match him drink for drink. The idiot had barely been able to stand when the meal was over, and would surely be in agony tomorrow, which served him right.

Richard raked his hand through his hair and reminded himself it was foolish to feel jealous. Was it not the way of the world for husbands and wives to take lovers, especially when a marriage was forced? Had he not written about that several times in his plays? Was that not the case with his own unfortunately joined parents? It did not matter that he had long ascribed that activity to moral weakness and vanity; he had not been forced into marriage himself then. He knew better now.

Didn't he?

He wondered if Elissa had fallen asleep yet. As a rule he detested sitting alone in the near dark, unless he was writing. He sighed and wished he had pen, ink and paper with him now, for writing always kept the bad memories at bay.

Tonight, however, he felt it necessary to sit here like some sort of contemplative monk, until he was too tired to feel desire for his wife so that there would not be a repetition of the humiliating scene last night. He also wanted to ensure that he would be in control of his temper the next time he saw her, for he did not want to give her the slightest inkling that he could be made jealous.

He would never again allow other persons to hold his happiness in the palm of their hand, to be disregarded at whim or fussed over when it suited them, to never know when he was in favor or out, whether he would get a kind word or a slap across the face . . .

He thought of little Will, and hoped the child had been too tired to sense the tension at dinner. He silently vowed to make certain that, whatever the difficulties between himself and his wife, the boy was spared as much as possible. He had grown up in a house full of hate and secrets, and he would not want Will to share a similar fate.

"Oh, here you are, my lord."

He shifted to regard Martha, who had come

from the kitchen and now stood regarding him with a sultry smile and predatory eyes.

Suddenly deciding that whether Elissa was asleep or not, it was time to retire, he rose at once and snuffed the rushlight. "Good night."

"No need to run off. I was just going to close the shutters."

She sauntered toward the windows, her hips swaying in what he knew she meant for a provocative manner. She reached up to close the shutters, the movement causing the fabric of her bodice to stretch over her voluptuous breasts.

He was quite sure she knew that, too. Then she latched the shutters, blocking out the moonlight so that they were alone in the dark.

If his wife did not welcome him, this woman would. Surely he had had enough confusion and refusal lately. Any man would understand that he had needs that should not be denied.

And yet the thought of coupling with this willing wench filled him with revulsion.

He heard her move closer and laugh softly. "You've grown up, Richard."

"You should address me as 'my lord,' " he noted, backing up carefully because it was difficult to see in the dark.

Suddenly Martha grabbed him and pulled him against her, grinding her hips blatantly against his body. She kissed him lustily and as her tongue invaded his mouth, her hands sought his manhood as if she were the most experienced whore in Bankside.

He tried to pull away gently, but Martha held him in a grip of iron. Gentleness would not do.

With considerable force, Richard shoved Martha aside—and at the same moment, beheld Elissa standing on the stairs, a sputtering rushlight in her hand, her hair loose, and a robe held closed over her chemise.

"Elissa!"

"Richard," she said, only the slight downturn of her lips giving evidence of any reaction to finding her husband in another woman's arms. "I thought perhaps you had fallen asleep. I see I was quite wrong." She turned on her heel. "Good night."

"Elissa!" he cried again, taking a step toward her.

Martha grabbed his arm. "If she don't mind, why not? I'm willin.' "

"I am not," Richard growled as he shook off Martha's grasp and hurried after his wife.

He caught up to her as she was about to enter the bedchamber. "Elissa!" he whispered intently.

She paused and regarded him steadily. "What is it? Would you like the light?"

"No!"

"Then good night."

He took hold of her hand. "I would speak

with you. Downstairs, so we do not disturb
anyone."

"I do not think we have anything to discuss."

"I do."

He thought she might refuse again, but she
must have sensed his determination, for she
nodded. "Very well. I shall light the way."

She led him below as majestically as the
king's chamberlain.

Elissa tried to keep her hand holding the
rushlight steady. She didn't want Richard to
know how upset she was to have found them
together.

*I will take my pleasure when and where I will,
and there is not a thing in this world you can do
to stop me.*

William Longbourne's words ran through
her mind over and over again, along with all
the pain of his numerous betrayals and the
shock of her discovery of the decadent, immoral nature of the man she had married.

How could she forget that lesson? Because
she was still a weak fool, perhaps. Because she
had allowed herself to forget that this man
was Richard Blythe, friend of the lascivious
king, notorious playwright and chronicler of a
licentious age. She should not expect morality
and decency from a sophisticated man of London and the court, where adultery was considered something to be enjoyed, not condemned.

Taking lovers was nothing more than a game to play, and marital fidelity a joke.

Although it was not right, and she would never believe it was, she would not give him the pleasure of condemning her for a naive country bumpkin.

Fortunately, Martha had left the main room of the inn, Elissa noted as she sat on the settle near the hearth and set the rushlight on a nearby table. Richard took the chair opposite her, the flickering light playing about his angular face, his eyes deep in shadow, and his expression grim. Even then, and despite what she had seen, she found her body warming beneath his steadfast gaze.

"I have done nothing wrong," he said softly.

"No?"

"No."

"Because I interrupted at an inopportune moment, or because you do not consider betraying your wife a sin?"

"She was trying to seduce me."

"How troubling for you," Elissa replied, not believing him for an instant. How could she, given his reputation? "And you stayed down here so late trying to dissuade her, I suppose?"

"No. I stayed down here rather than come to bed with you."

If he had struck her across the face, he could not have hurt her more. "I regret that seems such a horrendous fate, my lord. Perhaps you should have noted this to the king when he made his proposal. I am quite certain he would have sympathized with your plight and spared us both. Unfortunately, you did not, and he did not."

She rose to go, but he also stood and took hold of her arm to stop her. "Why should I be in any hurry to have you refuse my conjugal rights again?"

"I did not refuse you," she retorted, twisting away from him.

"Elissa, listen to me, and listen well," he said, his voice low and intense, his dark eyes gleaming in the dim light. "I am a proud man who does not take kindly to being treated like a flea under your petticoat."

Her lip curled with scorn. "If you wish to find some excuse for your immoral behavior, do not look to me. I have done nothing wrong."

"Not yet."

"And I never will!" she cried hotly. She stepped close to him, so that she could see his face, and he hers. She would have him see that she meant what she said. "I will not dishonor myself by committing adultery."

He raked his fingers through his disheveled hair. "Leave me."

"Do you think I am your servant, to be so summarily dismissed? I am your *wife*, and deserve to be treated with respect. I am not one of your whoring actresses. I realize that although you are a nobleman and friend of the king, you have been exposed to—"

"You have no idea what I have been exposed to," he growled, "and I will not grovel because a woman finds me attractive."

She straightened her shoulders. "And that is to be your clever, witty excuse? You will conveniently forget your fidelity to your wife upon such occasions? I daresay I should be grateful for the warning."

"Madam, spare me the martyr's pose, since you cannot play that role convincingly. There was nothing of the martyr about you on our wedding night—or have you conveniently forgotten that? No doubt you will next accuse me of dragging you down here against your will like some kind of barbarian."

"If you will excuse me . . ."

He grabbed her arm as she went to leave. With the strength of a cornered animal, she wrenched herself free.

"Don't you *ever* put your hand on me like that again!" she snarled.

Richard stared at her, shocked by the fierce look in her eyes. "Elissa," he cried, aghast. "I didn't mean to hurt you. I only wanted—"

"Yes! Yes, *you* only wanted! What of me, my lord and husband? Is there any thought of what *I* might want in that handsome head of yours? Can you even conceive that others have suffered disappointments, too?"

Surprisingly, his coal-dark eyes softened. "Obviously not well enough," he said with a gentleness she would never have imagined he possessed. "I should have."

"Yes, you should," she muttered, nonplussed by the sudden change in him.

"I fear I have been a selfish beast. Can you forgive me?"

"If you have done nothing wrong, there is nothing to forgive."

His lips slowly curved up into a genuinely pleased smile. "I assure you, Elissa, I am blameless tonight," he whispered. "Why should I want Martha when you are my wife?"

And then he pulled her into his arms and kissed her.

For a brief instant, Elissa's mind rebelled against the sensation of his mouth against hers, but only for an instant, as his tender kiss and warm embrace seemed to melt her fury and frustration.

She wanted to believe his explanation for what had transpired here. She did believe it.

Her robe fell open and she could feel the pounding of his heart through her thin chemise. Her own blood throbbed in her ears, pulsating through her body, heating her like the passion of his kiss.

As suddenly as he had started, he broke the kiss and swept her up in his strong arms.

"Where . . . where are you taking me?" she whispered.

"Somewhere we do not have to be quiet."

Leaning her head against his chest, she

clung to him, wanting him to make love with her, remembering their wedding night and the incredible way he made her feel.

And there was more. In Richard's arms, it was as if all the miserable years of her un-happy marriage had never been. She was at the beginning again, only this time, with no illusions, no silly, girlish ideas about men and love.

This time, she would not be a naive slave to a man's desires. She would fulfill her own.

They went through the kitchen and a nar-row door to a small, dark room that must be a storeroom, for a multitude of familiar odors greeted her, apples, flour and spices the most strong.

He paused a moment, then set her down on a soft pile of something in rough bags. Flour, she suspected.

Then he closed the door, plunging them into complete darkness and silence.

No, not complete silence, for she could hear herself breathing. And him, too—fast and heavy, perhaps from carrying her. Perhaps from some other cause.

He moved and she held out her arms, seek-ing and then finding him, catching him by the hand. As he had wanted her the night before, so she wanted him now, with an urgency she would not hide or deny.

She lay back on the soft pile, pulling him down beside her. Twisting, she kissed him deeply and tore off his jabot. Her fingers fumbled with his buttons, undoing his shirt, and then she slid her hands inside to caress him.

His arms encircled her and held her close as a low moan escaped him. That sound made her feel suddenly powerful—as if she, a woman, could command him. That she, not he, could control their lovemaking, instead of being made to feel that she had no right even to enjoy it.

Heady with delight, desire, and excitement, she gently pressed the tip of her tongue against his lips. When they parted, she exulted.

Her tongue dancing with his, excitement built within her and she hiked up her chemise before slowly straddling him, pushing him back against the rough bags.

His erection pressed against her warm, moist cleavage, his shirt and breeches no real barrier at all. He sighed raggedly as his hands found her breasts and gently kneaded them.

Moaning softly, she started to move back and forth, only a little, yet the sensation—

She gasped as she seemed to explode with a throbbing, pulsating feeling the like of which she had never experienced, not even on her wedding night.

"I have to take you," he said hoarsely, reaching down to swiftly untie his breeches. He yanked his shirt out of the way as she lifted her hips. Grasping him, she guided him, and with a growl, he buried himself deep inside.

Placing her hands on either side of his head, she started to rock.

Breathing heavily, whispering encouragement and half-muttered endearments, he tugged at the knot at the neck of her chemise. Once it was undone, he slowly pulled it beneath her breasts, then raised himself so that he could take her nipple between his lips. She leaned closer as his tongue brushed against her, sending wave after wave of pleasure surging through her.

Tension built again, as if every sinew of her body was being drawn tighter. And tighter. And tighter.

And then they both cried out as the tension peaked, burst, and slowly, slowly ebbed away.

Elissa laid her head against his chest and listened to his rapid heartbeat, which was like the pounding of savage drums.

As it slowed, it became as comforting as the rhythmic swishing of the scythes of the laborers cutting the grain in harvest time.

"Good God," Richard said with a ragged sigh. "To think all the times I played in this place as a lad, I never knew how truly exciting it could be. The bordellos behind Covent Garden might consider decorating a room with sacks of flour, baskets of apples, and jars of spices. I know I shall never react to the scent of apples or cinnamon the same way ever again."

She started to ease herself away from him.

"No, don't go," he cried softly. "There is no hurry, surely."

"We should be abed, my lord."

"I could become quite used to that form of address—except from my wife."

"Perhaps you would enjoy it from the denizens of a Covent Garden bordello?"

He regally held out his hand. "I have never had to pay."

"Sadly, all this activity has tired me, my lord."

Richard cringed as he cursed himself. "Forgive me again, Elissa, for forgetting that you don't understand that such talk is only meaningless banter. Now, since you have left me nothing save an exhausted husk, I must beg your assistance."

"We are not in London anymore."

He rose immediately and with swift, agitated motions, tied his breeches. "Elissa, I cannot change my habits of speech overnight," he said with more than a hint of frustration. "I will do my best to govern my tongue, but zounds! You must have some patience. I have been amongst actors, courtiers and their women for fifteen years. This sort of talk is common in London. However, I shall try to amend my habits."

When she still did not meet his gaze, he

reached out and gently took her hands in his. "Elissa, Elissa, my sweet, my wife, I do want to become the perfect country squire. Gad, that has been my goal for fifteen years."

"Truly?"

He lifted her hand to his lips, then gazed at her with seductive, yet sincere, eyes. "I am sorry if my impetuous speech upset you, and I know I have much to learn from you in that regard."

She flushed, and it was not just from his gentle kiss. "I think I have much to learn from you, too," she said softly.

"Well then, wife," he whispered, pulling her back down to the pile of flour bags, "we shall teach each other."

Chapter 10

"What is the matter?" Elissa asked the next day as the coach came to an unexpected halt.

She looked at Richard, who was seated opposite her, beside the slumbering Mr. Sedgemore.

"I have no idea," he said, shrugging his broad shoulders and giving her what for any other person would be a small, friendly smile.

The look in his eyes, however, was far more than friendly and she blushed like a young girl in the first throes of romantic love as Will clambered up on the seat beside her to look out the window.

Meanwhile, Mr. Sedgemore dragged open his bleary eyes and yawned prodigiously.

The coachman's head appeared at the window, an apologetic look on his face.

"I'm sorry, m'lord," he said. "We've got a bit of a hill to get down and the road's mud-slick, so I'm going to have to ask you all to walk."

"I remember doing this when I was a boy," Richard replied. "I think a walk in this fresh country air will do us all good, especially poor Mr. Sedgemore."

"Yes, indeed," Mr. Sedgemore murmured groggily. He was obviously the worse for too much wine last night.

Elissa was in no particular humor to walk, either. She was rather fatigued due to a lack of sleep, as Richard should well remember. Unfortunately, last night's activities appeared to enliven her husband instead of tiring him.

At least the way was not overly muddy, so there was not much chance of slipping, she noted as she disembarked, wincing slightly. Their nocturnal adventures had done more than weary her.

Her husband stood near the heads of the lead horses, surveying the road. Over in a nearby meadow, a flock of sheep ignored them.

Will jumped down, wobbling a little. "Is our house very far?"

"Over the next hill," Richard said without looking back. "I could walk from here."

He took a deep breath. "I have been too long in the stench of London," he murmured. "And I believe that could be the very same flock of sheep I passed when I left home fifteen years ago. By God, they could be the same sheep."

"It is five miles yet," Elissa noted, not joining him in praise of the clean country air or amusing observations concerning livestock. "That is too far for the rest of us to walk."

A five-mile ramble might be nothing to him, but it would be to her son, their fellow passenger, and her. Obviously, for all his playwriting, her husband lacked the ability to imagine walking five miles when one was only six years old, or suffering from a surfeit of wine, or wearing a petticoat and heavy skirt.

"I believe you are right," he replied, sauntering toward them. "Indeed, I fear some of us will hardly be able to reach the bottom of the hill."

He glanced at Mr. Sedgemore, who, with his hand firmly clasping the door of the coach, slowly got out of the slightly rocking vehicle. He staggered over to the ditch and promptly lost his breakfast.

"Men like that should stay away from wine," Richard remarked without pity.

"Did the wine disagree with him, Mama?" Will asked.

"Yes, dear, it did," she replied. Will was too young yet to hear much about drunkenness, and she gave Richard a look intended to convey her thoughts in that regard.

Her husband merely smiled and turned back to look down the hill. "Come, let us proceed. There is a chestnut tree along this stretch of road I used to climb as a boy."

"I shall see if Mr. Sedgemore needs any help," Elissa said.

"I think he should reap what he sows. If he cannot deal with the result, he should stay away from—"

Will interrupted by pointing excitedly toward a huge chestnut tree a short distance away. It was about ten feet from the edge of the road and had enormous branches. "I want to climb it! I want to climb it!"

"I shall take care of him, my sweet," Richard offered. "It is an easy tree to climb, if memory serves. Of course, it has grown somewhat."

"Come on, then!" Will cried, running down the hill and toward the tree.

Its low, wide branches did seem created solely for the pleasure of small, adventurous boys.

"Very well, but don't go too high," she called after him.

She looked at Richard. "We must get on our way soon. I shall assist Mr. Sedgemore."

"Do you think it wise to reward drunkenness?"

"Reward?" she asked, puzzled.

"If I knew you would play nursemaid, I would not have filled my cup only half full."

Her eyes widened. "Is that how . . . ?"

His grin was devilment incarnate. "I learned to drink with the best." His voice dropped to a seductive whisper. "I could teach you that, too."

Blushing, she cleared her throat. "Should you not help Will?"

"Of course." Richard strolled down the hill and toward the tree as if the road were the Banqueting House at Whitehall.

He really was too attractive . . .

"Lady Dovercourt," Mr. Sedgemore called weakly.

Suppressing a frown, she hurried to help him. Fortunately, it seemed he had already found the best remedy for his ailment, for he appeared somewhat better.

"Forgive me," he murmured with an apol-ogetic smile as they began their slow progress down the hill. "I should have realized that I could not imbibe as much as an experienced cup man like Richard Blythe."

He nodded at Richard and Will. "Do you think that wise?"

"Will has been climbing trees since he could walk," she replied, slowing her pace to make it easier for Mr. Sedgemore to keep up.

Its wheels shrieking from the brake, the coach slowly drew near behind them. Ahead, Richard easily boosted Will onto a bottom branch as thick as Richard's muscular thigh.

"No, I mean letting your son be so friendly with him."

As the coach passed them, Elissa paused and looked at Mr. Sedgemore, unhappily reminded of her own dread in that regard. "Why?"

His eyes full of condescending pity, Mr. Sedgemore spoke in a confidential whisper. "Because of the man's reputation. Who knows what he might teach your son?"

"I shall take care that he not corrupt my son."

"And what of you?"

She gave Mr. Sedgemore a sharp glance, wondering at his odd tone and if he had peeked into the storeroom of the inn last night, a thought which was more disgusting than any she had ever had regarding Richard. "Do you think I can be corrupted?"

He looked truly shocked. "No! Never! I meant, I hope he does not make you unhappy. Everyone knows the kind of man he is, and then there is the unsavory history of the whole family."

"I know that his uncle sold his estate without his permission," Elissa replied.

Sedgemore put his hand on her arm, and she halted. His brown eyes gazed into hers.

"Then there is much more you don't know about the Blythes," he said with quiet intensity. "More that everyone around Owston knows. The stories have died down somewhat, of course, since his uncle left, yet surely they will be remembered when *he* comes back."

"What sort of stories?" she asked warily, trying to listen to Sedgemore and keep her eye on Will as he disappeared up into the chestnut tree.

"I should not wish to taint your lovely ears . . ."

She lost sight of her son in the denser foliage of the higher branches.

"Will, come down," Elissa commanded. She hurried toward the tree, Sedgemore momentarily forgotten. "Richard, tell him to come down."

"He is quite all right," Richard replied, his head tilted back to look up into the tree.

"Mama! Look at me! Look at me!" Will shouted. "I think I can see our house!"

"Will, you've gone quite high enough! Come down immediately!"

"He is like a seaman in the crow's nest spotting landfall, is he not?" Richard observed evenly.

"He is not a seaman. He is a little boy who has gone much too high," Elissa declared.

"He will come down in a moment, after the thrill has worn off a little."

"A London playwright who has no children of his own can hardly be an expert on what is safe for small boys," Elissa snapped.

"I'faith, I know that full well, madam," Richard replied with a slight bow, "which makes the anticipation of having children of my own all the more delightful."

Elissa flushed hotly, swallowed hard and turned her attention back to Will. "William

James Longbourne, come down *at once!*"

The boy wisely started to obey.

"Would you have me cut a switch?" Sedgemore offered helpfully.

Elissa hadn't realized he had come so close. "There is no need for that."

"It would likely ensure a speedier obedience the next time he ignores you," Sedgemore said. "Little boys should not be allowed to run so wild."

"Was that the method of correction applied to you?" Richard inquired gravely.

"At least *some* of us were given proper discipline by our parents, so that we could grow up to be decent members of society," Sedgemore huffed.

"What are you implying?"

Sedgemore blinked and blushed. "I suppose you were given such discipline as your father was capable of," he muttered.

Richard took a step closer.

"What exactly do you wish to say, sir?" he demanded in a low voice that Elissa could scarcely hear—yet she heard the menace clear enough.

"I need help!" Will suddenly called out. He stood upon a thick branch about five feet from the ground. "Or should I jump from here?"

"No, no, don't jump!" she cried, reaching up to try to take hold of his ankles. "I shall help you."

"Here, allow me," Richard said. "Jump, Will, and I shall catch you."

"No! It's too far—" Elissa protested.

"Mama, let go of my ankles!"

"The boy will break his head," Sedgemore warned.

"I can do it! I'm not afraid!"

"I assure you, my sweet, I shall not let him be hurt."

"Mama, let go! I want Richard to catch me!"

"Mistress Longbourne—Lady Dovercourt! Are you going to let your son speak to you in such a manner?"

"If you do not back up, sir, I shall not be responsible if I knock you over," Richard growled.

Suddenly Will jumped. Elissa sighed with relief as Richard deftly caught him and spun him around. Sedgemore quickly moved out of the way, his expression one of disbelief and disgust, while Will laughed giddily.

Richard set Will down and watched as the dizzy lad wobbled.

"Zounds, Mr. Sedgemore," he noted dispassionately, "my fine, adventurous stepson looks exactly as you did when you got out of my coach at the top of the hill, except that you did something other than laugh."

"The coach is waiting," Elissa said, her relief making her speak a little sharply as she took her son by the hand and led him back to their vehicle.

"A whipping would do him good," Sedgemore muttered.

Richard ran a slightly scornful gaze over the man, then smiled. "That is precisely what I was thinking. Now, then, Mr. Sedgemore, where may we deposit you? I trust it is not far."

After they left Mr. Sedgemore at the livery stable in Owston, a small village of stone and half-timbered buildings with thatched roofs, Elissa would have been hard-pressed to say who was more excited to be nearing Blythe Hall: herself, her son, or Richard.

After all that had happened in the recent days, she wanted to be back in a familiar place, among familiar people. Will, who had as much difficulty remaining seated now as he had on the boat on the Thames, was obviously anxious to tell anyone who would listen of his great adventures, and to announce the arrival of a stepfather who was a duelist, as well as a great friend to the king, no doubt in that particular order. He would probably leave out Richard's literary efforts, as they did not conform to Will's notion of the heroic ideal.

As for what Richard himself was expecting, she almost dreaded to know. She thought of warning him of her late husband's renovations, yet she couldn't bear the thought of dampening the boyish impatience he was displaying, despite his attempts to hide it.

To be sure, if there was ever a competition
for hiding excited anticipation, Richard would
surely win. Only his tapping foot and surrep-
titious glances out the coach window betrayed
him. Nevertheless, they were enough to tell
her he was not nearly so blasé as he was trying
to appear.

She let herself imagine him as a boy, which
wasn't that difficult to do at this particular moment. He was probably a mischievous scamp,
climbing trees, enjoying imaginary battles, giving his mother no end of scares. Maybe being
away from London and the influence of the
king's decadent court would lead to a pleasant
alteration in Richard's worldly and world-
weary manner.

"Just past these trees now," Will said, "and
we can see the drive!"

"Some of the wood has been cut down,
then," Richard observed calmly, although she
noted he inched forward slightly on the seat.

"A few trees, to make a better view, my late
husband thought," Elissa said.

Richard suddenly moved back from the
window. "It's still there," he murmured.

Elissa looked out again and discerned the
corner of the Banqueting House peeking
through the trees. It was a small stone building
about twenty by thirty feet in size, built early
in that century, overlooking the little river that
ran near the main house. Many country estates
had such buildings, none on the scale

of the Banqueting House of Whitehall Palace, of course. They were intended to be a place to enjoy wine and fruit after the main meal on a warm summer evening.

The Banqueting House of the Blythe estate had not been used for years, however, and its ornately carved parapets and narrow circular towers were falling into disrepair.

Elissa supposed its state explained the despair that had crept into his voice.

"There's our house," Will announced, causing Richard to sit forward again.

He stared with unmitigated shock.

"What the devil has happened?" he cried angrily. "Was there a fire?"

Will stared at him with dismay and Elissa put her arm around him.

"He remembers Blythe Hall as it used to be, dear," she said comfortingly, "before your father rebuilt it. He is surprised, that's all."

"Surprised? I am horrified. Disgusted," Richard declared. "I never thought that I would return to find the stately house built during the reign of Henry the Eighth destroyed and replaced by some kind of modern monstrosity that looks like a pagan temple devoted to the god of poor taste."

"I shall explain the changes when we are preparing for supper, Richard," Elissa offered, glancing at her son and then giving Richard a censorious look.

She was right. Despite his extreme anger

and dismay, there was no reason to upset Will.

Yet what reason could there possibly be to tear down a house made of fine red bricks, with pretty oriel windows and strong oak floors, beams, and timbers, and replace it with this stone edifice? Two terrible projections stuck out from the colonnaded front of the new manor house, and a large portico totally dwarfed the formerly majestic entrance. A cupola like some sort of large bird cage sat in the center of the slate roof. The only thing Richard could find in the new house's favor was that there were more windows, and that there had been some sort of attempt to achieve a harmonious balance.

If something had to be razed, why not the cursed Banqueting House?

Maybe it was a good thing the house was gone, with all its memories—but he should have been the one to decide its fate, not some stranger whose only right to it had come from the size of his purse.

They passed through the gates and went up the drive, which passed the house and went around to the yard in the back, where the stables, gatehouse, and back entrance were. As the coach rolled to a stop outside the house, several servants came to stand in a welcoming line, which indicated a certain level of income. Either William Longbourne had been a very rich man, or Elissa was a good steward—for a woman.

"I had no idea the estate was so prosperous that you could afford so many servants," he noted, trying his best to sound calm.

"Let me get out first and introduce you," she said.

After Elissa and Will got out of the coach, she faced the servants, cleared her throat, and smiled. "I am so glad to be home and pleased to see that you are all well."

Their eyes suddenly widened in surprise and she heard a collective sharp intake of breath. Glancing over her shoulder, she saw the reason, for Richard disembarked from the coach like a conqueror making a triumphal appearance before the vanquished.

She thought he had looked regal the first time she had seen him. At present it was as if he had twice that arrogant attitude, and whatever emotions he had felt upon beholding the new house were either overcome, or very well hidden indeed.

She opened her mouth to make the introduction, yet before she could, Will cried, "That's my new papa! The king picked him himself, and he fights duels!"

The servants' eyes widened even more.

"I thank you, Will, for the finest introduction I have ever had," Richard declared evenly. Then he bowed slightly to the servants, who stared at him as if he were King Charles stopping by for a short visit. "I am the Earl of Dovercourt, formerly Sir Richard

Blythe of Blythe Hall, and your mistress's new husband."

That elicited another murmur of surprise as the servants glanced at each other.

"It is quite true," Elissa said, unsure whether she was pleased or annoyed that Richard had taken it upon himself to clarify the situation, such as he had. "Lord Dovercourt and I were married in London. I know you will make him welcome."

Richard stepped forward expectantly and Elissa took his cue. She began to introduce him to the servants.

Will didn't wait for this ceremony. He hurried inside, calling out that he wanted to make sure his room was as he had left it.

"He doesn't like the maids to touch anything, even though I have explained time and again that they must if they are to clean properly," Elissa explained in an aside to Richard.

Her husband simply nodded and they continued down the line, beginning with Davies, the butler, then the housekeeper, the two footmen, three maids, the groom, the cook, and ending with the scullery maid and stable boy.

As the servants returned to their duties, Richard suddenly turned to Elissa and swept her up into his arms.

"What . . . what are you doing?" she asked, her mind swiftly returning to the last time he had picked her up.

"In the ancient Roman tradition, I am carrying my bride over the threshold," he replied as he carried her up the steps toward the open door.

"We are not in Rome!"

"Nor are you a Sabine, and I do not intend to rape you," he answered softly. "But I have had many shocks today. The least you can do is indulge the whimsy inspired by my classical education."

"I didn't know you had a classical education."

"I did. Sadly, Latin was a bit of a stumbling block. I was much better at Greek. I quite enjoyed Ovid, even though I suspect my tutor censored all the best parts."

At last they were inside, and when he set her down in the entrance hall, she felt strangely disappointed.

"I did not recognize any of the servants, and they didn't seem to recognize me," he noted as he surveyed the interior.

Elissa adjusted her slightly disheveled clothing. "My husband dismissed all the servants who were here before he bought the estate. He paid them well, and with the proviso that they leave the county."

"That sounds extreme."

"He could be . . . extreme."

"So I see." Richard frowned studiously. "This looks familiar."

"It should be. Part of the entrance is the main hall of the old house."

"Then that is the original hearth?"

"Yes."

"I am relieved something survived the destruction."

He strolled toward it and she watched as he slowly, almost reverently touched the childishly carved initials that he found without a moment's hesitation.

"It was the size and detailed decoration of the fireplace that saved this portion of the hall," she ventured. "Otherwise, my late husband would have torn it down, too."

Richard started as if he had forgotten she was there, then straightened. "He seems to favor an ornate style. I daresay that was why he saved the Banqueting House."

"Yes, at least he left that," she noted. Then she clasped her hands together. "I'm so very sorry, Richard."

"Why should you be sorry," he asked, turning to regard her with his dark, piercing eyes, "unless this razing and rebuilding was your fault?"

Her gaze faltered. "It was."

Chapter 11

Richard's eyes narrowed slightly as his gaze intensified. *"You* are responsible?"

"William was easily offended, but I didn't know that when I married him. We had been husband and wife for only a few days when I voiced a wish for new plaster in one of the chambers. Within a week, he had moved us to a cottage while he rebuilt Blythe Hall. He said he would not have his wife complaining all the time and telling people she was living in a hovel."

It was in that small, cramped cottage that she had truly realized the nature of the man she had thought she loved.

"You called Blythe Hall a *hovel?*"

She shook her head. "No. However, I fear your uncle had not maintained the property very well in your absence. The house was in need of several repairs."

"I'm surprised he left this impromptu addition to the hearth I made in a childish attempt to get back at my parents after they had upset me."

He glanced back at his juvenile handiwork for another moment, his expression one of wry self-deprecation. "I wanted to make my mark upon the world even then, I suppose."

"William did plan to have it repaired, until he was told how costly it would be. He decided that could wait."

In view of Richard's disappointment today, she was very glad he had.

"You did not have it done, either, although you seem to have prospered."

"No, I thought it made the house more like a home."

And in truth, she had been desperate for anything that gave her that sensation.

He left her to stroll around the hall, looking at the ornate plaster ceiling, the wide staircase that ran up the left side of the entrance hall, the balustrade, the polished floor.

"The house *is* more comfortable and modern."

"Yes, so I see."

His anger had disappeared, yet she was not sure what exactly had replaced it.

"William designed it so that the large withdrawing room is along that corridor to the right," she explained, "with my closet where I keep the accounts off of it. The new dining room is to the left, closest to the kitchen. There are two bedchambers on this floor for guests. The other bedchambers are upstairs, and servants' quarters above that."

He halted and sighed. "Well, so I am come home at last. I shall write to the king to express my gratitude, of course." He cocked his head and regarded her gravely. "Where is our bedchamber?"

Her mouth suddenly very dry, she swallowed hard as his lips curved in a slow, seductive smile. "I sleep in the westernmost chamber upstairs."

"Then that is where I shall sleep, too. Do you object?"

She didn't trust her voice to be steady, so she merely shook her head.

His smile grew and his dark-eyed gaze intensified as he approached her. "I confess I am delighted you do not wish to see me banished to another bedroom. It would be like being sent into exile again, and a far worse one than I have already experienced."

"I am glad you are not angry about the house anymore," she murmured, wondering if he was going to kiss her right here in the entrance hall.

Although he came very close to her, he stopped short of embracing her. "Would you mind showing me the way to our bedchamber? Otherwise, I shall likely get lost. While it would be an adventure, I think I have had enough excitement for one morning."

Stifling a surge of disappointment and reminding herself that she was a lady and should act with appropriate dignity, she led him up the stairs and down the corridor toward the bedchamber. She opened the door and waited for him to enter.

"After you, my sweet wife," he said, bowing slightly.

As they entered, she watched as he studied the large, timber-framed chamber. The maids had kept it scrupulously clean and tidy. The wool bedcover was smooth as glass, and the table, chair, chest, and bed polished to mirrorlike perfection.

He looked at the large, curtained bed for what seemed a very long time. Her heart started to race and she began to hope that he had recovered sufficiently from the shock of seeing the new house to indulge in other excitement. "So, this is where young Will was conceived."

She started. "No, it is not."

His expression inscrutable, he looked at her. "Not here?"

"Not here, and not in that bed."

"The cottage, was it? How bucolic."

Tears started in her eyes and she hurried toward the window, embarrassed by her foolishly emotional response.

She was too slow.

"What's this? A tear for the dear departed?"

She would not answer. She would never tell

anyone about the night Will was conceived, when her husband had thrown her to the floor to roughly take his pleasure of her.

Yet in a way, she was glad he had reminded her of that night, and all the other horrible nights with William Longbourne. She needed to be reminded where her folly had led before, so that she would not tread that path again.

No matter how different Richard seemed from her first husband.

"I am touched by this evidence of your soft heart. Is there anything else I should know about Blythe Hall or the servants or the tenants, or do you intend to continue surprising me?"

"If you will excuse me, I have many things to attend to. I shall have Will show you the house."

She hurried from the room as if pursued by hungry bears.

Richard muttered a curse. The notion of Elissa making love in that bed with another man had prompted him to speak without thinking, and he deeply regretted his remark about Will's conception. While courtiers would have smiled and made jokes, it *was* in poor taste.

Her tears had been extremely disturbing, too. Somehow, he had come to think her somewhat invulnerable, as if, unlike most women, she had an almost masculine inner strength. It was surprising to find a chink in her armor and unsettling to discover it was the obviously cherished memory of her late husband.

Richard wandered toward the window and looked outside. He had had a very different view from his childhood window, which had looked upon the Banqueting House.

Thank God he could not see that accursed building from here.

He leaned back against the sill and looked around the comfortable room. Instead of contemplating his long-anticipated return to his family's estate, however, he was thinking about Elissa.

Only now did he truly appreciate the hope that had blossomed into being on their wedding night, that she would come to care for him. When he was making love with Elissa, it even seemed possible that they would come to live in harmony, perhaps even love, despite the unusual circumstances of their marriage.

Now, he was not nearly so sure.

What if his hopes were not unfounded? What if there was a chance that he could find happiness in a marriage forced upon him by the king?

Or was that the deluded aspiration of a fool blinded by passion and the seeming regard of a lovely, spirited woman?

He might do better to believe the latter, protecting his heart as he had always done.

Yet if he were wrong . . . if Elissa did offer him an opportunity for such happiness that he had scarcely dared to dream of . . . surely only a greater fool would toss that chance aside.

Sighing, Richard pushed himself off the sill and went to find his stepson.

Later that evening, after an exhausted Will had gone to bed, Richard and Elissa sat across from each other on matching settles in the new withdrawing room. It had quickly become obvious to Richard that his wife was in no humor to talk as she sewed upon some kind of embroidery that looked large enough to outdo the Bayeux tapestry.

He reached for his wine, rather glad to have that beverage available. As a rule, he was not a man to rely on its relaxing ability; tonight, however, was an exception. "Perhaps tomorrow you would do me the honor of escorting me around the estate?"

"You grew up here, did you not? Surely you do not need to be shown anything."

"So much has been changed. You wouldn't have me fall down a well, would you?"

She shrugged her lovely shoulders.

"Does that mean you would? I know I have upset you, but how can I make amends if I am dead?"

The smallest of smiles lifted the corners of her lips, and Richard felt the same sense of triumph he did when an audience applauded.

He rose from the uncomfortably hard settle and sat beside her. She shifted slightly, but didn't move away—another cause for a triumphant thrill. "What is that you are making?"

"A tapestry for this room, to hang on the wall opposite us."

He followed her gaze, then turned back to see her bent over her work.

"You sew very well."

"Are you an expert in that, as well?"

"I am not an expert at much."

"You always speak with such authority, I assumed you must be."

"I am not the only one who makes assumptions."

"My late husband only changed the house. The rest of the estate is unchanged—save for the northern portion. Your uncle sold the wood to Mr. Sedgemore."

Sighing with resignation, he reached out and placed his hand over hers. When she looked at him, he softly said, "I believe I shall never be surprised by anything ever again where the sale or alteration of my family's property is concerned. However, I promise I shall not complain to you about it anymore. What happened in the past was not your fault.

"Please try to understand," he continued, regarding her gravely. "For a long time, I clung to the certain faith that one day, this estate would be mine. I was horrified when I learned that it had been sold while I was in Europe. My uncle had no right to do so, so when the king was restored, I hoped he would ensure that it was returned to me.

"Now, under strange circumstances, I am back home—to what is not my home. I was shocked and angry. Forgive me for speaking hastily, without tact, and for causing you any hurt."

She didn't look at him as she laid aside her handiwork.

"Thank you," she said softly, raising her eyes to regard him. "Thank you for your apology, Richard. It means a great deal to me. William never apologized for anything." A smile tweaked her lovely lips. "I do not think you apologize often."

He felt a surge of relief, followed quickly by happiness. "I confess you guess aright."

"I assume you instead wield your wicked tongue or sword."

"Alas, 'tis true. Yet a man often slandered must have some defense." He sighed. "Although I daresay you have cause for dread, given my scandalous reputation, rest assured, Elissa, that while I am no saint, I am not the black-hearted, lascivious rogue rumor and some verse attributed to me would imply. I write only a very little verse—none of it obscene. Anyone can use my name if they choose. There is no law to stop them."

Understanding lit her serious mien, then her brow lowered ominously. "That is terrible! There should be a law!"

A little smile played about his face. "Such a passionate defender! It is a pity you are not a lawyer."

"We have an excellent lawyer in Mr. Harding."

Richard's smile disappeared. "Ah, yes, Mr. Harding, champion of brides everywhere."

"I am sorry the agreement was so severe, but I had to protect myself and my son."

He rose and pulled her into a loose embrace. "I have another confession, Elissa."

"You . . . you do?" she replied, breathless with anticipation.

"The more I am with you, the happier I am that the king made us marry, regardless of that dastardly agreement."

Her fingers began to follow the pattern of the muscles of his back. "You have never been in charge of an estate, and I have," she explained softly. "I was afraid you might destroy all I have worked so hard to build."

"A justifiable dread," he murmured as he nibbled on her earlobe.

She had never experienced anything like that. "It is not as easy as one might think to run an estate. I had a very difficult time after William died."

Richard leaned back and put a finger to her lips. "I would rather not hear about him."

Her brow furrowed again. "He was Will's father. We cannot erase him completely."

"I understand. However, as your *new* husband, I order that we never speak of him in one particular room in this house."

"Which room?"

"Our bedchamber."

Elissa nodded. Then her delectable lips turned up in a small smile, too. "He never set foot in that room after this house was built, Richard. I began to sleep there after he died."

"I cannot begin to tell you how delighted that makes me," Richard replied, reaching for her hand. "Shall we?"

"What?"

"Shall we retire to that room where that man's name is not to be mentioned?"

"Is that an order, my husband?"

"It is a request," he answered, regarding her with desire burning in his dark eyes.

"Then I agree. But what shall we talk of?" she asked with a hint of mischief as she let him lead her out of the withdrawing room.

"I think we have talked enough."

"What, then, shall we do?" she asked as they entered the spacious hall, her tone innocent, yet the smoldering yearning in her eyes telling him a different tale.

"If you do not know, then I shall not tell you."

She laughed softly, the sound delightful to him. "Oh, *that*."

"Yes, my sweet, *that*—and more besides."

He halted, pulled her into his arms just as she had wanted him to do before and quite regardless of the fact that they were in the hall, where any servant might see them, kissed her passionately.

Then he picked her up and with rather astonishing vigor carried her up the stairs.

She laughed again, feeling as she never had before, cherished and safe and free.

He shoved open the door to the bedchamber with his shoulder and began to set her down. Enjoying herself, she took her time, slipping her feet slowly to the floor so that she slid against his body. "What more would you teach me, my lord and husband?"

With a low chuckle, he reached past her and pushed the door closed. "Why some folk refer to love-making as sport."

"Why do they?" she asked softly, running her hands over his chest, and lower.

"Because they play."

"How?"

"You are making it very difficult for me to remember," he murmured as he began explorations of his own.

"Never mind . . ."

He moved away, a droll smile lighting his features. "Oh, no. I want to play."

Frustrated, she crossed her arms. "What game?"

"Who can undress the fastest."

It was her turn to smile. "I don't think you want to play that."

His gaze raked her body. "I assure you, I do."

"I will win."

He laughed. "With all those undergarments?"

"Would you care to make a wager?"

"I will win," he warned.

"Then make the wager."

"Very well. But I have very little money of my own."

"I was not thinking of money," she answered merrily—and honestly.

His eyes widened and his smile grew. "Ah! Again, I underestimate my country-bred wife. What do you suggest?"

"I suggest that the loser must do whatever the other asks tonight."

"Whatever?"

She blushed. "Well, within reason."

"I might want to be unreasonable."

"Then I suppose I shall have to win," she observed, trying not to look at his knotted jabot, the several buttons of his shirt, the ties of his breeches or his calf-hugging boots.

He, meanwhile, surveyed her laced bodice, her overskirt and the petticoat peeking out from beneath its hem. "When shall we begin?"

"On the count of three?"

He nodded, and when she cried, "Three!" she swiftly reached behind her neck to untie the lacing of her bodice. She had not had a lady's maid since her marriage, William deeming that a frivolous expense, so she had long ago learned to lace and unlace her bodice itself, a skill proving handy now.

In a twinkling, it was undone and while Richard tossed aside his cravat, she was already wiggling out of her bodice and chemise, paying no heed to the fact that she was going to be half-naked.

She wanted to win.

She grabbed the ties at the side of her overshirt and pulled them undone, and just as quickly undid the ties of her underskirt and petticoat.

She was already stepping out them when Richard was still on his shirt buttons.

"Zounds!" he muttered as he glanced at her and saw how far ahead she was. He redoubled his efforts on his buttons.

She kicked her skirts aside and finished wiggling out of her bodice and chemise, while he was tugging on the tie of his breeches. "I win!" she cried, standing before him naked and triumphant.

"You think so?" he asked slyly as he gave up with his breeches. "I think I am the winner, with this view."

Giggling, she dashed to the bed and hurried under the covers. "You must agree I win the wager, so now you must do whatever I say."

"Gladly," he replied as he started to untie his breeches.

"Would you please pick up my clothes? I

shouldn't have left them in a pile."

His brow furrowed. "That isn't quite the order I thought you would be issuing."

"Really?" she answered mischievously. "What else did you have in mind?"

"You wish an example?" he said as he gathered up her clothes and tossed them in a heap on a chair. "If I had won, I would be asking you to kiss me."

"Very well, Sir Richard. Kiss me."

He strolled to the bed. "Should I finish disrobing first?"

"Yes."

Elissa had been excited before, just being in his arms or returning his kiss, but now a new thrill came into being that had nothing to do with Richard's body being slowly revealed to her.

William would never had allowed her to give any suggestions, let alone commands. He would have begrudged giving up even that little power.

But Richard—Richard was so different, in so many ways. What before had been an unpleasant, onerous duty was fast becoming one of the greatest delights of her life.

He climbed between the covers. "Now for that kiss."

Happily she put her arms around him and pulled him close.

But before his mouth touched hers, he hesitated. "On the lips?"

She blinked. "Yes, I suppose so. Where else?"

"There are many places for a kiss."

She should have recalled that. "First on the lips."

He obeyed at once, his mouth moving slowly over hers in a way that nearly made her senseless with desire, until he pulled away.

"What next, my lady?"

"Perhaps I don't want to give orders any more," she murmured truthfully.

"But I am enjoying this," he confessed in a low, husky tone. "Are you not?"

At his admission, she felt even more excitement course through her body. "Kiss me again and touch my breasts the way you did on our wedding night."

He laughed softly. "I hear and obey with the greatest pleasure, my lady."

Her breathing quickened with the delicious sensations his caresses aroused. Emboldened, she suddenly reached up and pushed him over, so that he lay on his back.

"Do I displease you, my lady?"

"Lie still."

"To hear is to—" He gasped as she straddled him. She bent her head and began to flick her tongue over his hardened nipples.

"Oh, yes, Elissa," he growled. He put his hands on her cheeks to pull her up for his kiss.

But she grabbed his wrists and shoved them

onto the pillows. "I won the wager, did I not? You are to do as I say."

Richard had never felt so aroused in all his life as she spoke with both authority and amusement. Never before would he ever have acquiesced to such a thing, not in bed or out of it.

But with Elissa he would, and gladly. A new sense of freedom was blossoming in her—and within himself, too.

So he gave up control. Allowing her hands to keep his still, he waited for what she would do next.

Which was to kiss and lick his chest until he writhed with the exquisite agony of it and thought he would die if they did not make love.

She moved off of him. "Sit up, Richard."

"What?" he whispered, not sure he heard aright.

"Sit up, please."

Disappointed because of what he had hoped she was going to do, yet apparently mistaken, he did as she asked.

"I saw a picture once that I cannot forget. I hope this does not disgust you."

He held his breath as she moved, positioning herself so that they were face to face, her legs around his waist. Then slowly she shifted forward and lifted herself, gently guiding his erection to her moist honor, so that they were intertwined and joined, hip to hip and chest to breasts.

His mouth found hers as he began to push. Sensations such as he had never felt before assailed him and overwhelmed him.

Their kiss deepened and their breathing quickened.

"Oh, Richard, yes," Elissa murmured as he kissed her jaw, her neck, her ear, while his thrusts grew faster and more powerful. "Don't stop. Please don't stop."

That was a command he couldn't have disobeyed if he had wanted to.

Too soon he felt the building tension reaching its peak. As they clung to each other almost desperately, Elissa bucked and panted with equal passion. A sound grew in the back of her throat and he felt her body grip him tighter yet, the sudden throbbing pushing him over the edge. He threw back his head and growled with the pure animalistic joy of release.

"Richard?"

"Yes?" he sighed as his body relaxed, and he held her close.

"I like your games."

He chuckled softly. "And I could come to enjoy losing."

The next morning, Elissa sat at her desk in the small room she used for an office. Her closet paneled in pale new oak was a few yards in dimension, lined with shelves for her books of account, and overlooked the yard and stables.

She rubbed her tired eyes and tried again to decipher her entries in the account book before her. Her handwriting really was abominable, and she had not blotted several entries before closing the book the last time she used it. The page looked like some kind of mysterious creature had walked over it and smudged the words and numbers.

Even though she smiled when she remembered why she was so exhausted, her fatigue was not making this study easier.

She never would have guessed marriage could be so exciting and liberating.

As she yawned again, she glanced up from the accounts to see the distractingly handsome Richard leaning against the door frame, a disgruntled look on his face.

"What is it?" she asked.

He sauntered into the room, which held little more than her desk and chair. "What language do these people speak?"

She quickly closed her book so that he wouldn't see her untidy entries. "What people?"

"The servants."

"English, of course."

"And the stable hands?"

"English," she replied, somewhat mystified. "You would never know it by the blank stares they give me when I ask a question," he muttered, picking up her pen and absently examining the worn-down tip.

"Perhaps your question is the problem," she replied, resisting the urge to grab the pen from him. "What did you want to know?"

He put down the pen and looked at her. "I merely inquired which horse I could ride."

"And they did not answer?"

"Not at first. First, they had to look at each other, then back at me several times," he said, turning his head from side to side in imitation. "Then they surveyed the stable and the loft as if the answer would be written by a celestial hand on the ceiling.

"Finally, after all this," he concluded with obvious exasperation, "the groom, who, I must say, looks more like an ox than any person should, mumbled something vaguely coherent about asking 'the mistress,' which would be you, I take it."

"Yes, that would be me," she answered, trying not to smile.

"Well, mistress, which horse might your husband ride?" he asked. "The black stallion that looks to have a mean mouth, the placid mare that will likely lull me to sleep with her easy gait, or the pony, which has no external flaws that I can detect, yet is a little short for me?"

"The servants are simply being cautious, Richard," she explained. "They don't know you, but they do know me. I can have a fierce temper when I am displeased."

"Zounds, I know that. I have experienced your temper myself."

"Well then, you should appreciate why they didn't want to give you an answer, in case it was the wrong one." She smiled placatingly. "After William died, I admit I displayed my temper more often than strictly necessary. It ensured respect for the bereaved widow."

"An excellent strategy. I think your flashes of apparent ire increased the king's respect, too."

"Well, I truly was angered by him."

"Then you are braver than many a courtier."

"I was afraid, too."

"Most monarchs have that affect on people. Fortunately, Charles is more genial than the general rule."

"I shall have to take your word for that. He was not very genial, to my mind."

"Then you should meet the king of France."

"No, thank you."

"Besides, you did have the distinct advantage of me, you know."

"*I* had the advantage? You are his friend."

"You are a beautiful woman. I'faith, I fear you are already winding me about your little finger. Why, I am all sweetness and light in your presence, and I was perilously close to running those stablehands through."

"Sweetness and light is not what I would

call you. Fire and brimstone, perhaps."

"Fire, at any rate," he agreed.

Despite his light and easy tone, passion smoldered in his eyes, firing her own blood. He reached out to take her hand and pressed his warm, firm lips upon it.

"I have much to do," she said, although she did not pull her hand away. "When I finish these books, I have to . . . have to . . ."

"Whatever it is, it does not sound very urgent."

"It is the middle of the morning," she protested weakly.

He smiled his devilishly bewitching smile. "I know."

He let go of her hand and she was most absurdly disappointed. "Well, if you would rather work on those musty books, I shall not stop you. In the meantime, I think I shall take Will riding with me. No objections to that, I hope?"

"No, not at all. Indeed, he will be thrilled. I cannot ride out very often myself," she said regretfully.

She would very much like to go riding this morning, but she dared not take the time until she had everything sorted out.

"I assume the pony is his?"

She nodded. "Of course, and the mare is mine."

"That tame creature? I thought a woman of

your temperament would want something with more spirit."

"I ride for pleasure, not a challenge."

"Whereas I enjoy a challenge." Richard's voice lowered to an intimate whisper. "Such as seeing how long I can hold out against your insistent, insatiable demands upon my poor person."

"Richard Blythe, it was your idea!" she cried, even as her body warmed with the memories of all the things they had done last night.

"And one of my better ones, I must say. My dear, the ladies at court could learn a thing or two from their country sisters, if you are anything to go by."

"If I am not allowed to speak my late husband's name in some rooms of this house," she replied rather primly, "I think you should stop mentioning the ladies of the court."

"Jealous?"

She rose from her chair and came around the desk to face him. "I have got you now, not them, and," she said, boldly and possessively caressing him, "I will not share."

"Good God, woman," he muttered, yanking her into his arms, "I believe I have married a cock-tease."

"Richard! Must you be so crude?"

Laughing softly, he kissed her lightly on the forehead before moving toward the door. "I am not the one attacking my spouse in the closet in the middle of the morning. However, since you profess to be so busy, I shall take myself to the stables."

"You are quite right about the stallion," she said with a sigh when she realized he was in earnest. "He does have a mean mouth. He was my husband's horse, and William was a cruel horseman. I have given up trying to sell the poor beast, for no one will take him. Oh, I nearly forgot!" She reached for a letter open on the desk. "Alfred Sedgemore has invited us to dine with him this evening, to welcome you."

Richard raised an eyebrow. "How neighborly."

"It is neighborly," she replied. "He has invited all the important families around Owston to meet you."

"There is no possibility of refusal, I take it?"

"Not unless you wish to be considered arrogant and rude."

"That is a tempting thought. Then nobody shall force their presence upon us with unwelcome visits."

"Richard, I think to refuse would be most unwise."

"Heaven forfend that we should insult the neighbors, especially the ferrety-faced Mr. Alfred Sedgemore!" he cried with mock horror. "I shall endure as best I can." He grew thoughtful. "I wonder if I shall know any of them, or they me."

"Sir John Norbert will be there, and his family."

"Sir John—of course! Is he as fat as ever?"

"He is . . . stout."

"He is married and had a girl, I seem to recall."

"Girls. He has three daughters of marriageable age."

"If they take after their father, I hope they have large dowries."

Elissa could not quite stifle a smile, for in fact the Norbert girls—young ladies, really—did take after their father, in girth, manner, and appetite. Fortunately for the Norbert girls, they would indeed have very large dowries. "They are very nice young ladies."

His mouth betrayed a certain skepticism. "I promise to be charmed." He grinned ruefully. "If I can put up with Sedley and his ilk, I should be able to endure your country society."

"I did not see that London society was so very special. In fact, I would say the opposite was true."

"You were not exposed to the best of it," Richard replied. Then he made a contrite face and bowed. "My apologies, wife. It is the habit of those in the city to disparage those in the country, and playwrights most especially. I shall endeavor to correct this grievous fault."

"Please do."

"For your sake only, of course. I cherish your good regard."

"You should seek their good regard."

He looked genuinely surprised.

"Don't you want them to like you?" she demanded.

"My dear madam, I don't care one whit if they like me or not. I don't particularly care if anybody likes me or not—except you and Will, of course."

There could be no mistaking that he meant exactly what he said.

Unsure whether she was impressed or dismayed by his attitude, she said, "Perhaps you know Mr. Assey?"

"I beg your pardon?"

"Mr. Assey. He is a very wealthy wool trader."

"He should take some of that money and purchase a new name."

Elissa stared at him a moment, then smiled and flushed with sudden comprehension. "I have never thought of that before. Now I shall never be able to look at him without blushing."

"Don't look at him at all, then. In fact, I don't think I like the notion of you looking at other men, ever."

"I shall have a very difficult time doing business if I cannot."

"Don't do business," he answered glibly. "That should be a husband's job anyway."

Her expression froze. "I have been handling the business of this estate for five years and have no intention of turning it over to anybody."

"Not until I prove myself, at any rate, eh?" Richard said lightly as he went to the door. "*Adieu*, wife."

She watched him leave, thinking that although she valued her hard-won independence, it was very tempting to let Richard take the more onerous of her responsibilities from her hands.

She heard Richard call for Will, and her son's boisterous and delighted answer. He had never been a quiet child.

She frowned as she thought of all the times his father had brusquely ordered him to hush, even when he was but a babe, incapable of understanding speech.

She went to the window, which was open to catch the breeze. She could see Richard and Will heading toward the stables. Will's excited voice reached her easily, and although she could not hear Richard's exact responses, she could catch his amiable tone as he matched his stride to the boy's.

He was very good with children, and she suspected that if he truly did not care what the neighbors thought of him, he did value Will's good opinion.

She put her hand to her stomach and wondered if he would continue to do so when he had a child of his own.

It was much too early to be sure, of course. A mere day or two. When she was absolutely certain, then she would tell Richard that she was carrying his baby.

Chapter 12

"Ah, Lady Dovercourt! How lovely you look this evening," Mr. Sedgemore cried as he hurried toward them in the grand entrance hall of his country home.

Like the late William Longbourne, Alfred Sedgemore had razed the original manor on his estate. Mr. Sedgemore had done an even more thorough job of this, however, for he had torn down the whole of the house and built afresh. The result was a country home of the latest design, featuring pediments and columns and massive chimneys on the outside and impressively decorated rooms on the inside.

"Your servant, my lord," Mr. Sedgemore said to Richard as he bowed.

"Your servant, sir," Richard replied evenly, inclining in his head.

Despite the smile on her husband's face, she was very much reminded of his arrogant attitude the first time she had seen him in that boat on the Thames.

Confused by his manner, she said nothing as he placed her hand on his arm. Together they followed their host into the huge parlor paneled in dark oak and hung with various portraits of what she assumed were Sedgemore ancestors, all of whom looked as if they suffered from chronic indigestion.

Apparently Mr. Sedgemore had invited every person who had any claim to gentility for several miles around. Despite the crowd, conversation halted in midsentence as they entered, and everyone turned to look at them.

Elissa had believed her arrival at her wedding would be her one and only sensational entrance. She was quite wrong. Apparently, however, Richard did not find this at all unusual, for he bestowed a magnanimous smile upon them all.

Nevertheless, she knew something was very wrong.

It was not that the women stared at Richard as if they had never seen a man before. Clad in his black velvet jacket and breeches, pristine white shirt, and lace jabot, Richard looked very handsome and elegant and worldly compared to most of the men of Leicester. He also had the aura of the court to add to his luster.

In contrast to the feminine admiration, however, many of the men's reactions were openly hostile and obviously scornful rather than envious, a reaction she would have understood. To be sure, a few of the ones she knew to be ambitious regarded him speculatively, as if already planning on seeking his influence at court, but in general, it was as if Richard had returned from London a leper.

She told herself most of these men would look down on anybody who had to earn their living by any means other than agriculture, and especially anybody in the theater.

Despite her attempt at rationalization, Elissa couldn't help feeling that there was more to their reactions than the snobbery of the righteous.

Appalled and confused, she glanced at Richard—and could scarcely believe the calm equanimity on his face, the merry mockery in his eyes, and the wry twist to his lips. That he might find the women's responses amusing was one thing, but how could he laugh at the men's?

"As I live and breathe, it's Sir John Norbert!" Richard cried suddenly, abandoning Elissa and sauntering toward the plump man who half rose from the settle, then apparently wished he had not. "It has been a long time, Sir John!"

Sir John scowled and sat heavily. "Richard Blythe," he huffed, growing red in the face. "You're back."

"Obviously," Richard replied with an elegant bow. "Back to the land of my fathers, the bosom of my family. You all missed me, I'm sure."

Elissa looked on helplessly as Sir John's scowl deepened.

"And here is the charming creature who finally managed to ensnare you after all those years of carefree bachelorhood," Richard went on, addressing the equally plump, bejeweled, and middle-aged lady beside him.

"Yes," Sir John said with no attempt at courtesy. "Lady Alyce, you remember Richard Blythe."

"Lord Dovercourt," Richard corrected with a genial smile and shrewd eyes.

Sir John cleared his throat. "Lord Dovercourt."

"And who might these nymphs be?" Richard inquired, turning toward Sir John's daughters, who stood clustered nearby.

Elissa hurried forward and made the introductions. She might have been invisible, for all the attention the young women gave to her.

Claudia, the eldest and the kindest, was unfortunately also cursed with a slightly crossed eye that she endeavored to hide by constantly keeping her head to one side. Livia would have been the beauty of the family, if she had ever learned to smile with fewer teeth and more sincerity. Antonia was undeniably plain, and yet she was unaccountably the vainest of the three. She thought of nothing save her hair and clothes, unless it was her effect on the male population of Owston. Now, she batted her thin eyelashes at Richard as if she had a piece of soot lodged in her eye.

"Your servant, ladies," Richard said with another elegant bow.

He did not linger, but moved on to the next man, glancing at Elissa expectantly.

It was Mr. Sedgemore's place to make the introductions, but Elissa, not sure what was going on, took over that function.

The introductions were nearly complete when she stopped in front of a well-dressed, middle-aged man wearing a curled peruke, very lacy jabot, and lemon-yellow jacket and breeches. "My lord, this is . . ."

Blushing, she hesitated, afraid she would do something undignified, like giggle.

"This must be Mr. Assey, of whom I have heard so much." Richard bowed. "Delighted, sir, absolutely delighted. Such an unusual name. French, I take it?"

Mr. Assey's homely face beamed with a broad smile. "Indeed it is, my lord. Indeed it is!"

"I thought there must be some explanation," Richard answered.

He turned and nearly collided with Antonia. "You must tell us all about the court," she simpered. "And the king, too. Is he as handsome as they say? As handsome as you?"

Sir John cleared his throat loudly, making Elissa jump. Antonia, however, seemed impervious to any hints of inappropriate remarks as she smiled coyly at Richard. "Well, is he?"

"I shall have to defer to my sweet wife on that subject," Richard replied gravely. "She is likely a better judge of the men of court. If it is the women you wish to know about, then by all means, I shall offer my humble opinion."

"Is the queen—" Livia began.

"What about the women of the court?" Antonia interrupted imperiously. "Are they so very beautiful?"

"They are very elegant and sophisticated, and naturally they dress very well," Richard replied. "As for beauty . . . well, it is in the eye of the beholder, is it not?"

One of the younger men shifted his feet and glanced about nervously before speaking. "And Lady Castlemaine? Is she as pretty as they say?"

"She is very pretty, as are all the king's mistresses. Very temperamental, though, Lady Castlemaine, but her other qualities more than compensate, or so I understand."

Richard strolled over to the settle and insinuated himself between Sir John and Lady Alyce. "Of course, Charles likes a certain variety. I lost more actresses to the king's desire than I care to recall. Zounds, I believe Charles thinks of the theater as a harem. It plays the very devil with my productions, I assure you." He waved his hand in airy dismissal. "I have given all that up, of course, for the bucolic delights of the ancestral estate, and my beautiful wife."

Elissa could only stare at him.

What was he doing? Had he no notion of proper behavior among normal people? This might be considered appropriate talk and manners for the court, but not here in Owston.

Did he want them to think him the worst sort of decadent dilettante playwright, as she had? Could it be possible that he didn't understand how he was embarrassing not just himself, but his wife?

He was too intelligent a man not to see that, surely.

Unfortunately, she couldn't very well demand an explanation while they were in company—but the moment they were alone, she would find out why he had decided to humiliate both himself and his wife by acting the gossip-mongering fool.

"Well, that was quite a performance," Elissa said as the coach rolled along the bumpy country road on the journey home. "You could not have done better if you were trying to make them all hate you."

"I commend you on your perception," Richard replied with a calmness he most certainly did not feel as he reclined against the hard back of the seat. "It *was* a performance." He gave her a bitter smile. "After my years in the theater, I know when the house is for or against me. Sometimes you can tell before the curtain rises. It was that way tonight, so there was no point to try to make them like me. They had all formed their opinion of me before I even entered the room."

"Not *all* of them wanted to hate you."

"No, not all. I had the women on my side."

"I thought you would be pleased by that."

"Why should I be pleased? I am like a circus performer to them, or a freak, Handsome Playwright from London, Intimate Friend of the King. Nothing more. To be sure, they waited until they saw me, but I daresay they were predisposed to be excited by my addition to their rude and rustic circle."

"They were not the only ones being rude," she noted coolly. "Or perhaps I should say, impudent. And not all of the men disliked you."

His behavior had really been too outrageous for her to forgive him quickly, no matter that his explanation for his behavior was not without merit, or how attractive he was or how close they were in the confines of their coach.

"Oh, no. Some clearly have hopes of a connection with the court through me, so they were polite enough. And your Mr. Assey, despite his numbing choice of color for his clothes, seemed gentlemanly. There is also the charming Mr. Sedgemore. He is so very keen to be our friend—or yours, at any rate."

"At least he did not entertain us by listing the latest adulteries among the courtiers."

"That is what they wanted to hear," Richard replied. "I have never yet encountered a person in England who doesn't want to hear the gossip of the court, and you cannot deny that they were all fascinated."

"No, I cannot—but it was as much the way you spoke as what you were saying."

"As I said, a performance."

She regarded him steadily. "Richard, you confirmed their worst expectations of you. Why? Why could you not have made them see that there is more to you than the worldly playwright?"

He turned to stare out the window at the night sky. "Perhaps there is no more to me than the worldly playwright," he said, once more taking refuge in mockery and scorn for others' opinions.

"I do not believe that."

"Very well. I could have played the cavalier soldier for them."

"There is no need to *play* anything for them. You should just be yourself."

"That was Richard Blythe, Elissa—a man who performs, whether for a room full of country landowners and merchants, or the king, or the audience in the theater."

Her brow furrowed. "Are you performing now?"

He shrugged his shoulders.

"When you make love with me, are you performing then, too? Is every move choreographed like a court masque? Do you quote lines you have written and rehearsed? How many times? With how many women?"

"Elissa, I—"

The coach jolted to a stop, and before he could say anything, she had shoved her way past him and disembarked without waiting for him to get out first.

He sat in the coach and watched her march inside. The driver gave him a puzzled look, which he ignored as he left the vehicle and entered the house, his pace quickening with every step.

He did not go to the bedchamber. Instead, he turned toward Elissa's closet off the withdrawing room. Then he did what he had to do.

Richard's sigh was both tired and winsome as he rode along the country lane the next morning.

This road was very much as he remembered it, unlike so many things. He thought of the times he had walked this way, sometimes at night, seeking the solace of the quiet darkness, more often in the daylight, when he could look out over the ripening fields, or watch the flocks of sheep.

The natural beauty of the countryside had been a balm to him, a balm sorely lacking after he had left home, for nothing he had ever seen in London or Europe surpassed the natural beauty of the land surrounding Blythe Hall.

He was tired because he had been up all night and winsome because, after much contemplation, he had come to the conclusion that he had erred. He should have been less the cavalier courtier, and more the nobleman who deserved his family estate.

He was also sorry he had not gone to Elissa and apologized sooner, with words and actions, instead of spending the night as he had. He would find her before he took Will riding, and he would make the best apology he could.

Humming to himself, he began to consider what he would say and do. It would not be choreography, as she had charged, he thought with a smile, but it was very pleasant and arousing to imagine how he would begin, whether with a kiss to her hand, or her cheek. Perhaps her lips, depending on the look in her charming eyes—

Suddenly, his horse shied, and as he struggled to control it, Antonia Norbert appeared like some sort of demonic spirit, shoving her way through the bushes that bordered the lane. Her large and unfortunately ugly hat was slightly askew and bits of greenery clung to her apparel.

Rather revealing apparel it was, too, for daywear. Her cloak was too small and gaped most amazingly, showing the gown beneath, as well as quite a bit of her bosom.

She smiled broadly, not a bit nonplussed as he struggled to calm his mount, and her eyes fluttered in a manner he supposed was intended to be alluring. "Oh, Lord Dovercourt! What a surprise!"

Truly, the boldest whore in the most notorious brothel behind Covent Garden was subtlety itself compared to her. "Tell me, do you often lie in ambush for unsuspecting travelers?"

She giggled. Loudly. "Oh, my lord, you are so droll!"

"What are you doing out here all by yourself? Surely a lovely lady like you is taking a great risk."

More giggles, and Richard couldn't suppress a shudder as she eyed him coyly. "You would come to my rescue, wouldn't you, Lord Dovercourt? We hear you are quite the swordsman."

"I keep my sword sheathed unless I am in imminent danger of death," he replied, falling into the tone he used to banter with the ladies of the court. "Otherwise, I might do myself an injury."

She sauntered closer, her hips swaying, and Richard was very glad he was on his horse. "That is not what we hear. Owston is not so very out of the way that we don't hear news from London. You are said to be a very great swordsman, and a duelist, too."

"In my youth, perhaps."

"But surely you retain the skill," she murmured slyly.

"Such skills as I possess will be for my family's benefit."

"How noble of you!"

"If you will excuse me, I really must be getting home. I am late to take Will riding. Good day."

He didn't wait for her to say another word, or—heaven forbid!—giggle again, but rode on.

Antonia shrieked.

As much as he wanted to get home, he couldn't help twisting in his saddle to look back over his shoulder.

Antonia was bent over, holding her ankle. "I fear I have sprained it," she cried piteously. "It hurts to walk on it."

Looking ahead at the road, he wished courtesy did not demand he offer assistance. He would rather kick his horse into a gallop as if a horde of screaming barbarians were chasing him. Zounds, he almost wished that would happen—anything rather than have to deal with the obviously lustful Antonia.

Unfortunately, courtesy did demand that he offer assistance, so he stopped scowling and dismounted.

"Oh, dear, I am so clumsy," she declared.

"No doubt the road is to blame," he replied flatly.

"What shall we do?"

"You must ride my horse and I shall take you home."

"I could ride behind you," she suggested eagerly. "After all, it is a long way to my father's manor."

Richard smiled wanly and wished he knew the fastest way there. Undoubtedly she would suggest the longest, most circuitous route. "I have been riding some time already, and my horse is fatigued. Two riders would be too much. I shall walk."

Antonia opened her mouth to protest, took a good look at Richard's face, then wisely shut it.

"Come and I shall help you mount."

"I . . . I fear I cannot. It pains me to walk."

Barely refraining from rolling his eyes, Richard went to her. "Lean on my shoulder, then."

Antonia threw her rather beefy arm about his shoulder, which made her cloak fall open all the more, perhaps coincidentally.

Her breasts really were amazing, Richard was forced to conclude. Some men would surely consider the opportunity to toy with them worth any amount of trouble.

He, however, had seen too many breasts to be impressed, and the finest of all belonged to his wife.

"Well?" Antonia sighed, her breath hot on his ear.

Putting his arm around her waist, he helped her to his horse. "I fear my foot is too swollen to put in the stirrup," she observed.

The last time he had felt this trapped, he reflected, was when he had been commanded to marry. That had turned out better than he had anticipated; he feared no similar good could come from Antonia's behavior.

"Then I shall lift you," he said, managing not to grit his teeth. "Put your hands on my shoulders and let us hope the horse stands still."

Antonia emitted a little squeal as he lifted her, her breasts brushing his chin. The horse shifted and she nearly fell, but with great determination, Richard got her safely aboard.

Panting slightly from the effort, he took his horse's rein.

"We go straight along this road until we come to a fork, then turn left," Antonia commanded.

Richard nodded and started to walk.

"I'm so sorry to be such trouble," she murmured. "I don't know how I came to do that!"

"We all stumble occasionally."

"But my dancing teacher says he's never known anyone who dances as good as me."

Since his back was to her, Richard permitted himself a scowl at her ungrammatical speech.

"Do you dance, Sir Richard?"

"Rarely."

"You must know all the court dances."

Elissa had been right. He never should have talked so much about the court. Now look where that had landed him. "I was not at court so very often."

"You are too modest, I'm sure."

"Is this the fork?"

"Yes. Go to the left—the left!" she repeated as Richard headed to the right.

"Are you quite sure?" he asked, turning back to regard her skeptically.

"I should think I know where my own father's house is!" she declared. Then she got that sly look in her small eyes. "I do believe you are up to no good, Lord Dovercourt!"

That was enough for Richard. "My dear young woman, I assure you my intentions are totally honorable, even if yours are not."

"My lord!" she protested.

"I have been pursued by women often enough to know all the tricks. You could strip naked and I wouldn't dally with you, and I don't think your ankle is twisted at all."

"I . . . I . . . you . . ." Her reddening face crumpled, and he suddenly realized she was going to cry. She started to dismount. "My ankle *is* twisted!" she declared, "and I think you're a loathsome beast to think I could be so deceitful!"

She winced as she stood on the ground, glaring at him.

Richard sighed. She was better at this game than he had thought. Unfortunately, she seemed to have forgotten which ankle was the twisted one.

No doubt if he abandoned her here, she would tell everyone what a callous, hard-hearted blackguard he was. While that did not trouble him in the least, he knew it would up-set Elissa.

"I beg your pardon," he said, trying to sound contrite. "I have been too long among theater folk, I fear. Allow me to assist you back onto my horse, and then we will go to the left."

"Your apology is accepted," Antonia said regally as he approached her.

Again, and trying to keep as much distance between them as possible, he helped her onto his horse.

Will stomped into Elissa's closet, an expression between a pout and a scowl on his face as he flopped onto the stool she used to reach the highest shelves.

Elissa blinked her heavy eyelids. She had al-most nodded off over the accounts. Of course, if one lay awake until the small hours of the morning tensely anticipating the arrival of one's husband who never came to bed, fatigue was bound to result.

She had tossed and turned all night not just waiting for him, but also thinking about what had happened. To be sure, he had upset her with his behavior, but she had lashed out at him with dismay and frustration, then disembarked from the coach like a petulant child.

As she had contemplated their brief married life together, she had quickly come to the conclusion that no matter how he acted when he was with other people, he was not acting when he was alone with her.

That was a very flattering notion. Indeed, she didn't think there was a better or more sincere compliment that Richard Blythe could pay. It only remained for her to try to make amends.

But first, her son needed her. "What's the matter?"

Will crossed his arms. "He's not going riding with me."

"Richard?" she asked stupidly, although she knew that had to be to whom he referred. Then a horrible feeling settled in the pit of her stomach. "Richard is not here?"

Will shook his head. "He's gone riding already, without me."

"Perhaps he had an important errand."

Will's expression was skeptical, as well it should be.

"We shall simply have to ask him where he went when he returns," she said. In the meantime, she would not allow herself to speculate as to her husband's mysterious absence.

"When?"

Elissa took refuge from her son's eyes by looking at her account books. "When what, dear?"

"When will he get back?"

"I don't know. I'm sure he won't be long."

That wasn't exactly the truth, but unless Richard took it into his head to return to London in a fit of pique . . .

Surely not!

"He promised we would go riding every morning that it was fine, and it's very fine today."

Elissa raised her eyes to regard her disgruntled child. "Did he *promise?*"

"He said he would!"

"That is not the same thing as a promise, dear."

"Bloody hell, it is, too!"

Elissa stared at her son, whose face suddenly—and quite rightly—flushed with shame. "William James Longbourne, we do not use such language in this house!"

Shamefaced still, he nodded.

"Where did you ever hear that coarse expression?" she demanded. It was not from the servants, and most certainly not from her.

Will's lips trembled as he tried not to cry.

She rose and came around her desk. She squatted down and took his shoulders gently in her hands. "Will, where did you hear that expression?" she asked quietly.

"In the . . . in the stable."

"From whom?"

Tears started to fall on his cheeks. "He was very angry." He raised his stricken eyes. "Not at me, Mama," he hastened to qualify.

"It was Richard?"

He nodded, then wiped his nose.

"I see. I shall have to tell him that I do not countenance that kind of language in our house. Anger is no excuse for profanity. You are never to use that expression again, Will. Do you understand?"

His head bowed like a prisoner at the bar, he nodded again.

"You will not go riding today, or for the rest of the week."

Her son looked up, shocked. "But—"

"But that way, you should remember that one way to tell if a man is a gentleman is by his language. Now go upstairs until I call you."

Still hanging his head remorsefully, Will slowly left the room.

By the time Richard got Antonia home, fortunately without further flirtation, he was bone-weary as well as disgruntled. Perhaps Antonia realized that, or perhaps she realized that she had pushed him far enough. Either way, she said not a word before hobbling into the house.

As he headed for home, he tried to forget Antonia and think about his apology to Elissa again. He let his mind drift, imagining that he would begin with a suitably contrite speech, then a gentle kiss or two, followed by a caress, then more kissing . . .

He caught sight of the Banqueting House.

God save him, he would have that torn down! he silently vowed, his genial mood destroyed.

Why could it not have been struck by lightning or ruined by some other natural cataclysm during his long exile? Why had Elissa's first husband, that apparent proponent of new and modern buildings, not taken a dislike to it and razed it to the ground?

With these disgruntled thoughts, Richard drew near the stables, but before he could even bring his horse to a halt, the groom practically pounced on him as if he had been waiting in ambush these several hours.

"Lady Dovercourt wants to see you, my lord," the fellow declared without so much as a dip of the head in greeting. "*At once!*"

Chapter 13

E lissa watched her husband stroll into her
closet, his hands behind his back, apparently as unconcerned by her summons as he
would be by the observation that it looked
about to rain. He did not seem a bit contrite
about abandoning her last night, or Will this
morning.

She commanded herself to be calm and
composed. She would imitate his manner and
not let her anger get the better of her. "Where
have you been?"

He leaned his hip against the desk and regarded her steadily. "Riding. Did you miss
me?"

"You didn't come to bed."

"And did you miss me?" he repeated with
one of his slow, seductive smiles.

"Since you are a man and my husband, you
do not owe me an explanation if you do not

care to provide one," she retorted, "but you didn't wait for Will."

Finally, a look of something like contrition appeared on Richard's handsome face. "I left before he was awake. Has he been waiting for me? Damn that Antonia!"

"Antonia? Antonia Norbert?"

She discovered Richard was capable of looking sheepish. "She ambushed me in the lane, then claimed her ankle was sprained so, being a gentleman, I was forced to help her home."

Help her home, or do something else? Antonia had made her fascination for Richard very obvious. Given his past, would he really refuse anything Antonia cared to offer?

"Believe me, Elissa, I would far rather have been sweeping the streets of London," he continued sincerely, as if he read her mind.

Mollified, she told herself she was foolish to feel jealous or suspicious. "It doesn't matter now. Will shall not be riding today, or for the rest of the week."

Richard straightened abruptly. "What is it? Is he ill?"

She shook her head. "No. He is being punished. He cursed this morning."

"He cursed?" Richard asked as if that wrong were as minor as leaving a button undone, and as if she were stupid to take any notice of it. "Is that all?"

"Considering what he said, I think a week's lack of riding a just punishment."

"What did he say that upset you so?"

"Something *you* taught him."

"Something I . . . ?" Sudden comprehension dawned on his face. "Ah, the stables."

"Yes, the stables."

"Did he tell you why I cursed?"

"He said you were angry."

Richard's lips jerked into a little smile. "I stepped in a pile of dung. My reaction was instinctive and, under the circumstances, quite natural, I think."

"I fail to find my son's use of such language, and yours, at all amusing, my lord," she replied. "Profanity is a sign of weakness."

If she knew the words *he* had been exposed to in his childhood, his choice would have seemed innocence itself, Richard thought. "It was only a moment of frustration, Elissa. Why did Will curse?"

"Because you had gone riding without him."

"Then I am to blame in more ways than one, and so I apologize to you, and I will to him also."

"Naturally I can't expect you to comprehend how appalling profanity is to civilized gentlefolk. Nor can a person who has never been a parent understand the responsibility one feels to a child, I suppose."

He tensed. "Do you think I don't understand the reaction to some words? I made my living by understanding the power of words."

"Perhaps you should not go riding with him anymore, or who knows what you might teach him."

"What exactly do you think I will do? Set his young feet on the path to sinful corruption?"

She did not answer. She pursed her lips and looked away.

He was in front of her in a stride and grabbed her by the shoulders. "Do you honestly believe me capable of such a thing?" he demanded harshly. "Do you truly think I would destroy a child's innocence as mine—"

A strange expression passed over his face before he backed away, turned on his heel, and left.

Trying to control the sudden explosion of emotions raging through him, Richard strode to the entrance hall. He halted and put one hand against the stone hearth to steady himself as he drew in a great, ragged sigh. If only she knew . . .

But she must never know.

He heard a sound and straightened, half hoping, half dreading to see Elissa when he turned.

Will stood on the stairs, his hands gripping the banister and his eyes wide with a combination of surprise and fear.

Whatever happened between Elissa and

himself, he would not burden this boy with it.

Putting a smile on his face, he walked toward Will, who managed a tentative smile in return.

"I fear I have caused some trouble," Richard confessed as he sat on the second-lowest step.

Will sat beside him. Despite his distress, Richard felt a tender, paternal feeling stealing over him as they sat thus, or at least how he imagined a father should feel.

Glancing about like a conspirator, Will spoke in a whisper. "Is Mama angry with you, too?"

"Very angry, I am sorry to say," Richard admitted.

Rather too angry, he suddenly realized. Then another idea assailed him—but it was really too ridiculous. She couldn't be jealous, not of Antonia.

"I shouldn't have said that," Will muttered.

"Neither should I," Richard replied just as mournfully. Then he smiled at the contrite little lad. "We must make a pact that no matter how frustrated we become, we shall always endeavor to speak as gentlemen. Will you agree and shake hands on it?"

Will nodded gravely, and like two mature men, they solemnly shook hands.

Will sighed. "She won't let me go riding for a week."

"I know."

"Is she punishing you, too?"

"No."

"Blo—" Will caught himself. "I mean, that doesn't seem very fair."

"A grown man's punishment takes different forms."

"Then I can hardly wait to be a grown man!"

Richard regarded the fine lad he would be delighted to call his son. Had his own father ever thought of *him* this way? Had his own father ever thought of him as anything other than the cause of all his woe, as if Richard had asked to be the reason the man was forced to marry?

He rose. "Will, do not wish for childhood to end quickly. That is a far worse torment than being denied riding for a week."

Will jumped up. "Where are you going? Can I come, too?"

"No. Where I am going, you do not want to come," Richard said quietly before he walked out of the house.

All afternoon Elissa waited for Richard, wondering where he had gone and determined to apologize for being so upset over Will's language, as well as for her childish outburst the night before. She also wanted to understand his unexpected reaction to her criticism, even though she had no idea how she would broach that subject delicately.

Whatever her worries this afternoon, she

certainly didn't want to have to deal with the inquisitive Mr. Sedgemore, too, but there he was, standing in her withdrawing room.

"Good afternoon, Mr. Sedgemore," Elissa said evenly, managing to hide her displeasure at the man's unwelcome arrival.

"Is everything well with you?" Mr. Sedgemore asked gravely. "You look ill."

"I am not used to late hours."

"No, no, of course not," he replied with a smile that did nothing to make him more attractive.

She took a seat on one of the chairs. "Is there some matter of business you wish to discuss with me?"

"Business? No, not today."

Her brow furrowed slightly.

"Perhaps my visit is inconvenient . . . ?" he inquired, rising as if to leave.

"No, it isn't," she lied courteously.

Whatever she thought of Alfred Sedgemore personally, he was a wealthy, influential neighbor. It would not be wise to offend him.

"I have a confession to make, Lady Dovercourt, about last night," he said as he sat back down. "I must say I was rather dismayed by your husband's choice of topic."

"He says he has never met anyone yet who didn't want to hear court gossip."

Mr. Sedgemore chuckled. "Well, at least Sir John's daughters were well contented with his stories. And with him, too."

"He can be very agreeable."

"He may have made himself *too* agreeable."

She attempted to smile blandly. "It is a habit with him, I think, from his years in London."

"Given his past, did his behavior not trouble you? The apple does not fall far from the tree, after all."

"I know very little about my husband's family," Elissa said, trying not to seem too curious as she regarded her previously most unwelcome visitor. "He seems reluctant to reveal it."

"With good cause."

"Is that so?"

"I have heard only bits and pieces."

Elissa tried not to feel disappointed. Then she noted that Mr. Sedgemore's smug smile had returned. Perhaps he was only attempting to make his information seem even more valuable.

She clenched her teeth, then decided this aggravation was the price she was going to have to pay for the knowledge Mr. Sedgemore would hopefully impart. "Maybe I should ask Sir John about my husband's family."

"Sir John would likely refrain from telling you, if most of the sordid stories I have heard are true." Mr. Sedgemore frowned gravely. "Perhaps I should as well."

"If you think so," she replied, sitting back and doing her best not to show her avid curiosity.

"Or perhaps you should know the back-

ground of the man to whom you are married,"
Mr. Sedgemore mused.

"I would appreciate that."

Mr. Sedgemore smiled his sly, smug smile.
Richard's smile could be knowing, or sardonic,
or mocking, but it had an appealing quality
totally lacking in Mr. Sedgemore's expression.

Alfred Sedgemore looked as she imagined a
toad would, if a toad could smile.

"When my family first came here shortly after the death of Sir Richard's father, I over-
heard some of our servants talking. It seemed
nobody was surprised that his brother, your
new husband's uncle, was willing to do your
husband out of his estate because of what his
father had done.

"He had, or so the rumor went, seduced his
own brother's wife."

Elissa emitted a gasp of dismayed surprise,
which made Mr. Sedgemore's eyes gleam with
barely hidden delight as he continued. "She,
in turn, ran off with the steward, who had em-
bezzled most of her husband's money. They
were never found.

"The uncle wouldn't have been able to sell
it at all, of course, if Sir Richard had not gone
to Europe to be with the king.

"After selling the estate, Sir Richard's uncle
sent a very small portion of the money to Richard, then sailed for the New World. He died
on the voyage."

"I had no idea," Elissa murmured truthfully.

"There was more," Sedgemore went on eagerly. "It was said that Sir Richard's mother was no better than her licentious husband. I could never find out exactly what she was said to have done, but there were whispers of a multitude of lovers."

Elissa's first thought was for Richard as sympathy and new comprehension filled her heart. What had Richard known of his parents' behavior? Quite a bit, she surmised, judging by what he had said this morning.

What kind of life had Richard endured with such sinful parents?

How could she offer him comfort and sympathy? He was a proud man, and surely if he had wanted her to know these things, he would have told her himself.

Was it so surprising that he would be a cynical and bitter man? Would a man with such parents hold marriage in high esteem?

A clever young man might even hide his hurt and arm himself against rumors and gossip by excelling at sarcasm and dueling.

What was truly surprising was that he would be so tender toward her, and toward her son.

Unless he was only acting when he was with them.

Then she remembered the horrorstricken look that had passed over his face when she had accused him of teaching her son base language. That had been no act, no pantomime for her benefit. She was sure of it.

And she was sure the affection she had seen deep in his dark eyes was not feigned, either.

Mr. Sedgemore deferentially cleared his throat. "I fear I have upset you. I confess I am surprised your husband kept this knowledge from you."

"You cannot think I would be glad to hear a recitation of old tittle-tattle, and I am quite sure my husband had an excellent reason for not telling me these incredible tales, which are surely unfounded speculation, if not outright lies," she replied sternly as a surge of protective determination came over her. "Everyone knows how servants talk."

She paid no heed to the shocked expression on Mr. Sedgemore's thin face. "Naturally you will not repeat these things."

"I have heard Sir John himself condemn both your husband's parents for licentious behavior."

"I should also remind you that my husband is known to have dueled over matters much less personal to him than this. I daresay it would be best if you did not repeat such hearsay and innuendo, lest he take offense."

Mr. Sedgemore tried to look wounded, but he didn't fool her for an instant. "I only mentioned these things for your sake."

"And I would not speak of them again if I were you—for *your* sake."

"Am I to assume, then, that you care about my safety?"

"Of course I do. I would hate to have anybody killed over gossip." She rose and gave him her most empty, insincere smile. "Good day, Mr. Sedgemore."

With every appearance of friendly concern on his weasel-like face, Alfred Sedgemore approached Richard in the Nag's Head Tavern in Owston that night. "Why, my lord, what brings you here this evening?"

Richard had already imbibed one whole bottle of cheap plonk trying to restore some measure of emotional equanimity after his confrontation with Elissa that day, and was well on his way to completing a second.

His drinking was in no way intended to lessen his shame or subdue his unhappy memories, because he already knew that was ineffectual.

"I'm getting drunk," he replied, blearily regarding his interrogator, and not aware of just how greatly slurred his speech was.

Instead, he attributed Sedgemore's confused expression to the dolt's lack of intelligence.

Sedgemore took a seat opposite him.

"When I decide to get drunk," Richard grumbled, "I prefer to do so without company."

Sedgemore's response was a ferrety little

grin as he leaned forward and softly inquired, "Unlike your dear mother?"

Richard lunged across the table and grabbed the lout by the throat, not caring that the tavern was filled with farm laborers finished with the work of the day. His only concern was shutting the man's mouth.

"I'd keep quiet, if I were you," he whispered through clenched teeth.

"You are making quite a scene, but I daresay that's second nature to a playwright," Sedgemore gasped, glancing around the room.

Richard tried to focus on the other customers in the taproom, but they all blended into a staring, openmouthed mass. Even in his current condition, he realized Sedgemore was unfortunately right, and hurting the fellow would surely give rise to more rumors and speculation. He loosed his hold and sank back onto his bench. "Shut your mouth and go away."

"You cannot order me about like a lackey."

"I can warn you . . . as a neighbor."

"Perhaps I should be warning *you*, neighbor, that you had better treat me with more deference, or I might tell your lovely wife what I know."

Dread washed over Richard, sobering him slightly.

He must dominate himself and his emotions. He must show nothing. He must reveal nothing. He must hide his shame and fear and anger as he always had when his family was mentioned. "What do you know about my parents?"

"I would rather not repeat it, and certainly not in a public place."

"Indulge me," Richard growled.

"It is getting late in the day."

Richard splayed his hands on the table and leaned close, so that he was nose to nose with Sedgemore, all the force of his intense personality brought to bear on the man before him. "Tell me!"

Sedgemore gulped, then looked about. Perhaps seeing safety in numbers, he answered, albeit in a whisper. "There have been tales of scandalous behavior."

"What kind of scandalous behavior?"

"Surely you cannot wish me to go into details?"

"My mother died when I was nine years old and my father when I was sixteen. They were never saints to me before their deaths, so I think there is very little you could say that would shock me."

As for what Elissa would think, he could not bear to consider it.

"I have heard of . . . things . . . happening in the Banqueting House."

"Come, man, have I not made myself clear? Do not dissemble. What *things?*"

"I'm sure you know very well."

He did.

Sedgemore's lips twisted into a scornful smile. "Your lovely and somewhat innocent wife might like to hear how your mother died."

"My mother died of a fever."

"Oh no, my lord and good friend of the king. She died of a disease commonly associated with whores, coupled with the effects of drink."

Richard crossed his arms. "A very interesting fairy tale based on no evidence."

Sedgemore seemed unmoved and unafraid, a confirmation Richard hated to see. "I have evidence. I had it from her physician, a very good friend of your dear departed mama, as so many men were."

Richard felt as if stone filled his stomach, for he did remember the doctor. He was a small, scrawny runt of a man who came whenever his mother summoned him, and then stayed an inordinate amount of time. "I fail to see how this information would please my wife."

"I do not think of pleasing her with tales of your family. I think of warning her."

He was only thinking of it; obviously, he had not yet spoken of these things to Elissa. His secrets were still safe.

"You are a most solicitous fellow," Richard remarked. Then his eyes narrowed. "If you are scheming to drive a wedge between us, I would council you to take care."

Sedgemore rose and looked down at Richard with another smug, triumphant smile. "Somehow, I begin to think I may not have to do anything. I perceive you might do it yourself without assistance, wallowing in a tavern while a beautiful woman waits for you at home. If all is well between you, what are you doing here?"

Richard slowly rose and put his hand on his fine sword. Then he grinned a grin that his enemies in London would have recognized—and feared.

"If you are a wise man, Mr. Sedgemore, which is something I very much doubt, you will say not one word about my mother or my father to another living soul."

Sedgemore's eyes widened with very real fear before he stumbled backward, turned, and hurried from the tavern.

Richard went back to his wine, certain the cowardly Sedgemore's silence was now safely assured.

Chapter 14

When the lights shining through the windows of Blythe Hall appeared in the darkness, Richard halted the mare. It was extremely tempting to find a convenient haystack and slumber till dawn. That way, he wouldn't have to face Elissa and explain where he had been, or why he had been there.

Nor would he have to decide whether or not to tell Elissa about his childhood.

It would be easier, he supposed, if he had learned to put the demons of his past behind him, and he had dared to hope that he had—until he had come home and seen the Banqueting House.

He gazed at it now, standing nearly hidden by the trees.

Clenching his jaw with sudden determination, he dismounted, leading the horse toward a low branch. He looped the rein over it.

The scent of the dew-damp trees and grass

filled his nostrils. As always, that smell took him back to that other night, when he had awakened from a dream and gone searching for his mother.

Despite the memories, he walked toward the small building, then stopped before the wooden door, trembling like a dog scenting danger.

I could go there now, he told himself. His parents were long dead and buried. Food for worms. Dust. Their souls roasting in hell, without a doubt.

He pushed at the door. It easily gave way, scraping open over the dirty wooden floor. Taking a deep breath, he did something he had never before dared to do.

He stepped inside.

The moonlight streaming in through the tall windows clearly illuminated the interior.

He instantly realized that almost nothing had changed. The heavy table that had held fruit and carafes of wine still stood in the center. Around the walls were the same low couches, their upholstery now rotting from damp and mildew. Plaster was tearing away from the walls, exposing the brick beneath. Under his feet, the floor creaked and groaned. He would have to watch where he stepped, otherwise he might go right through.

He took another step further inside and noted the sagging, water-stained draperies.

"Could you not have closed them?" he muttered as he started to make a slow progress around the room.

He spotted something behind one of the couches and pulled it out.

It was a large framed portrait, of all things, with not so much as a sheet to protect it. He carried it to the table and set it down, then stared at the face looking back at him.

Who was it? Richard wracked his brain trying to remember, for there was something vaguely familiar about the middle-aged man's full lips, slightly drooping eyes, and arrogant expression.

Unmindful of mildew or the possible presence of mice, Richard sat on a couch, then closed his eyes and leaned back so that his head rested against the wall as he tried to remember.

The answer finally came to him. This man had visited Blythe Hall before his mother died. To be sure, he had been young then, and this portrait was of a man later in life, but Richard was quite sure it was the same person whose name he could not recall.

Of course, that was not so surprising. Many men had visited Blythe Hall and sported with his mother. He should be impressed he could remember one face out of the multitude.

That did not explain the presence of this picture. Surely his father would not be likely to keep a portrait of one of his wife's lovers.

Richard sighed wearily.

Maybe he would.

When next Richard opened his eyes, sunlight, not moonlight, shone through the windows. He sat up stiffly and slowly, every muscle aching in protest at sleeping on the tattered couch.

The next sight to meet his eyes was the portrait, the man's scornful face seeming to laugh at Richard's sorry state.

Richard tore his gaze from the face and surveyed the interior of the Banqueting House in the light of day.

It looked even more decrepit.

"Richard!"

He started and turned toward the door to see Will standing on the threshold, surveying the Banqueting House with wide, curious eyes.

"Get out!" Richard cried, jumping to his feet.

Will didn't move, apparently too stunned or scared to flee.

Richard reminded himself that Will didn't know what had gone on in this place.

"I'm sorry to scare you," he said in as calm a voice as he could manage, "but the floor is rotting. It is not safe."

Will relaxed a little. "But you are inside," he noted gravely.

"That is how I know the floor is rotting,"

Richard explained as he straightened his disheveled clothes. "What hour of the day is it?"

"Just after breakfast." Will's brow furrowed. "Did you sleep here?"

"I fell asleep in here," Richard admitted.

"Really?" Will said eagerly. "I've always wanted to sleep here just for one night, but Mama won't let me. I'm not even supposed to—"

He fell silent and flushed as he stared at the floor.

"She doesn't let you come in here at all, I daresay, and now you know why. It is dangerous."

"Yes," Will mumbled.

Richard raked his hands through his unkempt hair. "You have eaten, then?"

"Yes."

"Has your mother?"

"I don't know."

"I hope my absence didn't worry her." Richard was not pleased that he was resorting to seeking information from Will, but he was anxious to know what Elissa might be thinking.

"I don't know."

"Perhaps you will join me anyway?" Richard asked. "I am famished. And I could tell you about the pirates I saw in London once."

"Oh, would you?"

"They were a very bloodthirsty-looking band of men, I assure you."

"I wouldn't be scared!"

Richard went to the table and picked up the portrait. "I found this last night. I daresay your mother has a good reason for keeping it here."

He glanced at the picture again—then almost dropped it as he recalled the disgusted expression that had been on Will's face that day in London when he learned Richard was a writer and not a soldier.

The man in the portrait was William Longbourne.

Richard's knuckles turned white as he gripped the portrait of Will's late father. "Do you know who this is?"

"No."

Odd that of all places she might have stored it, she had chosen this one. Could it be that she knew of her husband's past decadent activities there? Had he told her? Had he told her everything he had done there, and with whom?

Had he been guarding his secrets unnecessarily?

He realized Will was staring at him curiously. "It has occurred to me, Will, that your mother must have her reasons for wanting this portrait where it was," he said as he put it back where he had found it. "It may be presumptuous of me to move it without discussing the matter first. Come, let us get something to eat."

Together they left the Banqueting House.

"Oh, here comes Mama now," Will announced, pointing across the lawn. His voice dropped to a confidential whisper. "I think she must be looking for us."

Never in his entire life had Richard Blythe felt more like fleeing than he did on this fine morning as Elissa walked toward them over the lawns of his family estate.

And then, a miracle happened.

She smiled at him. A wary, tentative smile to be sure, but a smile nonetheless, and in that instant, he felt so relieved, his legs grew weak and he almost sank to the ground.

But he could not be truly relieved until he ascertained if that portrait was indeed William Longbourne, why it was in the Banqueting House, and most important of all, how much she knew about his parents.

"Here you are. I see Will found you," she said as she glanced at her son.

"I was late returning from the village and didn't want to disturb the household, so I slept in the Banqueting House," Richard explained.

In spite of her welcoming smile, he felt as if he were treading in a treacherous bog, where one misstep could lead to death.

"Then you must be hungry."

"I am. Will has consented to join me. I hope you will, too," he said.

"Yes," Elissa replied softly.

Will slipped one hand in Richard's, and the

other in his mother's. Richard glanced at his wife over the boy's head and for an instant, their gazes met and held.

As they did, Richard told himself not to be too optimistic until he had an explanation for her change in manner. Unfortunately, she had every right to be even more angry with him because of his absence last night.

They reached the house and halted inside the entrance hall. Richard surveyed his soiled, disheveled clothing. "I shall have to be excused a moment to make myself presentable, or no doubt the help will believe their master a vagabond."

"Will, please go and tell the cook to serve your stepfather his breakfast in the dining room. We'll be down shortly."

Will nodded and scampered off.

"No doubt he is planning to command a second breakfast for himself, too," Elissa noted, her expression frustratingly inscrutable as she turned toward her husband.

Richard waited for her to come beside him before he proceeded to the steps. "If it is any comfort to you, I did not have any dinner last night."

"It is not a comfort to me, although I would like to know where you were. I was worried about you."

No one had ever worried about him in his whole life.

"I went to the Nag's Head," he said, even

more remorseful as they continued upward. "Have I some cause to hope that you are not angry with me for behaving like a child who goes off to sulk?"

She paused and looked at him gravely. "No, I am not angry. I'm sorry I was so unreasonable yesterday."

"You were justifiably annoyed with me. Zounds, you should be even angrier with me now for not coming home," he said as they entered the bedchamber.

"I am sorry I berated you the way I did. You are, after all, my husband. I should not chide you like an errant child."

He went to her and placed his hands on her shoulders. "I am more sorry than I can say both for my actions and for worrying you. I promise I shall try to remember that I am a married man and so should not retreat like a wounded bear when I am upset."

He smiled very, very slowly, and his eyes seemed to grow even darker. "I'faith, I am a fool of a husband to spend the night freezing in the chill Banqueting House when I could have been apologizing to my justly angry wife and asking her forgiveness. Do you forgive me, Elissa?"

"Yes," she murmured as he bent to kiss her.

He kissed her tenderly, yet she sensed the thrilling, unbridled passion lurking, ready to burst into vibrant being.

She was so glad he had come home, and

that now she had some knowledge of his past to guide her.

Then she realized something was growling.

She pulled back. "I'faith, my lord, you *are* hungry."

"Aye, for more of this," he muttered as he tugged her back into his arms and pressed a fiery kiss upon her lips.

For a moment, she gave herself up to the pleasure he invoked, but only for a moment.

"Will will be wondering where we are," she said as she drew back. "Besides, I would not have you faint."

Richard's grin was wickedly attractive. "Indeed, I had best eat well today, for I am sure to need all the vitality I can muster tonight."

Elissa was already very warm; nevertheless she felt as if a tropical sun had suddenly replaced the one outside her window. She ran her hand over her lips. "And I would prefer you shaved. I fear I am chafed."

"I do not want to hurt your lovely skin," he said as he turned and went to the washstand. "Either there or"—he glanced back at her, the most devilish expression on his handsome face—"anywhere."

"I will be the one fainting if you keep talking like that," she said as she went to his chest to fetch him a clean shirt.

"I found a portrait in the Banqueting House," he remarked as he removed his jacket and tossed it on the bed.

She flushed, and not with pleasure. In truth, she had forgotten it was there, or she would have had a servant take it away and burn it. "It is of William. I didn't want to look at it after he had died, so I put it in there. And then I decided it might upset Will to have such a reminder of his deceased father in the house, so I thought it best to leave it where it was."

Willing him to accept this explanation, she pulled a clean shirt from the chest beside the bed. Richard removed his shirt and it joined the jacket.

In the light of the morning sun, Elissa could see that he had been telling the truth about dueling scars.

"Will looks a little like him," he observed as he began to wash his face.

Her hands slowly balled into fists. "I don't think so," she replied, trying to sound calm.

Her son was nothing like his father and never would be, if she could help it. He would be fine and honorable and decent. He would treat a woman with respect and dignity.

His face covered with soapy water, Richard cast a glance in her direction. "You are glad?"

Laying his clean white shirt on the bed, she struggled to sound matter-of-fact. "Will resembles me more, that's all. I thought we were not to discuss him here."

"But as you said, he is your son's father. I suppose I should know something about him. He was older than you by several years, I take it," Richard replied as he searched for his razor.

She spotted it under the square of linen for drying and handed it to him. "He was."

"How did you meet?"

"My father made his aquaintance in London and invited him to visit. I fear I was a very silly girl ready to fall in love and be married. William never spoke of his family or his friends, or very much of anything, really."

She should have suspected that this silence was not a good sign, but she had been too vain, anxious to hear only his praises of her grace and beauty.

"He was a reticent fellow, then?"

"Extremely."

"Despite this lack of conversational gifts, you fell in love."

Flustered by his piercing dark eyes that seemed to demand honesty, she turned away.

After a moment, she heard him begin to scrape the stubble from his face.

She slowly wheeled around and realized that he was watching her in the mirror even as he shaved. There was a terrible sadness in his eyes—and in that moment, she had a revelation.

"Richard, I thought I loved him, but I didn't know what love was. He flattered me and promised to make me happy. Regrettably, I soon discovered that what I felt for William Longbourne was only girlish infatuation."

Richard put down the razor and his hands gripped the edge of the washstand. Incredibly, his shoulders sagged with what looked like relief.

"Are you all right?"

He started to wipe off the remains of the soap. "Am I all right?" he mused aloud.

Then he threw down the linen and laughed, a rich, merry sound that she couldn't recall him ever making before. Wry smiles, sly chuckles—but never a laugh of such joy.

Still laughing, he faced her and spread his hands. "My lady, my wife, I do not think I have ever been so happy in my life!"

"Because I didn't love William Longbourne?"

He took one long step and tugged her into his arms. He bussed her heartily on the cheek. "Yes! I am ashamed to say I have been most abominably jealous. Even though you led me to believe he was no great lover, I still thought you cared for him very much."

She nestled her head against his chest. "I was jealous, too."

"Of Antonia?" he demanded, leaning back to regard her quizzically.

"Of any woman who looked at you twice."

"I must commend you on your inscrutability."

"I have been studying a master, my lord," she said, eyeing him significantly.

"Me?" he cried incredulously. "I am as easy to read as . . . as . . ."

"Our marriage settlement," she finished gravely, her eyes dancing merrily.

"Zounds, woman! Nothing about that document is easy!"

She leaned against him again, glorying in the sensation of his naked flesh against her cheek. Then she realized he was undoing the lacing of her bodice.

She jumped back. "Richard! What are you doing?"

His eyes widened. "I thought it was coming undone," he replied innocently.

In spite of his attitude, she knew that wasn't true, for the desire in his eyes betrayed him. "We have not time. The breakfast will be on the table and Will will be waiting."

He shrugged. "It is your fault."

"My fault?"

"If you were not so beautiful and desirable, I would not be so distracted," he answered as he put on the clean shirt.

"Perhaps I will have to make you sleep in the Banqueting House again."

He turned away and reached for his jacket. "I would rather we pulled it down."

Startled by the sudden gravity of his tone, she said, "I thought you would be glad to have one building from the original estate left."

"Not that one."

"Why not?"

"It is in a sad state of ruin," he noted as he pulled on his jacket.

"We could have it repaired. I think it rather pretty."

"I don't. Have you a hairbrush about?"

She went to the washstand, found the item, and gave it to him. "It seems a shame to destroy it."

"Then we shall not," he replied as he gave his disheveled hair a few quick strokes.

Elissa hurried to him and put her hand on his arm so that he looked at her. "Let us not quarrel about it," she pleaded.

His expression softened. "No, of all things, let us not quarrel about that."

"Cook sent me to fetch you," Will suddenly announced from the door. "She says everything's getting cold."

Chapter 15

At breakfast, Will ignored the bread and cheese before him to listen with rapt attention as Richard talked about the pirates he had encountered in London.

Elissa, however, wanted to hear more about his past. When she finally got the opportunity to broach that subject, he talked of the triumph of seeing his first play performed and well received.

"I confess that I had not known such pleasure and fulfillment in my whole life," Richard finished, glancing at her with a look that both sparkled and smoldered. "I have since, once or twice."

Elissa blushed hotly and tried very hard to subdue an embarrassed grin. "I suppose it was a great relief."

"Great relief? I should say so, for I knew that I wouldn't have to take to begging in the streets."

"I cannot imagine you ever begging for anything."

"You should have stayed a soldier," Will said, his tone implying that Richard had somehow allowed this distinctly better opportunity to slip his mind.

"That was not as enjoyable as the theater, and I had some battles there, you know."

Will frowned skeptically. "Sham battles."

"You say that only because you've never seen two actresses who want the same role. Women can be far more vicious than men, I assure you, especially ambitious women. For instance, it would never do to cross Lady Castlemaine."

"Who is she?" Will demanded.

"A very good friend of the king," Elissa answered.

"That is one way to put it," Richard observed.

Elissa gave him a warning look. "She is also related to the Duke of Buckingham."

"Another good friend of the king."

"Were they your friends, too?" Will asked eagerly.

"Heavens, no!" Richard replied. He made a mournful face. "They are too exalted."

"But you are a good friend of the king!"

"Not *that* good—and I would not want to be," he hastened to add. "Our sovereign, for all his excellent qualities, can be somewhat temperamental. You can fall out of favor quickly if you are not careful. I prefer to avoid having to walk such a tricky path."

"That would require diplomacy," Elissa added gravely. "Perhaps as much as maintaining peace among several actresses seeking . . ."

"Parts?" Richard amiably supplied. "Now that I am married, I am delightfully out of that fray."

"Lady Dovercourt, Mr. Rowther has come," a servant announced, drawing Elissa's attention away from her husband's seductive eyes.

"Why so glum at this arrival?" Richard asked when he saw Will's frown.

"He is my tutor," Will muttered.

"And a very good tutor he is," Elissa said.

"Come now, Will," Richard said jovially, "you are very lucky to have the opportunity to be educated. Indeed, some of my happiest hours were spent with my tutor, and his lessons stood me in good stead over the years."

"Did he teach you fencing?"

"Zounds, no! Latin and Greek, rhetoric, theology."

"Theology?" Elissa demanded incredulously.

His eyebrow raised, Richard said, "No need to sound surprised. I studied everything and anything Mr. Elliot cared to teach me."

Elissa flushed again. "I simply didn't realize you had such a broad education."

"Oh, I did, but there is some part of my education that I fear is sorely lacking. I do not know how to run an estate. Perhaps while you study with your tutor, Will, your mama will share her expertise with me."

As much as she might welcome some assistance, Elissa felt a little shiver of dread along her spine at the prospect of losing any of her authority and independence. Still, when Richard looked at her that way, it was difficult to resist his request. "Very well."

Richard smiled that slow, incredibly attractive smile of his. "Excellent. I promise I shall attend to your every word."

He glanced sharply at Will. "And I hope you shall do the same. There is many a valuable lesson that comes from books, Will—moreso than you can learn with a sword."

Will didn't seem convinced.

"Perhaps if you do well with Mr. Rowther, your lovely mama will allow me to teach you something of swordplay."

"Oh, will you? Will you, Mama?" Will cried, his eyes pleading.

Elissa looked from one male to the other and saw the boyish enthusiasm Richard was trying to hide. It was very tempting to acquiesce, but she was not sure she was ready for her young son to learn how to wield a rapier yet, however necessary it might become later in his life.

"We will not be using real weapons, of course," Richard added.

"We won't?" Will asked with obvious disappointment.

"Would you run before you can walk? No, first you must learn the proper stance, and how to move quickly. Many a duel has been lost because of clumsy feet."

"If that is the case, you have my permission," Elissa agreed. "Now, off to Mr. Rowther."

"And study hard!" Richard seconded as Will scampered away.

They heard his feet clattering though the entrance hall as Richard held out his hand. "Avaunt ye, my lady, and lead me to the ledgers!"

"If you insist," she said, rising, "but I must remind you that I do not intend to give up managing this estate entirely, no matter what may happen."

He frowned. "What are you expecting to happen?"

Too late, Elissa pressed her lips together. She did not mean to hint that she might be with child, for she still was not completely certain. She had been delayed by tension and fatigue before, and with the trip to London, it might be that way this time, too. "I may fall ill, perhaps."

"Perhaps," he replied as he escorted her from the room. "In which case, I shall be too upset to do any managing at all, the estate will fall into ruin, and I shall have to take up play writing again, but the taste of the fickle audience will have changed and I shall die starving in a London gutter."

She eyed him quizzically. "Does your imagination always run to such lengths, my lord?"

"Unfortunately, it does far more often than I would like. It is the writer's curse, I fear, as well as our blessing, to be able to imagine all sorts of consequences."

"I perceive I shall have to do my best not to fall ill or die."

He faced her. "No, you must not," he said gravely, and then he grinned again. "The king would not be pleased."

"And you?" she asked, keeping her tone as light as his.

His gaze seemed to intensify like the rays of the sun through glass. "I would be devastated."

She had to kiss him after that. Since they were alone in the corridor, she saw no reason not to.

Until her lips met his in passionate rapture. Then she knew that to kiss him here was something of an error, because she did not want to stop.

Fortunately, he drew back and cocked his head to regard her with a wry, sardonic smile. "Perhaps we should abandon the ledgers."

"It was your idea to look at them."

"I would rather look at you."

"And I would rather kiss you, but then nothing would be accomplished."

They slowly strolled toward the withdrawing room.

"An interesting word, *accomplished*," Richard reflected. "I can think of many things I would like to accomplish with you, Elissa."

"This estate cannot run itself."

"True enough," he said as they entered the withdrawing room and continued toward her closet. "I fear my concept of life in the country was comprised solely of lazy days in the garden out of the smoke and stench of London, not of hours spent hunched over a ledger book."

"We shall have some time in the garden, although I must confess it is in a sad state. I have been more concerned with farming than flowers."

"Now that I am here, perhaps you will have more time to spend with the flowers, although you are prettier than any flower I have ever seen."

She gave him a sidelong glance as she went to the cupboard behind her desk and drew out the ledger for the present year. "That doesn't sound like a very original compliment."

"I think my talent for flattery is getting rusty."

"I do not know whether I should be pleased or sorry about that," Elissa murmured as she opened the ledger to the last page that had writing on it.

"I suspect the problem is that I have not got

enough words to describe you, or the way you make me feel."

At his softly spoken, sincere reflection, Elissa swallowed hard and had to force herself to concentrate on the task at hand.

"Yes, well, I was about to enter the household expenditures for the week. This column is for income, and this is for expenditures," she said, turning the book toward him and pointing at the appropriate locations on the ruled page.

"I have heard that some people keep diaries in code. Do you keep your ledgers in code, too?" Richard inquired as he bent down and studied the page.

She gave him a puzzled look. "No."

"Then, madam, you have the most abysmal handwriting I have ever seen."

Blushing furiously, Elissa snatched back the ledger. "I suppose you have a better hand?"

"Indeed I do. I have often been complimented on my penmanship. Have you some paper and ink handy? I shall be happy to demonstrate."

Briskly putting back the ledger, she wordlessly got him paper, a trimmed quill, and a bottle of ink. With a theatrical flourish and apparently quite unconcerned by her peeved manner, Richard sat in her chair and proceeded to write.

She came behind and looked over his shoulder. "What is that you are writing?"

"You are unfamiliar with the works of Shakespeare?"

"Who?"

Richard made a long-suffering sigh. "Your education has been sorely neglected if you cannot write better than you do, and you have never heard of William Shakespeare."

"My education was in keeping house and household accounts, not the arts," she muttered as she gazed at his lean, strong fingers propelling the pen with such ease and artistry.

"Then I shall simply have to correct this sad neglect," he said, pausing to dip the quill into the ink with a singularly graceful gesture, "and, my sweet, I shall be delighted to do so."

"I have heard of Ben Jonson," she offered, now looking at the shape of his ear as he continued his work. Richard had very attractive ears.

"It is my opinion that Shakespeare's works will prove to have the lasting fame," Richard replied. "I would consider myself very fortunate indeed if I could achieve even a modicum of his understanding of human nature and to write so well."

"But writing is an unfit pastime for a gentleman of quality," she pointed out.

"Unless it is to fill ledgers. Now tell me, what do you think of my penmanship?"

Elissa tore her gaze from the smooth angle of his jaw to look at his paper. "This is the neatest hand I have ever seen," she said, duly impressed.

Her husband looked as pleased as Will when he remembered his lesson. "Then why do I not take care of the entries into the ledger?"

"I must admit that if all I had to do was read the entries and compare them to the bills and lists, my work would be a vast deal easier."

He pulled her into his lap. "Do you write many letters?" he asked, toying with a stray curl on her forehead.

She began to breathe a little faster as her arms stole around his neck. "Not many, but some."

"I offer my services as a secretary, too," he murmured, caressing her cheek. "I assure you, my dear, that I can write very charming letters when necessary—or most uncharming letters when necessary, too."

"You really are a devil," Elissa whispered as he began to kiss her neck, "to tempt me so."

"I would tempt you to more than that," he whispered as he began to undo the laces in the front of her bodice.

"Richard!" she protested, truth be told, half-heartedly.

"Yes?"

"What are you doing?"

He chuckled softly. "I am trying to tempt you."

"You . . . you are succeeding," she panted as his hand slipped into her bodice.

"Good."

"Here?"

"Why not?"

"But it is morning . . ." she murmured, her back arching as he gently fondled her breasts.

"I know what hour of the day it is." He ran his lips along the curve of her collarbone, the action making her squirm in his lap.

She was not the only excited one, she realized. "And we are in my closet—"

"With a closed door that can be locked, I think. Will you lock it, or shall I?"

Without a word, Elissa rose and went to the door, where she turned the lock. Then she faced him, leaning against the door for necessary support, for her legs trembled as he came toward her.

He took her hands in his, then pulled her into his embrace. He ground his hips in a circular motion that elicited another groan from deep within her throat. She reached up and grabbed his shoulders, then thrust her tongue into his hot mouth as he gently guided her toward the desk.

She blindly untied his jabot and insinuated her hand beneath his shirt. He tensed at the first touch of her fingertips on his bare skin, then relaxed as she stroked him. With more anxious need, he yanked the lace right out of her bodice and when it fell open, nuzzled her undergarment lower until her breasts were completely exposed to his lips and his astonishingly supple tongue.

Slowly, his hands caressed her as if he were attempting to memorize her shape by feel alone.

"Please, Richard," she panted, no longer willing to wait. "Take me now. At once!"

She reached under her skirt, hurriedly undid the drawstring of her drawers and wiggled out of them.

"That is a command I am only too happy to obey," he replied softly, watching her with hungry eyes.

He set her on the edge of the desk and untied his breeches just as quickly. He shoved up her skirt and moved between her legs, and she wrapped her limbs around his waist.

Then, with a low, animalistic moan, he pushed inside her. Splaying her hands behind her, she raised her hips, meeting thrust for thrust, panting, sighing, urging him on. Her legs tightened around him, pulling him against her. His mouth captured her nipples, his tongue caressing the tips until she thought he would drive her mad.

Suddenly a growl burst from the back of his throat as he stiffened. Simultaneously pressing her lips together to stifle a scream, exquisite tension burst and radiated through her.

Sighing, Richard laid his head against her

naked breasts as she leaned forward to embrace him.

"Zounds, Elissa, you rob me of all finesse," he panted.

She laughed softly, toying with his hair. "I do not need finesse as long as I have you."

Two weeks later, Elissa stood in her bedchamber looking at her slumbering husband. All around her there were subtle changes brought about by his masculine presence, from the musky scent of the soap he used for shaving to his jacket slung over the back of a chair and his black boots on the floor.

At one time, there had been the remnants of his writing life on the chair: a worn pen, a clay vessel of ink, and a page or two of paper. These, she noted with pleasure, were gone, further proof that he had indeed given up that unseemly pasttime.

Instead, she thought with another secretive smile, he was finding other ways to spend his days, either with Will, or helping her with accounts and correspondence, or distracting her with other, more delightful activities, or simply with his masculine presence and wry observations.

She had not thought herself lonely before they were married, but she knew now that she had been, and very much so. Richard was a wonderful companion, for both her and her son.

She sighed softly, appreciating how fortunate they were that Richard had come into their lives. He could not be kinder to Will if her boy were his own son.

She had never thought to feel this . . . this love. Yes, love, she realized with increasing happiness.

She loved Richard.

She studied his familiar face. When he was awake, there was often a wry mockery in his dark, sardonic eyes, but when he slept, he seemed again an innocent youth, except for his full, soft lips. They seemed less innocent, as if he were pouting for her kiss.

Nor could she ignore the sight of his naked torso. Although the rest of him was covered by the sheet, she knew full well what was hidden, and that thought added to the warmth coursing through her as she regarded him.

She put her hand to her stomach. Tomorrow, she told herself. Only one more day to be absolutely certain, for she would not want to be wrong and have to disappoint him.

Richard shifted, made a little gurgle at the back of his throat, then opened his eyes, squinting in the dim light that shone through the small opening in the drapery.

"Who goes there?" he muttered.

His hand suddenly darted out to grab her and she let herself be pulled onto the bed. "An assassin?"

She fell on him, an event he acknowledged with a grunt.

"If you are going to manhandle me like a ruffian, that is what you deserve," she said pertly as his arms stole around her.

"You crept upon me like a thief."

"I shall likely have a bruised wrist."

He took her hand again, gently this time, and as always, his touch made her burn with desire. "Then I shall kiss it better for you, shall I?"

His lips touched her wrist with a light, gentle, nevertheless arousing, kiss.

"There," he murmured, raising his dark eyes to look at her. "All better?"

"All better."

"I perceive daylight, do I not, my lark?" he said, still holding her hand as he shifted to a sitting position against the wooden headboard while she sat on the edge of the bed.

"Yes," she said, trying not to sound disappointed that he had moved even that far away from her. "It is nearly ten o'clock."

"I fear I keep court and theater hours."

"You have not been at court or the theater for some time now."

"But I was for years before this, my sweet." He sighed wearily, but his eyes smiled mockingly. "If I did not exhaust myself completely with certain delightful activities, I would not fall asleep until dawn."

"And these activities would be?" she asked with feigned innocence.

"You know full well, my wanton wife," he murmured, bending forward to kiss her lightly on the cheek.

"If I am a wanton, you make me so."

"I take that as a great compliment," he said with a sincerely pleased smile.

"At the risk of making you insufferably arrogant, you are a most astonishing lover," she confessed, blushing at the memory of the things they had done together.

He waved his hand in dismissal. "Simply experience."

"Yes. I daresay it is."

He shifted forward, frowning worriedly. "I assure you, Elissa, no woman has ever pleased and excited me as you do."

Still she did not look at him. "I must seem very ignorant to you," she said softly.

He reached out to cup her chin and lifted it so that she met his steadfast gaze. "Elissa, believe me when I say I greatly prize what you would call ignorance and I would not change one thing about you."

He cocked his head and scrutinized her. "Well, there is one thing I would change," he mused. "Your manner of doing your hair."

She put her hand to her sleek topknot.

"It is too severe. I would have you wear it loose all the time," he said softly, reaching toward her head.

She scooted backward. "Richard!" she warned, although not very severely. "I like it this way, and I do not enjoy fussing about my hair. I never have, and I do not intend to start now."

"Oh." He sat back abruptly.

"Now you're sulking."

"I am not."

"You are."

"Bold hussy!" Richard cried, lunging for her and pulling her into his arms. "I have dueled men for less!"

"Nevertheless, I am very glad Will isn't here to see you. He thinks you are the next thing to the king and I shudder to consider how his opinion of you would suffer if he knew you wasted one thought upon anybody's hair."

Their shared laughter soon gave way to a passionate sigh as his mouth swooped down upon hers.

After several minutes, Elissa drew back and fanned herself. "I'faith, sir, I need some air! You quite crush me with your embraces."

"Now who is sulking?"

"I'm not sulking. I'm panting."

"So am I," he said huskily. "For more."

She held up her hand to stop him. "I cannot waste all day . . ." She paused, searching for the right word.

"Fumbling about in bed?" he suggested, his voice low and soft. "Caressing? Kissing? Making love?"

"Richard!" she warned again, very weakly.

He grinned and moved away. "Very well. But please do not think me an utterly lazy lout, sweet wife. I had not counted on the absolute quiet of the countryside. I wake up in the night and cannot sleep for the silence. I think I shall have to import some hawkers and criers and dung collectors and watermen to provide the appropriate barrage of noise."

"Is that why you wander about in the dark?"

Richard regarded her pensively. "I did not think I was disturbing you."

"I am a light sleeper," she answered truthfully, glad of this chance to find out what he did at night when he left her. He went downstairs, but she never heard him leave the house.

And she had listened very carefully.

"Obviously." He assumed a furtive expression. "I go to the kitchen and eat."

"You will grow stout."

"Not if I continue my evening exercise. The king claims tennis keeps him slim, but I believe his other physical activities account for it, too, and in that, I intend to heed our sovereign's model," Richard replied virtuously.

Elissa rose, shaking her head. "You are incorrigible, but I can see why people enjoy your company."

With a grunt, Richard climbed out of bed, gloriously, marvelously naked. "Zounds, it would be better if Will did not want to practice fencing so much! I am as stiff as a post."

"So I see."

"Wanton wench!"

"I am not the one parading about undressed," she retorted as he sauntered toward the washstand with a casual, yet regal, air, as if he were attired in a king's raiment. "Will's muscles have been sore, too. Perhaps you should not work so hard."

"Perhaps."

"Speaking of company, we are invited to dine with Mr. Assey this evening. I have already sent word that we shall."

Richard frowned.

"I thought you liked Mr. Assey."

He poured water from the pitcher into the basin. "I do, as much as I can like any acquaintance whom I must endure when I would rather be alone with you."

"We cannot lock ourselves away like hermits," she said as he began to wash his face. "The neighbors—"

"Will be offended. I understand." He grabbed a square of linen with which to dry and glanced at her. "Are we to be his only guests?"

"I doubt it. I would expect Sir John and his family, and Mr. Sedgemore."

"Wonderful," he replied sarcastically. "I had better arm myself against another ambush by

Antonia the Amazon. Do you think my sword will be sufficient?"

"A mask would be a better choice, I think. You are far too handsome. I understand vizards are very fashionable now."

"If I wear one, so must you." He went to his chest and pulled out some drawers and breeches and put them on.

With a blush, Elissa thought this something of a pity, and hiding his features would be, too. "They sound uncomfortable."

"They are," he agreed. "Another nuisance some fashionable fool decreed necessary because he wished to be disguised so no one need know when he was about unsavory business. That is precisely why they appeal to several members of our illustrious court, and not to me."

She was glad to hear that. "We don't have to go, if you really don't want to."

He faced her, a wry, self-mocking smile on his face. "Lord and Lady Dovercourt will be neighborly, and perhaps the only weapon I need is my obvious devotion to my wife. There is a condition to my attendance, however."

"A condition?"

"You must wear your hair loose."

"Loose!" she cried, again putting her hand to her topknot. "I can't! I have never—"

"If the ladies in the king's court can wear their hair about their shoulders in the evening,

I see no reason my wife cannot." He smiled seductively. "It would please your husband very much. Sadly, we shall have to trim the sides a bit, but only a little and I promise I shall save a lock to wear beside my heart."

She felt herself weakening and then she decided this was a small request for a loving wife to honor. "Unfortunately, I do not know how to curl it at the sides, as the ladies at court do."

Richard grinned. "I have been a student, a soldier, and a playwright. I am willing to add lady's maid to my list of accomplishments. Lord knows I have watched enough actresses fussing over their hair to have some notion how curls are accomplished."

"I do not have curling tongs."

"My lady, leave that to me," he replied with a flourishing bow. "Surely a servant can be sent to purchase them in the village."

"I would not count on that," Elissa said dubiously. "Owston is not a large place. There is not much call for curling tongs."

"My lady, please!" he cried, putting his hand to his bare chest as if mightily offended. "There must be a blacksmith in the village. I will go myself on this important mission."

He threw himself down on bended knee and dramatically declared, "My lady, I swear by yonder moon—"

"It is daylight."

He glanced at the window, grimaced, then raised his hand toward the window. "I swear by yon glowing orb that you shall have tongs before night falls or I am no true knight!"

"Whether you are a true knight or not remains to be seen," Elissa replied skeptically as she went to the door. He would no doubt make better progress getting dressed if she left. "And I think you should have been on the stage yourself instead of writing for it."

Chapter 16

"**Y**ou are going to destroy all my hard work," Richard chided as he caught Elissa touching the cascade of curls that fell down her cheeks as they approached Mr. Assey's withdrawing room. "And after all the trouble I had persuading the blacksmith to make the tongs. You would have thought I was asking him to make a suit of chain mail."

"The curls tickle."

She had insisted upon doing most of her hair in her customary style, but he had taken out several locks on either side and curled them. She wasn't sure of the effect; however, he seemed very pleased with his efforts.

"Those that frame the cheek are called *confidantes*," he explained. "Those farther back are *heartbreakers*, and you shall break my heart if you tug on them again."

"I would call them all nuisances."

"I declare them absolutely delightful and I

am fearfully jealous of the way they are able to caress your cheek while I can only look upon it," Richard whispered so that the liveried servant leading them toward the withdrawing room could not overhear.

Richard ran an admiring gaze over her gown of pale violet silk made years ago, before she was married. It was not in the newest fashion, although it did have a low, rounded bodice. "That color suits you to perfection."

His low, intimate words reconciled her to whatever discomfort she might endure over her hair for the rest of the evening, she decided.

The servant held open the door and they entered the withdrawing room.

Mr. Assey's house was old, made with comfort rather than ostentatious fashion in mind. The rooms were small and cozy, and the withdrawing room, with its cheerful fire to ward off the chill of the evening, seemed to welcome them.

There were fewer people here than at Mr. Sedgemore's dining party. Sir John, Lady Alyce, their daughters, and Mr. Sedgemore were the only guests.

In other respects, this evening proved to be far more satisfactory than the other had been. Richard spoke very eloquently and intelligently about the continuing troubles with the Dutch, and then about developments in the New World. She had not expected him to be so knowledgeable about political or military matters, although she supposed she should not be surprised that he was aware of the personalities of the men who ruled England. After all, he had met most of them, either at court or the theater.

The male guests seemed impressed, too. Regrettably, the same could not be said of the ladies. Lady Alyce yawned prodigiously throughout the discussion, and her daughters seemed happy to talk quietly among themselves and generally ignore the men.

Elissa supposed Sir John had taken them to task after Mr. Sedgemore's dinner—and quite rightly, too! She wondered if he had heard about Antonia's allegedly twisted ankle, or if his daughter had wisely chosen to keep that to herself. She rather suspected the latter.

As for her own behavior, she could hardly keep herself from staring at Richard. He looked handsome and elegant in his black velvet, his hair brushed neatly back and tied, so much better than the perukes the other men sported. Most attractive of all, though, was the secretive little smiles he gave her when nobody else was looking.

She had never felt so overheated at a dinner in her life, and yet she would not have changed anything for the world.

As the evening went on, Antonia began to converse almost exclusively with Mr. Sedgemore, who likewise disengaged from the men and their discussion. Their quiet whispers caused Elissa to speculate about a possible match between them. That was not a bad notion, she thought. Mr. Sedgemore had wealth and a fine property; as the younger daughter of minor nobility, Antonia could do worse.

Indeed, the more she thought about it, the more the idea pleased her.

Let Antonia glance occasionally at Richard then, she thought benignly, for *she* was the one who got to go home with him, a prospect that made it more and more difficult for her to attend to the conversation.

That, and her decision to tell Richard that she thought she was carrying his child. She had been tempted to do so as he had curled her hair, but the fact that they had to leave shortly held her tongue.

Later, she vowed, when they were alone and in bed, when she had ample time to enjoy his surely pleased reaction, then she would tell him.

Antonia detached herself from Mr. Sedgemore and strolled over to where Elissa sat beside the obviously slumbering Lady Alyce, some distance from the rest of the company.

Clad in a tight gown of bright and unflattering green, Antonia was difficult to ignore, and as she drew near, Elissa recognized the nasty gleam in Antonia's eyes.

She must have heard some new, probably

condemning gossip from Mr. Sedgemore and was anxious to impart it. "I must say it is always a pleasure to see a woman who is so *happily* married. You look as content as a cow in a pasture."

Elissa didn't like Antonia's tone, but she betrayed no reaction. "I am content, and very happy."

"I hope you continue to be so, with *such* a husband," Antonia retorted boldly, straightening her shoulders in a way that seemed to thrust her large bosom forward in emphasis.

Elissa suspected Mr. Sedgemore had not heeded her advice to guard his tongue about Richard's family. "I assure you, I shall be."

"Well," she drawled, "I daresay *some* women would even be quite proud to be wed to a man like Sir Richard—oh, I beg your pardon, the earl—who is so used to commanding the attention and admiration of many ladies. Surely he continues to require that admiration, even here. And after all, it is the nature of aristocratic men to take mistresses, is it not?"

"And who would you cast in that particular role?" Elissa inquired gravely. "Yourself, perhaps?"

Antonia could not subdue an angry frown. "I would never do anything so low!"

"Then who are you suggesting?"

Antonia moved far too close to Elissa for her liking. "It could be almost anyone except my mother, my sisters, and myself. The whole county should condemn you for bringing that man here."

"If anyone is upset that he has returned to his home, they should take their complaints to the king, who is, after all, responsible."

"Do not condescend to me, Elissa Longbourne!" Antonia snarled.

"Lady Dovercourt," she corrected.

Antonia's lip curled with disdain. "If your handsome husband has not already taken a mistress, his fit of morality will not likely last much longer. We all know his past and the sort of people he associated with in London. Not only is immoral behavior in his blood, he enjoys it!"

Elissa ran a cold, measuring gaze over the young woman. "I would keep your foolish, ignorant opinions to yourself, if I were you, Antonia, and I would keep my jealous, spiteful mouth shut!"

Lady Alyce snorted and opened her eyes. "Oh! What? Dear me!"

"I am bidding you and your daughter good night," Elissa said with a fraudulent smile as she rose from her chair.

"Oh, good night, good night," the befuddled woman murmured.

"Good night," Antonia said without troubling to hide a sneer.

Elissa hurried to Richard's side, as determined to leave this place as she was not to let Antonia upset her.

She would not believe that her husband would betray her. He loved her. He had not said so in so many words, of course, but she didn't doubt it.

She hadn't doubted William Longbourne's love, either, when he asked her to be his wife.

"What is it, my sweet?" he asked, looking at her with surprise, and then concern. "Are you ill?"

"No," she replied with a more genuine smile at their host. "I think it is getting rather late. I believe we should thank Mr. Assey for a wonderful evening and go home."

"Very well," Richard agreed, and the coach was ordered at once.

"I thought I would be the most anxious to return home tonight, since I like nothing better than being alone with my beautiful wife," Richard observed when they were on their way home. "Or is it that I embarrassed you again?"

"Not at all!"

"Did the curls tickle too much?" he asked softly, moving close beside her on the seat and reaching out to brush one back from her cheek.

His touch made her sigh with barely suppressed desire, and she was suddenly certain

Antonia's words came from spiteful jealousy. "No."

Perhaps now would be a good time to tell him about the baby . . .

She never got the chance, for Richard suddenly pulled her into his arms, and his mouth captured hers in a rapturous, heated kiss. She responded eagerly, the pent-up desire she had felt all evening suddenly liberated.

Leaning into him, she felt his chest heave with his breathing, sensed the growing tension in his taut muscles, and yearned to run her hands over his naked skin.

As she fumbled with his jabot with quick, impatient movements, he untied her bodice. While his tongue explored her willing mouth, his hand plunged inside her loosened gown. Cupping her breast, he teased her pebbled nipple with his thumb while a low groan of sensual pleasure rose from his throat.

His body pressed hers against the back of the coach as her hands clutched his shoulders. The swaying motion of the coach added to her excitement in a way she had never foreseen.

Then she felt him lift her skirt. "Now?" she panted.

"Not that," he answered in a low whisper. "Not yet."

His hand found her honor and with slow, incredibly arousing thrusting motions, he caressed her. At the same time, his tongue flicked upon her naked flesh. Between that sensation and the other, all she could do was give herself over to the pleasure he aroused.

She had to clamp her lips shut to stifle the scream of pure animal pleasure when he brought her to completion just as the coach rolled to a stop outside the stables of Blythe Hall.

"We are home," he whispered, quickly pulling down her skirt.

Hastily retying her bodice, she could think of nothing to say as the waves of pleasure slowly subsided, unless it be a request to go on a long—a very long—drive.

The coachman opened the door and Richard leaped out, then held out his hand to help her. She stumbled slightly as she got down and he swept her into his arms, glancing back as the startled driver and stable boy exchanged looks.

"Lady Dovercourt is a little dizzy," he explained as he carried her toward the house.

Her arms tightened about his neck. "They will think I am drunk," she chided in his ear.

"Would you rather they knew what we had been doing in the coach?"

"No," she said as he carried her toward the stairs. "You may put me down. I am quite capable of walking."

"I am in a great hurry," he replied as he started up the steps.

"Am I not too heavy?"

"You are as light as goose down."

"I am not."

"Do you doubt my strength?"

"No."

"Good."

He continued toward the bedchamber, kicked the door open, quickly crossed the floor and laid her on the bed.

"Now then," he said in the most seductive tone of voice Elissa had ever heard or imagined, "my turn."

"Yes," she replied just as provocatively as she reached up and pulled him down onto the bed beside her. "It is."

As she sat in her closet, Elissa sighed, then leaned back in her chair and rubbed her eyes. Zounds, if she did not get more rest, she would soon be too fatigued to do much of anything.

Unfortunately, the only way she would get more rest, she suspected, would be to exile Richard to a different bedchamber, a far from satisfactory solution.

Yawning, she resumed her search of the desk for ink and a new pen. She was sure she had put those items in here when they had been delivered a few weeks ago.

Should there not have been more paper, too? Or had Richard used it all for letters?

She would have to remember to speak to him about that.

Sighing, she acknowledged that she was becoming very forgetful these days, or perhaps too easily diverted by her handsome, virile husband.

She had been so distracted by him last night, she hadn't told him about the baby. She would do so the minute he finished fencing with Will.

She glanced down at her desk and spotted a letter that must have come by messenger sometime last evening while they were at Mr. Assey's. She picked it up and, recognizing her lawyer's plain, neat hand, tore it open.

Dear Lady Dovercourt,

I hope this letter finds you in good health, and enjoying some happiness regardless of the unfortunate circumstances of your marriage.

Elissa smiled. Some happiness? She had never been happier.

I regret I have some bad news with which to trouble you, but I must, for to do otherwise would, I fear, be criminally irresponsible: I am sorry to have to report that my clerk, Mr. Mollipont, has been involved in some questionable dealings.

I am very, very sorry to have to tell you that he

has been copying and selling certain legal documents referring to your legal affairs.

"My legal affairs?" Elissa murmured in bewilderment and a growing sense of dread.

The copies in question were sections of your late husband's will, as well as portions of your marriage settlement with Mr. Longbourne and some details of the sale of the Blythe estate to him.

The cold finger of fear which this letter had already laid upon her became an icy grip.

The pertinent sections of your husband's will concern what will happen to the Blythe estate should your son predecease you.

You may not know that this question caused your late husband some consternation, but since he had no living relatives, your father and I were eventually able to persuade him to accept the following terms in that regard. If your son meets with an untimely death, the property in its entirety reverts to you.

I should also remind you of the terms of your current marriage settlement. If the earl outlives you, and you die without further issue, all your property becomes his, including anything that you yourself may have inherited.

I confess that such an eventuality did occur to me, and yet taking into account your son's

*robust health, your own youth and obvious ability
to bear children and, although this ought to be no
excuse, the haste with which it was necessary to
draft the document, I thought this an unlikely
enough event and so did not change the usual draft
of marriage settlements that I make for my clients.
In hindsight, I should have taken more care with
this portion of the document and ask your forgiveness for not doing so.*

*Unfortunately, as of yet Mr. Mollipont refuses
to name the person interested in this information.
All he will say is that he was compelled to this
criminal activity because of gambling debts. My
lady, I am shocked and aggrieved that my trust
and yours has been so utterly betrayed and will do
all in my power to force Mr. Mollipont to tell me
all.*

*I am confident that I will eventually be suc-
cessful.*

Elissa could well believe this. Mr. Mollipont
would not be able to keep his secrets from the
stern, persistent Mr. Harding forever.

*Although I do not wish to cause you undue alarm
or pain, my lady, I must point out that while I
know of no specific incidents in your current husband's past to make him a suspect in this matter,
he would be the one most obviously to benefit from
the death of your son.*

Until we can know the identity of Mr. Mol-

*lipont's accompliss, I would suggest that you take
all possible care of your delightful child.*

I remain, very faithfully yours,

Robert Harding

Stunned by the contents of this epistle,
Elissa didn't know what to do. His first im-
pulse was to summon Richard ... but then
again, maybe that would not be wise.

Yet Richard had not been to London since
he had returned to Blythe Hall, so he could
hardly be in league with Mr. Mollipont.

On the other hand, he could write letters,
and he had many acquaintances in London
who might act as his agent in this business.

Oh, surely Mr. Harding was wrong to suspect Richard of any involvement in such a terrible scheme. Mr. Harding likely suspected
everybody of everything—

"My lady! My lady!"

She started at the servant's alarmed cry,
then hurried to the door.

"What is it?" she demanded of the dis-
traught footman who stood at the door of the
withdrawing room.

"There's been an accident!"

She gripped the door frame. "Who—?"

"It's your son. They was fencing and—"

"Not with real swords!"

"He said the tip come off and—"

"Oh, sweet heaven!"

At that moment, Richard appeared at the door to the withdrawing room.

One look at Elissa's pale, terrified face, and he silently heaped more curses on his own head.

"Will is fine, Elissa," he hurriedly assured her as he came into the room. "I blame myself for not taking better care, but I promise you it isn't a bad cut—"

"Where is he?"

"In his room, play—"

"Did you send for the doctor?"

"The wound is not serious enough for—"

"I shall be the judge of that!" she snapped, brushing past him.

Was it possible she was as wrong about Richard as she had been about William Longbourne? Could he be planning to take her estate by the horrible means Mr. Harding's letter suggested?

I never should have agreed to let Richard teach Will anything about swordplay, she thought, as she hurried to the stairs. Will was going to be a country gentleman; he didn't need martial skills. He need know only how to keep accounts and manage the laborers and tenants, how to bargain with the wool merchants . . .

What if Will's wound became infected? What if the injury became gangrenous?

Tears filled her eyes as she ran up the steps as fast as she could. If anything bad had happened to her darling son, she would never forgive herself.

And she would never forgive Richard, either.

Would Richard have taken such a risk with a child of his own? Was this accident merely the result of a momentary lapse of good judgment?

It must be! Richard was good and kind to Will, as if he genuinely cared about her son.

Or he acted as if he did.

She had seen for herself what a very good actor Richard was.

What of his wish to help her with the ledgers and other business of the estate? Did he really want only to be helpful, or was there another, more sinister reason for his assistance?

Then a great and terrible question took precedence over all these: Had she put her beloved child in jeopardy by allowing herself to be blinded by love yet again?

With a self-recriminating sigh, Richard hurried after his perturbed wife.

It was not that he feared for the boy's health. The cut on the boy's arm was a minor one. However, he was responsible for ensuring Will's safety. He had failed, causing Will pain and upsetting Elissa.

He never should have acquiesced to Will's oft-repeated plea to try "just once" with real rapiers. He should have insisted they continue with the sticks.

He was nearly to Will's bedchamber when he heard the lad's excited voice. "So then, Mama, he *burned* it!"

Richard cringed. "I *cauterized* it," he corrected as he entered the room.

Will stood in the middle of his bedchamber, his sleeve rolled up and his arm thrust out. A few of his wooden toys were scattered about on the floor. His small rope bed was in the corner, a table and chair near the window, and a washstand beside the door. His bandage had been removed and now lay on the bed. Elissa knelt beside him, carefully examining his injury.

Richard recognized the lad's attitude: He was like a brave warrior recounting his battlefield exploits, or like King Charles when he told of his narrow escape from Cromwell's men. The king took great satisfaction in describing how he had spent an entire night hiding in an oak tree. In truth, he never seemed to miss an opportunity to talk about it.

"He never even whimpered," Richard remarked, not hiding his admiration for the lad's bravery.

"I told you I didn't cry, Mama, even though it hurt like bloo—"

Will looked at Richard and flushed guiltily.

"Even though it hurt very much," he amended. "And Richard says I'm going to have a *scar!*"

"Yes, I think you are," Elissa agreed as she began to rebandage the boy's arm.

Will grinned with unmitigated delight.

"I'm sure it's not serious," Richard said placatingly.

"Since you have not studied medicine, I think we must defer to the doctor's opinion."

Richard noted the way Will's face fell, and his uneasy glances from Richard to his mother.

"It was just an accident," Will said. "I jumped and knocked the end of his sword with my blade and they scraped together and I was afraid I had hurt his sword so I went to see and Richard didn't realize and he lifted the blade and there I was!"

"Do you mind if your mama and I go downstairs for a few moments, Will?" Richard asked. "You will be all right by yourself?"

Will nodded.

"I think I should stay—"

"I do not," Richard said, using the same tone of voice he used to command his actors when they balked at a bit of staging.

Like his actors, Elissa wisely realized this was not the time to balk.

But she did not meekly obey. She lifted her chin and, with all the majesty of a queen, strode from the room. "We shall speak in my closet."

Richard knew there would be no lovemaking this time.

Chapter 17

Elissa whirled around to face him the moment they were in her closet. "How could you take such a risk?"

"Obviously, I didn't consider it a risk," Richard replied, trying to remain calm.

Hopefully, that would help Elissa to see that this accident was not so very terrible. Will was not likely to suffer any ill effects, unless one counted a possible vain addiction to showing off his scar.

He sat on the edge of the desk and shrugged. "I was too lenient, or lazy—whatever you wish to call it. He was so eager and persistent, I gave in. I promise I will be wiser in the future."

"But to use real swords!"

She crossed her arms over her chest and glared at him. "Or does your vivid imagination not extend to dangerous pastimes?"

"The swords were tipped. It was an unforeseen accident."

"With children, it takes but a moment for disaster to strike. You encouraged him to climb that tree, you let him play with real swords—"

"You let him climb the tree, too," Richard protested, straightening.

"I would never have allowed him near an unsheathed sword," she retorted. "Perhaps I am asking too much of your imagination. You are not a parent. Still, I am shocked you could be so reckless."

"I am not a child, Elissa, so do not speak to me as if I were."

"You acted little better than a child."

His expression hardened. "I have not acted like a child since I was eight years old and had that luxury taken from me. I made a mistake, and I will try not to repeat it. That is all I intend to say on this matter."

"If I am in the wrong to upbraid you, how dare you chastise me for caring about my son? I am his mother!"

"I may not have the privilege of being a parent, but by God, my lady, did you not see that you were upsetting Will with your own childish display of temper?"

She realized with a flush of guilt that he was right. But even if he were trustworthiness personified, he still did not understand a mother's feelings, and he had no right to be so patronizing.

"Where have you been going at night?" she demanded.

He started at her abrupt change of subject, then his eyes narrowed. "Why do you ask that?"

"Why not? Surely I have a right to know where you go at such an hour. And what have you been doing with pens and papers and ink? I thought you were giving up writing—or have you a secret correspondence?"

"To whom do you suspect I have been writing?"

"That is for you to tell me, since you have been using goods purchased with my money to do so."

"I am not accustomed to being interrogated, my lady, as if I were a criminal."

"Then you should not sneak about in the middle of the night like a criminal, or take things without asking like a thief. Or an unfaithful husband."

As he flushed hotly, dismay and shame flooded through Richard. That she would accuse him of this, after all he had said to her—things he had never said to a woman before.

For once he had dared to trust a woman, to feel something beyond lust or the challenge of seduction, to fall in love . . .

To fall in love.

How ironic that he, Richard Blythe, so fa-

mous for his witty, caustic plays about the fol-
lies of love, should find himself so hopelessly
and foolishly in the throes of that emotion,
only to discover that the object of his love believed him capable of base deceit and duplicity
and betrayal.

That she did not love him as he loved her.

At the sound of an approaching coach, they
both glanced at the window.

"Are you expecting someone?" Richard demanded. "The neighborly Mr. Sedgemore?
The unfortunately named Mr. Assey? Heartless Harding, perhaps?"

"I am not," she answered briskly, going to
the window.

He followed her and looked over her shoulder, trying to ignore the subtle aroma of her
perfume.

Then he recognized the coat of arms on the
coach door.

"Bloody hell!" he cried. "It's Neville! What
the devil is he doing here?"

"Making you use the sort of language you
said you would not, if nothing else. Am I to
assume this is a friend of yours?"

"Lord Farrington is my dearest friend, save
Foz. Now if you excuse me, I daresay our
quarrel can wait."

Preferably forever, he thought, as he
marched from the room.

When he exited the house, he put a welcoming smile on his face.

"Neville!" he called in greeting as his friend stepped out of the vehicle under the portico.

"Lo, the country squire cometh!" Neville, Lord Farrington, cried in response. Then he made a very dramatic bow.

Country living seemed to agree with the man Richard had secretly considered the epitome of urban sophistication. There was a healthy glow to his cheeks and a brightness in his eyes Richard had never seen in London. To be sure, Neville was as fashionably attired as always, and like Richard, he had never donned a wig.

"You scoundrel, what brings you here?" Richard asked.

"You know I am but melted wax to be molded by my wife's lovely fingers," Neville replied.

"What, has Arabella come, too?"

He had his answer in a moment, as Neville helped his obviously pregnant, pretty, and smiling wife down from the coach.

"Forgive us for not waiting for an invitation," she began as soon as her feet were on the ground, "but I shall not be able to travel much soon, and your estate is not so very far from ours . . ."

"I am *delighted* you have come!" Richard cried as he kissed her on each cheek. "And I must beg your forgiveness for not inviting you sooner. I have been rather . . . busy."

"I can see why," Neville replied in low,

knowing tones as he nodded at something behind Neville.

Richard spun around, to see Elissa marching
toward them. "Yes, my wife has..." He
paused, then began again. "That is, she..."

"Ods bodikins, I don't believe it! He's
speechless!"

Richard subdued a scowl as Foz's muffled,
sleepy voice issued from the coach. Then his
friend, wig askew, stuck his head out of the
window and grinned. "I never thought I'd see
that day!"

"If it were any other man, Foz, I'd knock
your head for saying that," Richard warned.

"I only meant it as a joke," Foz mumbled,
pouting.

"I know that," Richard answered genially as
he faced Elissa.

His good spirits were quite destroyed, but
one would never have known it from his expression. "Elissa, my sweet, allow me to introduce Neville, Lord Farrington, his bride,
Arabella, and I think you will remember Lord
Cheddersby."

Her expression was infuriatingly inscrutable
as she curtsied. "Delighted to meet you. Welcome to our home."

"We shall only stop a little while," Arabella
explained hastily.

"Nonsense! You must stay for at least a
week," Richard replied.

Foz grinned happily, but Neville and Arabella glanced at Elissa, then each other.

"You join me in wishing that my dearest friends stay some time under our ample roof, do you not, Elissa," Richard said, and it was not a question.

"If you wish."

"We can only stay one night," Neville said firmly. "Now that I, too, have an estate to manage, I cannot stay away for long. And my father gets positively peckish when Arabella is away. He will be riding roughshod over the servants until she gets back."

"That I can well believe," Richard agreed. "Very well, one night only it shall be."

"If you will all excuse me, I had better alert the servants," Elissa announced. Then she turned and swept into the house.

Neville's brows rose. "I knew we should have sent word first."

"This is all my fault," Foz moaned. "I was bored out of my skull in London with nothing to do and nobody to do it with, so I thought I'd take myself to Neville's estate, and then we got to talking about you and you did invite me but only me—"

"It is my fault," Arabella interrupted. "As newly married myself, I should have remembered that you two might not want company just yet."

"Nonsense!" Richard repeated, his tone slightly defensive. "I am very pleased you have come. You have caught Elissa unawares, that's all, and she doesn't like surprises."

And that, he was sure, was no lie.

"Perhaps we would do better to stay at the inn in that village we came through," Neville suggested.

Not where he had gotten drunk! "No, no, I insist you stay here."

"Then she is not angry?" Foz asked worriedly.

"No! Taken aback, perhaps, but not angry. You are my friends, I am delighted you have come and I insist you stay here. There is no more to be said."

Again, Neville and Arabella exchanged wary glances.

Foz, on the other hand, giggled. "Then it is just as I said it would be. I knew it would be so, after watching all your plays."

Richard raised a brow in puzzlement.

"I said you would be the master here. It is a perennial theme in your plays that only a fool allows his wife to command him."

"Is that so, Richard?" Arabella asked pointedly.

Richard suddenly wished he had not been so forceful in espousing certain sentiments in his literary pursuits. "I fear I am forgetting my manners, Lady Farrington, letting you stand here so long. Come, let us all go inside for some refreshment."

*　　*　　*

"So there I was, slumbering peacefully through the third act," Lord Cheddersby continued that evening, equally oblivious to the tension in the dining room as to the final course of the meal before him.

"Peacefully?" Richard interrupted. "I daresay your snores were audible throughout the house."

The handsome, well-dressed Lord Farrington and his pretty wife smiled at that, as they had smiled at so much since their unwelcome arrival, Elissa thought sourly as she silently consumed her pudding and tried to ignore the banter about things of which she knew nothing.

"They were not!" Lord Cheddersby protested.

"I have heard you snore, Foz, and trust me, they probably were," Lord Farrington said.

Elissa glanced at the man with his easy, charming speech and manners. He wore a suit of finely tailored dark brown brocade and an ecru shirt with a touch of lace. His naturally curling hair fell about his broad shoulders.

He was, she supposed, the most conventionally handsome man she had ever seen, and yet there was no challenge in his eyes, no hint of fierce determination or bold self-confidence in his features. Indeed, it was easy to believe that had he been less intelligent, he would have made a fine fop in the king's court.

She tried not to look at Lord Farrington's

young, merry wife at all and cursed herself for
the jealousy she could not subdue.

Yet she was not jealous of Arabella's looks,
fine velvet gown, jewelry, or pretty hair rib-
bons. She was jealous because Lady Farrington
seemed to be having the happy, carefree life
that had been denied to Elissa. What did this
woman know of suffering, denial, or fear?

If she had experienced what Elissa had,
would she be so pleasant and ever-smiling?

As for Lord Cheddersby, his friendship with
Richard was truly a puzzle, for he seemed exactly the kind of buffoon her husband would
scorn or make sport of.

Perhaps he did, and the man was too stupid
to know it.

She also wondered if they were secretly noting the plainness of her plate and linen, the
simplicity of their meal, the lack of French
wine or the champagne that was all the rage
at court, and pitying their friend.

"Snores or not, that is still no reason for that
saucy Nell Gwyn to throw an orange at my
head," Lord Cheddersby complained. "The
wench could have killed me."

"Indeed," Richard replied with a wry smile,
"she might have killed you, for she is a very
healthy young woman."

"Healthy? Ods bodikins, she is an Amazon!"

"That is not the Nell I know," Neville remarked. "She is too petite to be a warrior."

Elissa glanced at Lady Farrington and was surprised to see that the woman didn't so much as blink.

Was she a fool, that she didn't suspect her husband of an illicit liaison with this Nell? Everyone knew that the young women who sold oranges at the theaters were also prostitutes—and Lord Farrington had used the harlot's first name.

Then she flushed to think that if Lady Farrington were a fool, she herself was a greater one, for surely her own husband had had numerous encounters with such creatures.

"Well, she could be a miniature Amazon, couldn't she?" Lord Cheddersby asked after a moment's thought.

"Nell is an impertinent wench, but I doubt she meant to hurt you," Lord Farrington said.

"I hope you are right, for she is a pretty little thing. Mind, I've still got the bruise." Lord Cheddersby started to lift his elegant wig. "Look here—"

"By all means, yes," Elissa confirmed. "Display your wound to my husband. He is a veritable marvel when it comes to injuries, although an attack with an orange may be beyond even his expertise."

Their company looked at her with some surprise—as if they were taken aback to realize she was there, Elissa thought coldly. As for Richard, she didn't care how or if he looked at her.

"My wife's son had a slight mishap with a sword," he explained. "Nothing serious. It was no worse than the cut Buckhurst gave you in Whitehall that night when you saved Arabella from him."

"Ah, yes. That night," Lord Farrington said, giving his wife a secretive and loving smile.

A lump came to Elissa's throat. Just last night, Richard had looked at her that way and she had rejoiced.

But that was last night. So much had changed in so short a time!

"Where is your stepson?" Lord Cheddersby asked. "I would like to meet him again. I swear, he was quite the finest little chap I ever set eyes on, as I said at the time. Didn't I, Richard?"

"My son is in his bedchamber. He is far too young to keep such late hours," Elissa replied.

She knew she sounded pert and petulant, but she told herself she didn't care what these people thought of her.

Lord Cheddersby sighed as if his life were a vale of tears. "I tell you, Richard, there has not been a decent play since you have left London—and I am not the only one who says so."

"You flatter me, Foz."

"No, I don't! They are all lacking wit, or humor, or anything entertaining."

"You mean no one has realized that for a play to be popular, there must be an excuse for an actress to display her legs?"

Lord Farrington chuckled. "I seem to recall you wrote one play without that requirement."

"And a dismal failure it was, too."

"I feel so responsible for that!" Lady Farrington said with a sigh.

She smiled at Elissa. "Did he tell you about his failed tragedy? Sadly, I understand I was his inspiration. Perhaps you will prove a better one."

"I think not."

Richard cleared his throat. "I have given up writing."

"Foz told me some such nonsense," Lord Farrington replied, "but I couldn't believe it."

"If so, I do think that would be a pity," Lady Farrington said.

"You've only seen one of my plays," Richard said to her.

"It was very amusing."

"You didn't think so at the time."

As Elissa listened to their conversation indicating an acquaintance of long duration and some intimacy, another cold, frightening, dreadful thought crept into her mind.

Just how intimate had Richard been with these people, especially Lady Farrington, for whom he had written a play?

Elissa rose abruptly, shoving her chair back so hard, it audibly scraped the floor. "Since it is growing late and I have never been to the theater, I think I had better make sure that Will is safely in bed."

As she marched from the room, his obviously confused friends simultaneously turned to regard Richard.

Richard knew full well that his guests suspected there was trouble between himself and his bride. Zounds, how could they not? Elissa had certainly made it plain enough. Even Foz now sensed the tension between them, just as surely as Will would tomorrow. The old pattern was repeating itself, something he had vowed to avoid at all costs.

As the awkward silence continued, he felt compelled to speak. "She is a very concerned mother," he said, not willing to reveal anything of his true feelings, even to them.

"I knew that the first day, too!" Foz cried triumphantly.

"When is the baby due?"

Shocked and not quite comprehending, Richard stared at Arabella. "What did you say?"

Arabella flushed and glanced at her husband. "I thought from her glowing complexion . . . I assumed she was with child."

Richard recovered himself sufficiently to speak with a measure of calm. "You are mistaken. She has not said anything of that to me."

"Oh, well, I must be wrong, then," Arabella replied with a weak smile. "Perhaps it is only that I want the two of you to be as happy as Neville and I."

"Since this marriage came about by the king's command and not through any mutual desire, you surely cannot expect such felicity here."

"No, but we had hoped to find it nonetheless," Neville said quietly.

Arabella rose. "If you gentlemen will excuse me, it has been a tiring day. I believe I should retire, too."

"I'll go with you," her husband said, also standing. "Good night, Richard. No need to see us off in the morning, for I think we shall leave very early."

Richard slowly got to his feet. He would hide how upset their obvious sadness and disappointment made him, just as he had always hidden his past, his hopes, and his dream of having a home full of love, respect, and happiness instead of hatred, immorality, and hypocrisy.

"It is not as if I keep London hours here," he said, trying to achieve his usual sardonic tone. "I shall see you in the morning."

"Good night," the couple bade him, and they left the room.

"Yes, well, I suppose I had better retire, too," Foz muttered, toying with the lace on his cuff as he, too, got to his feet.

"What, no more gossip to share over a glass of wine?" Richard said, determined to act as if all were well. "I have missed the scandalous doings of the court."

Foz shrugged. "It's only more of the same. Squabbles between the king and Lady Castlemaine, the queen is not yet pregnant, the Dutch are making trouble . . . you know. I, um, I am very tired, Richard. I think I should go to bed."

"Good night," Richard said evenly.

Foz started toward the door, then hesitated and turned back. "Richard?"

"What is it?"

"You recall my particular forte?"

For a moment, a wild surge of hope seemed to burst into Richard's heart. "I recall that is unrequited love."

Foz nodded. "Yes."

"Do you see evidence of that here?" he asked, trying to sound unconcerned.

"No."

Disappointment—stupid, childish, utterly ridiculous disappointment—momentarily possessed him.

"But there is something between you and your wife." Foz rubbed his forehead. "If I were not such a dolt, I could describe it."

"Would you call it animosity?"

"Ods bodikins, no!"

"Then give me your closest approximation."

Foz frowned. "I don't think you will agree."

"Tell me."

"I think you are both afraid."

"What?" Richard scoffed, crossing his arms over his chest. "Me, afraid of a woman?"

"Of *that* woman," Foz said quietly.

"Why?"

Foz sighed and this time, rubbed his chin. "I think you care very much about her, and her opinion of you."

"I have never given a fig for anybody's opinion of me!"

"Perhaps not—until now," Foz answered quietly.

"You're mad!"

"No, I'm not." Foz came closer and regarded his friend with pensive, sincere concern. "And I think she's afraid of you."

"That is the most insane thing of all! Why would she be afraid of me? I would never hurt a woman!"

"Of course I don't mean you would ever lay a hand on her. It's something . . . something quite different."

"If this nonsense is all you have to say, I give you good night!"

Foz shook his head, then silently left the room.

Chapter 18

The next morning, after waving farewell to his friends and watching their coach wend its way down the drive, Richard marched to the bedchamber.

He had not slept—or done anything—with Elissa last night, of course. Instead, he had made his bed on one of the settles in the withdrawing room, and a most uncomfortable bed it had been.

His visage grim and fiercely determined, he shoved open the door.

Elissa, who was in bed but not asleep, sat up, drawing the bedclothes up to her neck as she eyed her husband warily.

He said not a word, but went to his chest and threw open the lid. Still wordlessly, he pulled off his wrinkled jacket and tossed it over the nearby chair. He removed his linen shirt and threw it on the floor.

"What are you doing?" Elissa demanded,

staring at his naked, muscular back.

"I am changing my clothes," he said, beginning to root about in the chest.

"Where were you last night?"

"What is that to you?"

"You are my husband."

He gave her a scornful glance. "To your eternal regret, I am sure."

He pulled out a clean white shirt. "Nevertheless, I might have expected you to respect me, or my friends. I'faith, it seemed even mere politeness was too much for you."

"It was hardly polite of them to come without an invitation."

Richard's lips turned down into a petulant frown. "I invited Foz before we left London."

"You didn't tell me."

"They are my friends, and that should have been enough to ensure them some courtesy. But take heart, Elissa. You shall not have to put up with me or my friends any longer. I am going back to London."

The part of her rational mind that believed he could conceivably have a hand in a plot to take control of the estate told her she should be relieved, yet she was not. His words were like a dagger in her heart. "To London?"

He pulled the fresh shirt over his head. Then he started tossing his personal belongings into the chest, including the discarded shirt. "I grew up in a house of hate, and I will not live in one again."

Hate? He hated her? She put her hand to her throat as if stifling her anguish.

How could he speak of hate after what they had shared—unless he had never loved, or even liked her.

Unless he had deceived her even more cruelly than William Longbourne had.

"I shall return to where I belong. Where I am appreciated. Where I should have stayed."

"I believe you are right. You do belong back in that hellhole with your lascivious theatrical cronies," she said as she got out of bed. "Then there will be no need to write so many letters, or have them do any favors for you."

"I have not written any letters," he muttered.

She ignored the shock of the cold bare floor beneath her foot as she wrapped her arms around herself, and not just for warmth. "Tell me, will Lady Farrington be waiting for you there? Or your other *close* friends? Of course, one can only speculate *how* close."

He went as still as a stone, then slowly wheeled around to face her. "What do you mean by that?"

"I mean that you must have had a very special friendship with Lady Farrington if she inspired you to write a play," she said, determined to show nothing of her pain, a lesson she had learned from one husband and that stood her in good stead now.

"She is my friend's wife."

"And that is supposed to reassure me? How stupid do you think I am?"

"Do you honestly believe me capable of betraying one of my oldest and dearest friends for a few fleeting moments of passion?"

"I am afraid that you are capable of anything to get what you want. Is selfishness not the way of the fashionable world, of the court?"

"It is not my way and has never been my way."

"Oh, spare me your righteous protests!" Elissa cried. "I can only wonder what other weeping, wailing, brokenhearted woman will come looking for you when you are gone. Antonia? Or maybe there will be more than one woman who has sported with you in the Banqueting House after receiving a passionate note?"

His face flushed.

"Oh, now you display some small hint of shame? I compliment you on your acting skills. Perhaps I am stupid after all, for you certainly had me fooled into believing that you cared about me as something more than a companion for your bed."

He crossed the floor in an instant and grabbed her by the arms, glaring into her face with blatant hostility. "You think I have been meeting with women in that cursed place?"

"Why else would you leave our bed so often?"

"How dare you accuse me of such behavior!"

"I dare because of who you are! I dare because of your past! I dare because someone has paid Mr. Mollipont for copies of my marriage settlements and my late husband's will. I dare because I want my son to be safe!"

His hands fell to his sides and he stared at her, his brow furrowed both with animosity and confusion. "I know you think I am as lecherous as the worst rogue at the king's court, but what is this about marriage settlements and wills? And what the devil has Mr. Mollipont to do with anything?"

"He has made copies of certain papers at someone's behest," she said, fighting to maintain her rapidly diminishing self-control, "papers concerning what will happen to this estate if Will were to die before me."

His face turned ashen. "You think that I could want Will dead in order to have back this estate?"

"Wouldn't you? Wouldn't you give anything for that? You were willing to marry a stranger for it. Why not kill her child, too?"

He staggered back as if she had struck him. "My God!" he gasped. "My God! *This* is what you think of me? That I could . . ."

"I don't know what to think!" she wailed helplessly, suddenly fearful her suspicions were based on unfounded and utterly unsupported speculations. That her imagination had run rampant with disastrous results.

Then Richard shuddered as if a bolt of lightning shot through him, and he assumed an air she well remembered from the first day she had set eyes upon him, an air of arrogant invincibility. "Bloody hell, madam, I think it is a good thing I am going. Send my things to London. I will not bide here another instant."

He went to the door, then paused and looked back at her, his lip curling with disdain. "The king himself told me of that provision before we were married, and as I told him, this estate would never be worth a child's life."

He marched out, slamming the door shut behind him.

Elissa sank slowly to the floor and covered her face with her trembling hands.

She didn't know what to do. Who to believe. Who to trust.

Mr. Mollipont's crimes, the missing writing materials, Richard's late-night sojurns . . . were they linked? Should she listen to Mr. Harding's warning, or trust in her husband?

How could she, when she couldn't even trust herself?

She had misjudged a man once before and followed her foolish heart. If she made the wrong choice this time, she might pay for it with more than her own pain and suffering.

She might pay for it with her son's life.

*   *   *

The news that Lord Dovercourt had ridden off to London spread through Owston as quickly as such news could, giving rise to avid speculation and rampant rumors.

And in one case, triumphal joy.

Two days later, Elissa raised her eyes from the neat columns written in Richard's familiar hand. She was not surprised to see Alfred Sedgemore come like a vulture to pick over the ruins of her life. Indeed, she had expected him before this, but that did not make his appearance any more acceptable.

She wanted to be left alone, for she was still trying to decide what to do. Her heart urged her to go to London after Richard, yet what if Mr. Harding was right to suspect him? What if Richard had tricked her? Just because she thought she loved him didn't mean that he reciprocated and that he was worthy of her trust.

If she made the wrong decision, more than she would suffer.

More than she was suffering already, she knew. Will had hardly smiled or spoken since Richard's abrupt departure. Instead, he wandered about the house like some sort of mournful spirit.

She remembered what Richard had said about upsetting Will with her behavior, and she wanted to explain why Richard was gone. Unfortunately, every time she started, she felt the tears come to her eyes. She was determined that her son not see her anguished uncertainty, so explanations would have to wait until she was in better control of herself, or had come to a decision.

Now, as with Will, she forced herself to put on a pleasant face that had little to do with her inner turmoil. She had known rumors would fly after Richard's sudden exodus; better to deal with them and be done, as much as she could be. "Good day, Mr. Sedgemore."

Regarding her with a pity Elissa found intolerable, Mr. Sedgemore toyed with the broad brim of his hat. "I fear I have heard some most upsetting news, my lady."

Although she would rather order him leave, she gestured toward the chair opposite her. "Please, sit down. I daresay you are referring to my husband's departure for London?"

"I gather it was a hasty departure." Mr. Sedgemore leaned forward, his feral eyes full of sympathy and something else, something that made a shiver run down her spine. "I am so sorry!"

"Why?"

"Am I to assume, my lady, that you are not sorry to see him gone?"

He regarded her so expectantly, she felt compelled to answer. "If I am sorry for anything, there is no need for you to be."

He leaned back, and she suddenly thought he seemed far too comfortable in that chair, as if he felt he belonged there. "Perhaps the only person who really should be sorry is your dear departed—yet living—husband, and the king, for making you marry. And oh, yes, Sir John."

"Sir John?" she asked, genuinely puzzled.

"Yes. It seems his intention to take his daughters away from temptation has instead sent them straight into it, for they left for London the day before yesterday, too." He rubbed his chin thoughtfully. "Rather an interesting coincidence that they go there at the same time as your husband, wouldn't you agree?"

"Why should they not? Oh, you must miss Antonia."

His expression grew puzzled. "Antonia?"

"I was under the impression that you were quite taken with her."

"My lady, please!" he cried, and she saw that he was sincerely shocked at her suggestion. "I have no interest of an amorous nature in that woman, I promise you." He frowned. "I fear I am not doing a good job of this."

"Of what?"

"Offering my assistance to you in this time of need."

"Thank you for the offer. I shall let you know if I require any assistance."

He put his hands together as if she were a saint to whom he was praying. "I don't mean to upset you further. I want only to give you comfort."

She didn't reply.

He smiled kindly. "I understand your desire to appear unaffected by this disastrous alliance. So would any woman of spirit. However, it is not necessary. We all know about Richard Blythe."

She raised her eyebrows questioningly. She didn't think anybody really knew Richard Blythe, not even his wife.

Obviously taking her silence for acquiescence, he leaned forward again and spoke conspiratorially. "Why, one need only know Blythe consorted with theater people to understand his moral laxity, but in his case, there is the added natural immorality of his family. Imagine having orgies in the Banqueting House."

"*Orgies?*" she gasped.

"You had cause to send him packing and you did not know about that?"

"My husband participated in orgies?" she asked weakly as a host of thoughts and emotions collided in her mind.

"Not lately, that I have heard of, but probably before he went to Europe. Like father, like son, after all. And like mother, like son, too."

Her stomach turned as she struggled to comprehend what this horrid man was saying to her. "You . . . you know this for certain? You have proof?"

"It was said Richard's father built the Banqueting House to have privacy for their bacchanals, away from the servants."

"And Richard . . ."

"One can only assume."

He said he lost his innocence at an early age.

He loathed the Banqueting House.

He wrote of lascivious, immoral people at the mercy of their lust.

How could a man exposed to such baseness at an early age love except with the passion of lust, a passion shallow and fleeting?

But even as the questions came to her mind, her heart answered. Or perhaps, for the first time since he had left her, she finally listened.

He was bitter and cynical, but still capable of love. She had seen it in his eyes, heard it in his voice, felt it as he held her.

He loved her. He would never hurt her, or Will.

It had been her mistake to mistrust him. She had been too quick to accuse him based not on what she knew of him, but from her own experience.

Richard loved her, and she loved him, let Sedgemore say what he would, dredge up whatever stories of the past he could, spread terrible rumors—

"I'm sure your brilliant lawyer will be able to get this unhappy marriage dissolved," Sedgemore remarked, "if his marriage contracts are anything to judge by. They are truly legal marvels. I never would have believed it possible to have a woman's property so well protected after marriage, and then to render one's husband essentially unimportant in the daily running of an estate . . . truly, I am all admiration."

Her limbs weak and shaky, holding on to the desk for support, she got to her feet. "Please go away."

"My dear Elissa!" Mr. Sedgemore hurried to embrace her. "Let me help you."

"Let go of me!" she cried, his very touch abhorrent to her. "Please, I would like to be alone. Thank you for your sympathy, but please leave me."

He moved away. "If you wish."

Still leaning heavily on the desk, Elissa raised her eyes to regard him. "I do."

"Good day, Lady Dovercourt. Perhaps another time . . . ?"

"Yes, another time," she murmured, saying anything to make him go.

Finally, he departed, the ever-comforting, ever-helpful Mr. Sedgemore, who looked at her so greedily and whose land bordered this estate's and who should have no knowledge at all about either one of her marriage settlements.

She sat down and stared at the closed door. "Oh, dear God," she whispered. "What have I done?"

In the next instant, her indecision vanished, replaced by sudden, determined resolve. She jumped to her feet and began calling for Will and her maid.

She was going to London to see her husband, and she would take her son with her.

Robert Harding looked up as Richard Blythe, his gaze openly hostile, marched into his office and halted, arms akimbo. Barely visible behind him, Dillsworth, the new clerk, stood palefaced with fear, obviously totally incapable of preventing the man from entering his employer's office unannounced.

The lawyer's eyes widened for a brief moment before settling into their usual imperturbable, steadfast gaze. "To what do I owe the honor of your visit, my lord?" he asked calmly.

"It is a fine thing to hear you speak of honor," Richard said sarcastically.

He had been in London for days, yet he had never come to face his accuser before this. He had finally thought himself capable of remaining calm, but as he faced the man who had made Elissa believe he could be capable of murdering her son, he felt his precarious self-control giving way to anger. "How dare you make base allegations against me?"

"That will be all, Dillsworth. Kindly close the door," Harding said with infuriating composure.

Clearly curious as to what this startling arrival heralded and perhaps afraid that an attack on the lawyer would precipitously end his career, Dillsworth nevertheless did as he was told.

"You seem surprised to see me," Richard growled. "Did my dear wife not write and tell you I had absconded to return to my life of infamy and debauchery?"

"I have heard nothing from Lady Dovercourt."

Richard felt as if the floor had suddenly tilted. She had not informed her lawyer of his departure? What could that mean?

"Won't you take a seat, my lord?"

"Not until you tell me why you thought fit to accuse me of the most greedy, disgusting scheme any man—"

"Please sit down, my lord," Harding interrupted, his tone one of martial command. "I was not *born* a lawyer. My methods of persuasion are not refined, but they are effective, as the unfortunate Mollipont discovered."

Richard couldn't believe the man's aplomb. Heartless Harding indeed, for most men he knew would be quaking in their boots at the very thought of encountering an angry Richard Blythe—and with very good cause. "Are you presuming to threaten me?"

"If I must. Now, please sit down, my lord."

Richard sat.

"The evidence would indicate your wife revealed the contents of my letter to you."

"Did you have any evidence at all to accuse me of plotting to do her son harm?"

"I can understand how upsetting my letter must have been, but surely you can understand that I felt it my duty to warn my client."

"To turn her against her own husband, you mean."

"The copies of the selected portions of the will and the marriage settlement that I found in Mr. Mollipont's lodgings did look very suspicious, and the man was clearly too terrified of whoever was paying him to reveal the fellow's identity for some time. He finally saw the wisdom of telling me all, but only yesterday. I immediately wrote to your wife."

Richard let out his breath, feeling that he hadn't drawn an easy one since his argument with Elissa. Thank God she would soon know that he was innocent of plotting against her.

But that still did not absolve the man sitting in front of him of precipitating a disastrous argument. To be sure, he and Elissa had their troubles—what newly wedded couple didn't?—but he didn't doubt they could have worked them out had Heartless Harding not accused him of such a dastardly plan.

Nor did it alter the fact that *somebody* was intent of carrying out that plan.

"Unfortunately, I did not want to take the risk that harm might befall your stepson during the interim, so I wrote the first letter. I beg your pardon for any needless discomfort I have caused."

"Discomfort? I'faith, Harding, I have suffered more than discomfort."

At last a look of slight remorse appeared in the lawyer's cold gray eyes. "I shall endeavor to set things right. I have not only discovered who was paying Mollipont for the information, I believe I know why."

"Who?" Richard demanded, jumping to his feet and splaying his hands on the desk before him. "Who was it?"

"If you are going to continue to act in this hostile manner, I fear I shall be inciting murder if I tell you."

"Do you expect me to be calmly rational under these circumstances?" Richard retorted.

"If you cannot be, I shall not tell you. I will send the king's men for him and have the fellow charged appropriately."

Richard's brow lowered ominously. "You do not have to tell me. I can guess. That ferret, Sedgemore. He wants my wife and he wants the estate, too, no doubt."

"I will not confirm or deny anything until I am quite certain you do not intend to take the law into your own hands."

In the face of the lawyer's stern and unyielding expression, Richard let out his breath slowly, then sat again. "Very well. I shall be calm."

"Good."

"It is Sedgemore, isn't it? Just tell me, and I will give you my solemn word that I shall let the king's justice decide the matter."

"I would rather wait. If he knows he is suspected, he might flee the country."

Richard sighed. "Then I am forced to yield."

"In this instance, yes, I think you must."

"You did not wait to accuse me."

"I didn't accuse you formally. I merely sought to warn your wife. Indeed, I confess I had my doubts that you could be the perpetrator of the plot almost from the beginning."

"You didn't manage to convey any doubts to Elissa."

"It is not my place to offer doubts, but to protect my clients, especially ones in very vulnerable positions."

"Whoever the guilty party is, marrying a woman and then murdering her child seems an extreme way to raise money or obtain property."

"I fear you underestimate your wife's charms and the value of the estate, which is one of the most prosperous in the county." Heartless Harding's expression changed ever so slightly. "Can you think of any other reason a man would want your family estate in particular?"

"Other than its beauty? No." Richard shook his head. "This scheme seems incredible."

"For a man who writes often of human greed and folly, I am surprised that you find this so difficult to believe."

"It is one thing to make up evil characters.

It is quite another to know that there is actually a human being capable of acting in such a despicable way. What made you first question my involvement in the plot?"

"I doubted you were capable of this sort of scheming, or you would have stopped at nothing to get your estate back as soon as you returned to England. Instead, you waited for a legal and just course of action."

"I waited a very long time, too."

"And were amply rewarded for it."

Richard cocked his head slightly and wondered if Mr. Harding's concern for Elissa's welfare was merely business, after all. "You might have told her that conclusion. I could never hurt Will."

"I believe you."

As he regarded Mr. Harding, Richard sensed that this man's trust was not something easily earned and was glad to have done so.

If only Elissa trusted him, too.

"I care for her very much," he confessed. "I love her."

The lawyer actually smiled. "I am glad to hear it. She deserves to be loved, and to be happy."

"Then I must confess myself surprised that as her concerned advocate, you didn't prevent her from marrying me when the king commanded it," Richard remarked, not quite revealing his avid curiosity on this point.

"I considered it the wisest course of action,

given that the king was determined. Should I assume you will be returning to Blythe Hall shortly? If so, I will write another letter and let you take it to her."

Before Richard could answer, or even think of what he should do next, there came a very soft and tentative knock on the closed door.

"What is it?" Mr. Harding called out.

A subdued Dillsworth stuck his head inside the room. "I'm very sorry to disturb you, sir, but there's a lady come who wishes to speak with you. It's urgent, she says."

Chapter 19

"**D**id this lady not give a name?" Mr. Harding inquired.

"She says her name is Lady Dovercourt, sir."

"Elissa is here?" Richard cried. He rushed to the door and shoved the startled clerk out of the way. "Elissa!"

Elissa let go of Will's hand and jumped up from her place on the bench where she had been waiting. "Richard!"

"Papa!" Will cried, then clapped his hand over his mouth, his face flushing.

Elissa looked down at her son, surprised by his choice of words, then returned her gaze to her husband who, for the first time in their acquaintance, looked doubtful and unsure.

Mr. Harding, however, was not. He strode forward. "Lord and Lady Dovercourt, please avail yourself of my office. Dillsworth, Will, and I shall go for a walk."

Elissa stopped staring at Richard, whose gaze finally wavered. "I beg your pardon?" she said.

"I said, Dillsworth, your son, and I shall leave you two alone for a little and take a walk. Come along, Will. *Dillsworth!*"

Mr. Harding addressed the clerk with some emphasis, for the young man, his mouth agape, had apparently gone hard of hearing.

"Please, Will, go with Mr. Harding," Elissa said softly.

Although she, too, was feeling far from confident, she was grateful for this sudden and unexpected opportunity. She needed to speak to Richard alone.

Mr. Harding went to take Will's hand, but he moved away, looking uncertainly from his mother to his stepfather.

"I'm sorry!" he suddenly cried with an air of desperation.

"You're sorry?" Elissa repeated, concentrating on her obviously distressed son. "Why should you be sorry?"

"For making Richard go away." Tears filled Will's eyes as he looked at Richard. "I promise I won't touch another sword ever again as long as I live if you'll come home."

"Oh, Will," Elissa cried, guilt-ridden that she had never considered what reason her son might imagine for Richard's departure if she did not explain it.

"Will, my leaving had very little to do with

that," Richard said softly, but with firm conviction as he went to the boy and knelt before him, putting his hands lightly on his shoulders. "Please believe me. You are not responsible for the, um, difficulties between your mother and me."

"No, you're not," Elissa confirmed. "I am. It was my fault Richard went away."

Richard rose and regarded her steadily. "It was my fault."

Suddenly Mr. Harding cleared his throat. "We shall leave you two to mend your quarrel, shall we?"

To her surprise, Elissa saw what might have been a sparkle of amusement in the solicitor's eyes as he came forward and took Will's hand.

Will still seemed hesitant.

"It's all right," Elissa said softly. "We'll be here when you get back."

"Yes, we will," Richard agreed. "Both of us."

"I know a very fine pastry shop in the next street," Mr. Harding remarked to no one in particular.

The lad looked somewhat mollified, and finally went with the others, leaving Richard and Elissa alone.

"Forgive—" she said at once.

"I'm sorry—" he began simultaneously. Then they both fell awkwardly silent.

Elissa smiled tremulously. "Let me speak first, please."

Richard shook his head. "No, Elissa," he said, taking her hand and leading her into Mr. Harding's office. "I have been silent about some things too long, and it has caused us no end of trouble and pain. Hear me out, and then perhaps you will understand."

"Very well," she replied as she sat down, "as long as you first know this one thing. I trust you absolutely, Richard, and I know you would never hurt Will or me."

"Oh, God, Elissa, I am glad to hear it!"

"Then I shall listen to anything you want to tell me, although perhaps I should also say that I may know more than you think."

His brow furrowed. "About what?"

She flushed but did not look away. "About your parents. Alfred Sedgemore was very eager to tell me about them."

"Ah, the accommodating Mr. Sedgemore!" he replied with a sneer.

"Who knows far more about my legal affairs than he should," Elissa added. "I think if we suspect anyone of criminal activity, it should be—"

"That worm. I think so, too. Heartless Harding is being very coy with his information, yet I believe Sedgemore's days of freedom are definitely numbered."

"I am so sorry for accusing you, Richard! I should have listened to my heart, and trusted in you."

"Given what you heard of me, I cannot

blame you." He leaned against the desk. "I daresay Sedgemore painted a disgusting picture."

"Yes."

Richard shoved himself off the desk and walked around it, dragging his fingers over the scarred surface. "My parents *were* disgusting, and my home an unhappy one, Elissa. Indeed, it was miserable, but I didn't know how miserable until I was older and came to understand that not all families were like mine. Not every son tread carefully lest he upset his mother or his father, or immerse himself in his studies to find sanctuary. Not every child lived with a nearly unbearable tension when his parents were in the same room, or flinched to hear them speak to one another in the meanest, cruelest, most vulgar terms when the servants were not within hearing. And when the servants were within hearing, did not have to marvel at the complete change in their manner toward each other."

He glanced at Elissa. "I learned about hypocrisy at a very tender age, although I did not have a name for it."

He sighed and sat in Mr. Harding's chair. "Forgive me for what I am going to tell you next, for it is not fit for a lady's ears, but I would have you know all, so that you might understand why I am the way I am."

Elissa nodded, trying to listen without betraying either foreknowledge, shock, or dismay, even as her grip tightened on the arms of her chair.

"So, now you know the loving atmosphere in which I existed," he said, continuing to regard her with steady intensity. "But there was more, and worse, to discover.

"One night, when I was eight years old, I was awakened by a bad dream. I had many bad dreams, but this was worse than most, I assume, although I don't remember what it was.

"At any rate, I wanted my mother." His bitter laugh was terrible and sad to hear. "Why I wanted her when she either ignored or berated me during the day, I don't know, but I suppose any mother is better than none when you are a frightened child.

"So I looked for her. Neither she nor my father were in their bedchambers. I heard some music and went to the window, where I saw light in the Banqueting House.

"I knew they often entertained their friends very late in that place, so I decided I would seek my mother there."

He sighed again and passed a hand over his forehead. "I remember I felt as if I were on a great adventure, creeping outside in the summer's night. I remember the dewy grass wetting my feet, and how the moon shone. I was a little frightened of the shadows, but I was filled with curiosity to learn what a grown-up party was like."

He paused and looked away. "There were times I wished I had been stricken blind rather than see what I did when I looked through the window of the Banqueting House. I saw sweets and wine spilled on the table as if pigs had rooted there. I saw decor that wouldn't be out of place in a sultan's harem."

His voice dropped to a barely audible whisper. "I saw naked bodies intertwined, couples and threesomes and more, like snakes writhing in a pit.

"And then I saw my mother with a man who was not my father, and my father with a woman I had never seen before."

"Oh, Richard, how terrible for you!" she said softly, rising to go to him. She knelt beside him and gently put her arms around him.

He sat completely still, as if incapable of movement, until he sighed raggedly and looked at her. "I was literally sickened by what I had seen," he confessed. "I stumbled back to the house, too shocked to comprehend the full import of what I had witnessed. The next day, they acted as they always had, as if they were like anybody else, and moral, upright gentlefolk. To know that at night, they could be so different—and then to suddenly understand the sly glances that passed between them and their guests."

"Richard, I am so sorry," Elissa whispered.

He regarded her with mournful eyes. "I think this was how they endured their loveless marriage. Each was free to take lovers and to indulge in whatever carnal exercises they could devise.

"Unfortunately, after my mother died, my father acted with less care and subtlety, so when I heard he had seduced my uncle's bride, I could well believe it." He sighed again and raked his hand through his hair. "I wouldn't put it past Sedgemore to claim I participated in such disgusting things."

"He implied it," she admitted.

"Damn him, I knew it," he muttered, kneading his fist. "I was but a child!"

"I wondered . . . I feared that you were forced."

His expression softened. "No, Elissa, no," he replied gravely. "I saw, but nothing more. That was enough to make me lose all respect for my parents, but even they were not that base."

"You said you were robbed of your childhood."

"Not that way."

He put his hand over hers. The mask of wry, worldly invincibility he had worn for so long started to crumple as hot tears burned his eyes. "It was enough to see . . ."

Elissa rose and pulled him into her comforting embrace.

"Shh, my love, shh," she crooned as he finally wept for his lost childhood, comforted at last as he had never been in his lonely, bitter life.

"Oh, Elissa," he whispered as he tried to choke back the wretched sobs.

He looked into her sympathetic eyes. "I need you. You and Will are the best things that have ever happened to me. I would rather kill myself than hurt either of you. Please forgive me for doing anything to make you hate me."

"Hate you?" she repeated wonderingly. "I don't hate you. Oh, my darling," she cried softly, regarding him with a gentle, loving smile. "Don't you see? I was not upset because I hate you. I was upset because I had come to love you so much. Too much, I feared."

A look of sudden comprehension came to his eyes. "Foz said you were afraid. I thought he meant that you were afraid of me."

"I was afraid of what I felt for you, its power and strength. I was afraid my love for you made me weak."

"Not you, my dearest. Never you. I would find it easier to believe a mountain would crumble to dust in a day than you would weaken."

"Perhaps if the mountain came to love someone as I do you, it would—especially when the lover left. And what should I forgive you for? For keeping your parents' shame a secret? I could not fault you for that. I have done the same. I didn't want anyone to know about William Longbourne."

"I already know about his . . . propensities. I recognized him from his portrait." Richard's lips twisted in a sardonic smile. "He was one of my mother's many friends."

Elissa's eyes widened. "Then he was a decadent man long before I knew him," she said wearily. "I wish there had been some outward sign of his inward corruption. Unfortunately, there was not, or if there was, we were all too naive to see it. He tricked everyone in Owston with his outward friendliness, but he really hated everyone and believed himself superior. In private, he could be terribly cruel.

"I don't think he even loved his own child, except as a potential heir and proof of his virility. I regret I ever met him and curse myself for a fool for marrying him. The only thing I cherish about my first marriage is Will."

Richard sighed. "Deception appears in many guises, and such people are, I fear, all too common."

He gave her a little smile of commiseration. "I have met some very gifted actors in my time, but none as good as some of the actors I have encountered elsewhere."

"I also discovered the shame of being a silly, vain young woman who fools herself into believing she loves an attractive, flattering, admiring man who talks of love and marriage."

Richard took her hand in his. "You are not the first to learn this lesson, Elissa, and I daresay you won't be the last." His brow wrinkled.

"I cannot bear to think of anyone laying a hand on you."

"He didn't beat me, although he was often rough. His words could sting worse than a blow. And he was so hard to please! Especially in bed. Then, one night when he had chastised me as a stupid cow unworthy of him, he said he would have to teach me all about love. Not the kind that poets drone on about, but exciting, passionate desire that could be sated any number of ways, with any number of partners." Her voice fell to a whisper. "Of either sex."

"Oh, Elissa," Richard said softly and sympathetically.

He put his knuckle under her chin and gently raised her face so that she could not look away. "Elissa, you know that I am a man of the world. There is not much of the worst of human nature that I have not heard about.

"Did he force you?" he asked quietly, thinking of this proud, spirited woman humiliated and ashamed, yet all the while marveling that she could still be so strong.

"No. I told him I would never degrade myself in such a manner and I was disgusted that he would not only engage in that licentious debauchery, but that he would try to corrupt me, too. He did not laugh at that. He became angry and told me that he had married me because he wanted a son. He would make love with me for that purpose, and only that purpose, from then on, and he would have his sport elsewhere."

She sighed again and laid her head against Richard's shoulder. "As time passed, I became grateful that he at least had enough decency to engage in his disgusting pursuits away from Owston."

"There were no rumors of his . . . activities?"

She raised her head and reached out to brush a stray lock of hair from his forehead. "There are always rumors. You are aware of that."

"Yes, I am well aware of that." He put his hands loosely about her waist. "Now you know why I was so cynical. It was impossible for me to put my faith in anyone after my childhood, until now." His expression became both happy and yet unsure. "Elissa, I swear upon my life, I love you with all my heart."

"As I love you." She leaned toward him and kissed him tenderly. "When you come home, we shall raze that horrible building to the ground." Doubt appeared in her lovely eyes. "You will come home?"

He laughed with true joy. "Of course I will!" His eyes shone as he felt her waist. "Is there not another reason I should return? Or would you try to tell me you are merely growing plump?"

"Oh, Richard, I should have told you I was with child sooner, but I wanted to be sure. I didn't want you to be disappointed."

"Should I be disappointed?"

Her smile was all the answer he needed.

"Elissa, I am truly the happiest man in England."

"Married to the happiest woman."

"When the baby comes, I shall do my best to make sure Will does not feel overlooked or unimportant, as I did."

"You are wonderful."

He smiled ruefully. "Zounds, wife, too much praise will go right to my head. Perhaps you had best leaven it with a criticism."

"Very well," she said, scrutinizing him.

"You agreed rather rapidly," he noted.

"You are not a very good lady's maid," she said gravely, the attempt at seriousness quite destroyed by the happiness in her eyes. "You are far too virile for it."

"I must have been mad to leave you!" he cried, embracing her. "And now I confess I am anxious to return to—" He paused.

"What is it?" she asked, the dearest little wrinkle of concern appearing between her eyes.

"I fear I must stay a day or two in London. You see, my sweet wife, I have a new play opening this evening, and I may have to make some changes, depending upon its reception."

"A new play so soon?"

He grinned. "Yes. All those nights you thought I was dallying with other women or writing to mysterious henchmen—"

"I was wrong to think that!"

"Well, in one sense, I was deceiving you, and for that I beg your forgiveness. I was writing a play."

Elissa's brow contracted. "I thought you hated being a writer and that it was beneath you."

"Alas, I must confess that I thought so, too, only to discover that I quite enjoyed it after all. There is something truly exciting about making people up." He gave her a thoughtful look. "I suppose it is one way to make people do exactly what I want."

"You mean you enjoy being in command."

"Would you rather I tried to command *you?* I would sooner throw myself upon the mercy of a drunken, dissatisfied audience."

She assumed a pert, aggrieved air. "I think I manage very well."

"Now that you have a clerk with a good hand."

She leaned her head against his chest. "Yes." She lifted her head to regard him quizzically. "There is one thing I still don't understand, Richard. If your life was so terrible at Blythe Hall, why did you want so much to go back there? I should think you would never want to see it again."

"Why did you not leave it when your husband died?"

"Because it was my son's home."

"And Blythe Hall was mine. My parents were not the best, to put it kindly, but I loved the estate. I would go for long rides and rambles, and the beauty of the countryside never failed to comfort me.

"Although I left home seeking escape when I was old enough, if I had known that to do so would mean it would be years before I could return, I might have found the strength to stay."

"If you had, we would never have met."

"Zounds, you are right!"

"And if the king had not forced us to marry, we might not have fallen in love."

"I obviously owe His Majesty a great deal," he murmured while his hands tentatively began to explore her body. "Have you any plans for this afternoon, my love?"

As he pressed light kisses along her cheek heading toward her lips, she sighed softly and nodded, embracing his lean, hard body.

"Too many to count," she whispered huskily, boldly caressing him.

She felt his chest shake with the low rumble of a chuckle. "I was merely going to ask you to come to the play."

With a sly smile and darkly intense gaze, he gently positioned her against Mr. Harding's desk. "Although since you are so willing, perhaps we need not wait for nightfall."

Whatever Richard might have been thinking, the noisy return of Will, Mr. Harding, and his clerk effectively prevented anything more than a quick, yet very passionate, kiss.

Taking Elissa's hand, he led her to the outer office, where they discovered Dillsworth diligently attempting to wipe traces of pastry from Will's collar and Mr. Harding regarding them with something akin to curiosity.

"All is well, Mr. Harding," Richard announced jovially, giving Elissa's hand a squeeze.

"I am glad to hear it," the lawyer replied evenly.

"My new play opens later today, Mr. Harding. I would be honored if you would be my guest and come to see it," Richard said.

"Regrettably, I have little time for the theater," Mr. Harding replied.

"But surely you can make an exception!" Elissa cried.

The lawyer's stern visage softened a very little. "Perhaps today, I can make an exception," he agreed.

"Excellent! Come to the stage door at Lincoln's Inn Fields Theatre. You and Elissa will have the best seats I can commandeer."

"What about me?" Will piped up. "Can't I go, too?"

"Oh, I don't know . . ." Elissa began hesitantly.

"I don't think there is anything terribly scandalous in *The Vicar's House*," Richard said thoughtfully.

"Then of course he may go," Elissa replied.

Richard's smile was nearly as broad as Will's before he grew studious again. "I confess I am afraid the audience will be disappointed. I am not sure the tone is quite even. I was in a rather magnanimous mood when I started it. Then I rewrote it as a tragedy when I was in a blacker humor. Then I recalled the dismal failure of my last tragedy and went back to the original version, scowling at every rehearsal, I'm sure. I don't know whether it is a comedy with dramatic overtones, or a drama with comic overtones."

"Whatever it is, I'm quite sure it will be marvelous," Elissa said proudly.

"Oh bloo—" Richard began. He glanced at Will. "Zounds, I nearly forgot! Where are you staying? I am afraid my lodgings are rather small for three."

"You must all stay with me, then," Mr. Harding said. "In fact, I insist."

"Thank you, we will," Richard agreed, "but it will only be for a short stay before we go back home. Now, if you will excuse us, Mr. Harding, we must make haste if I am to pack my things and get to the theater in time for some last-minute instructions."

He made a wry face. "I fear my actresses are all angry at me. I was as fierce as a bear with them yesterday." His eyes shone with happiness as he sighed with feigned dismay. "I can't think why."

"I believe Will and I should come along with you, perhaps, to protect you from the wrath of your actresses," Elissa remarked with equally feigned gravity.

Richard cleared his throat. "Perhaps we should save the introductions until after the performance. The female performers are always nervous with a new play."

"If you think that best," Elissa replied.

Richard grinned his devilish grin. "Besides, I am far too happy when I am with you, and to have them see me thus will surely destroy my reputation."

"As a happy husband?"

"No, as the greatest cynic in London."

"I did not realize that was your reputation."

He sighed melodramatically. "I have been working on that impression ever since I arrived after the king's restoration, and now it may all be for naught."

"That was not the only kind of reputation you were earning."

"Elissa!" he cried in protest.

She smiled. "Besides, I have spent quite enough time away from you lately, so I fear your reputation will simply have to suffer."

"If it must, it must," Richard agreed with a philosophical air.

"We'll go to a theater?" Will asked excitedly.

"We shall," Richard confirmed. "I'll have

the property master show you all the stage weapons, if you like."

"Oh, yes, please!"

"Richard!" Elissa protested.

"I promise on my love for you that we shall be very, very careful. Will you trust me?"

"In everything," she replied gravely.

"Then come, Will, Elissa, let's go to the theater." Richard said with a smile as he took Elissa's hand and placed it on his arm, then took hold of Will's. "See you anon, Mr. Harding."

"Indeed."

"Good-bye!" Elissa said, and Will added his farewell.

The moment the door closed behind him on the crowded street, Will said, "Shall I really get to see the swords and things?"

"And the powder they use to make explosions, if Henry is in a good mood," Richard confirmed.

"Who's Henry?" Will asked.

"The property master, and a very grumpy fellow he can be."

"I shall be very good," Will vowed.

Richard let go of the boy's hand to ruffle the lad's hair. "I'm sure you will be."

Elissa suddenly halted so abruptly, Richard nearly knocked her over. "Mr. Sedgemore!" she cried.

As Richard followed her startled gaze, Sedgemore stepped out of an alley and smiled as he looked from Elissa to Richard to Will and back to Elissa. "Lord and Lady Dovercourt. What a pleasant surprise."

"I doubt it," Richard said evenly, running his gaze over the well-to-do squire who was so uncharacteristically and plainly dressed. "What are you doing skulking about the alleys of London?"

"Did you follow me here?" Elissa demanded suspiciously.

"No, of course not!" he replied, his expression incredulous and cautious. "This is merely a . . . a pleasant coincidence. I came to the city on business. I often do. There is nothing wrong with that, I trust."

"I'faith, this is a most convenient coincidence," Richard said, gently removing Elissa's hand from his arm, "since I have something to discuss with you in private."

"I don't believe you do," Sedgemore replied warily.

Richard glanced at Elissa. "I shall be happy to explain, if you will come along with me to Mr. Harding's office."

"I regret I cannot," Sedgemore said, backing away. "I . . . I have an appointment."

"Yes, you do—with my husband and our lawyer," Elissa said. "For one thing, you can explain how you come to be so familiar with my marriage settlements and my late husband's will."

"I knew it!" Richard cried triumphantly as Sedgemore began to turn.

He reached out and grabbed the man's shoulder. "Come along, Sedgemore. I think you must explain yourself to Mr. Harding, and the constable, and to me."

"I'm not going anywhere with you!" Sedgemore declared as he twisted out of Richard's grasp and marched hurriedly away.

"Go back to Mr. Harding's and wait for me there," Richard commanded Elissa and Will, his hand moving to the hilt of his sword as he started forward.

"But I want to—" Will protested.

Richard glanced back at them over his shoulder. "No," he said simply before regarding Elissa grimly. "Take Will back."

As she complied, he hurried after the fleeing Alfred Sedgemore.

Chapter 20

Sedgemore disappeared down an alley,
but not before Richard saw where he
went. Paying no heed to the curious onlookers,
he drew his sword and began to trot through
the malodorous alleys and back lanes after
him.

Once or twice he nearly lost his prey, but
Sedgemore was not familiar with these pas-
sages. Richard was, and knew to stop and listen when he lost sight of his quarry.

Whose rapid footsteps always gave him
away.

No matter how Sedgemore twisted and
turned in his route, it was steadily south, obviously making for the Thames. If he got to a
boat, he could be away before Richard could
catch him or summon help.

Richard started to run flat out, his drawn
sword signaling to people better than any vocal warning that he was not to be trifled with

in his pursuit. They made way—and then he almost shouted with triumph when he saw that Sedgemore had blundered into an alley with no exit.

His quarry whirled around, his eyes darting like the trapped rat he was. Richard had seen men look thus before and knew desperate men could be extremely dangerous.

"You are caught, Sedgemore," Richard said, his sword at the ready as he approached him cautiously.

"Let me go! I haven't done anything!" Sedgemore protested as he backed into the wall.

"Then why did you run?"

"Because you threatened me!"

"I only said I would take you to Mr. Harding. If you are innocent of any crime, you have nothing to fear."

"Prison is nothing to fear? They will throw me into Newgate whether I am innocent or not! As you are a man of the world, you know this as well as I." Sedgemore took a step forward and held out his hands in a pleading gesture. "What is it you think I have done?"

Richard raised his sword a little more. Just because he could see no obvious weapon didn't mean the man did not have one, either in his sleeve or his belt or his boot. "Plot murder."

"Me? Who am I supposed to want killed?"

"My stepson, and then you would need to

dispense with me to clear the way for you to try to become Elissa's husband."

"That's absurd."

"Then why try to discover what becomes of the estate if Will dies before his mother, and she before her husband?"

"This is the most ridiculous thing I ever heard!"

"Naturally I concur that it is ridiculous to think Elissa would ever contemplate marrying a piece of dung like you."

"Who are you to insult me?" Sedgemore cried. "You are nothing but a decadent, immoral writer of rubbish! You debase yourself and all you touch with your disgusting ways."

"By all means, spare my tender feelings and do not reveal your true opinion of me," Richard said sarcastically.

"If there is a plot afoot that involves your stepson, surely you are the more likely suspect. You are the one who always wanted the estate, and you come from a despicable family. A man like you would do anything necessary to get what he wants."

"I am a man of honor, as Mr. Harding already knows, or I would have tried to get back my estate by base means before this."

"Elissa knows the kind of rogue you are!"

"I would prefer you refer to my wife as Lady Dovercourt," Richard answered. "And she certainly knows me better than you do."

"I will call her whatever I want, and when

you are dead, I shall call her my wife."

Richard's lips twisted into a menacing grin. "Even if you managed to kill me, do you honestly believe she would ever marry you?"

"After Longbourne, I should have been her husband. I waited long enough. Curse the king—and God curse you!"

"I am not the cursed one here, for I could never do such a despicable thing as kill a child for some acres of land. Come, Sedgemore, surrender, for your game is over."

"I won't go to a filthy, stinky, diseased prison!" Sedgemore cried, desperation growing in his eyes as he recognized Richard's resolve. "And I won't be hung! Let me go, Blythe!" he pleaded as he sank to his knees, spittle appearing at the corners of his mouth. "I will pay, and gladly."

"Yield, Sedgemore. It is finished," Richard said, keeping his eyes on Sedgemore's hands, so that he saw the dagger as Sedgemore pulled it from his belt.

He turned away in time to avoid the blow, then just as quickly twisted back and slashed his opponent's arm.

Sedgemore dropped his dagger and clutched the bleeding gash. "I shall say you tried to kill me so I wouldn't tell what I know about you!"

"What nonsense is this? What can you tell that you have not already spoken of to everyone you know?" Richard demanded as he waited tensely for the man's next move.

Sedgemore lunged for the dagger. His fear made him fast, and he grabbed it, then jumped up and ran at Richard.

Who was prepared. He neatly deflected the dagger with his sword, sending the man sprawling in the stinking muck.

Sedgemore got to his feet, his dagger still in his hand. "I will not die in a prison—that is where you should be. It is where our father should have been!"

Richard stared at him, dumbfounded.

"You know what he was like—the liaisons he had. Like you, he would bed any woman that he could, including his brother's wife. Nobody knew what happened to her, did they? Well, I know—because I am her son, and your father's bastard."

"Why didn't you tell me? I would have—"

"What? Made my shame as well known as yours? At least I made something respectable of myself. *I* never stooped to writing for a bunch of wealthy fools. I deserved Blythe Hall more than anyone! More than you, more than Longbourne, more than Longbourne's brat."

"Oh, God," Richard groaned.

He could see the resemblance now, the angles of the man's face a slightly altered, less attractive version of his father's features. He recognized the bitterness in his voice, and the pain beneath.

God help him, he had felt the same himself.

Taking advantage of Richard's momentary distraction, Sedgemore struck. Instinctively, without thought, Richard defended himself, lunging forward to stab his bastard brother in the chest.

With a low moan, the man crumpled to the ground. Richard kicked away the fallen dagger, then knelt beside him.

"I could have had her, and the land," Sedgemore snarled weakly. He took painful breath. "Well, I would rather die here than in Newgate."

Richard stifled a moan of anguish, for now he could hear an echo of his own sardonic tone.

"Let me take you to a doctor," he pleaded. He thought it futile, but he had to do something.

Sedgemore grimaced with pain. "No!" His breathing grew more strained. "She died in labor, my mother. Your uncle's steward changed his name to Sedgemore and raised me as his son. I always knew I was different . . . special . . . noble. He told me the truth before he died, and I found out what I deserved—and what you, a base, lascivious rogue who could lower himself to write plays, did not."

"Don't talk anymore. Let me help you."

But there was no more time, and no more help to give. The man's last breath rattled in his chest as he closed his eyes, and died.

With a weary sigh, Richard slowly sheathed

his sword and retrieved Sedgemore's dagger, then stared down at the body in the dirt.

One more sin to lay at his father's feet. "Pray God this be the end of it," he murmured.

Then he lifted his half-brother's body over his shoulders and made his way to the back of Mr. Harding's office. Nobody questioned him or tried to stop him. One look at Richard's grim, pale face, and they left him alone.

Once there, he laid his burden down and covered Sedgemore's face with his jacket before going into the office.

The moment he entered, an anxious Elissa immediately noticed the blood on his white shirt and hurried toward him. "What happened? Are you hurt?"

"Did you have a duel?" Will demanded eagerly, and the young clerk's expression was as keenly excited.

With a slightly puzzled frown, Mr. Harding came to stand in his office door.

"No, not a duel. Come, Elissa, I must speak with Mr. Harding, and you shall know all, too. Will, please wait here. We shall not be long."

Somewhat to Elissa's surprise, Will obeyed without a hint of protest—but then, she would have instinctively obeyed Richard's softly spoken command, too.

Once in the office, Richard threw himself into a chair. Elissa stood beside him, taking firm hold of his hand, while Mr. Harding sat behind his large desk.

As Richard related what had happened, Mr. Harding listened with inscrutable patience, and Elissa with exclamations of surprise and dismay.

"And so I could think of nothing else to do but bring his body here," he finished wearily. "It was self-defense, pure and simple, but I daresay I shall have to answer for it."

Elissa's grip on his hand tightened. "He won't have to go to prison, will he?" she asked anxiously.

"I very much doubt it," Mr. Harding replied. "I shall bring the matter before the proper authorities, but I am sure it will be easily resolved. Sedgemore was indeed the person who paid Mollipont for the information. I think I can make a strong case that no charges need be brought against you, and should any judge think otherwise, I believe His Majesty will want to intervene."

"Once again, I must be grateful that I can amuse our sovereign," Richard muttered.

"Yes, you should be," Elissa seconded firmly.

Richard ran his hand over his sweat-streaked face. "I should have guessed my father's sins would outlive him. I should have supposed he would have left a bastard or two or ten."

"His sins were his, my love," Elissa said softly. "Let the guilt be his, not yours."

"If only I could be sure this was the end of

it," Richard replied with a weary sigh. "I cannot help thinking there may be other painful discoveries yet to come."

Elissa squeezed his hand. "But there will be no more secrets between us, at least."

Her husband managed a wry smile. "Yes, no more secrets between us, at least. Thank God."

Mr. Harding cleared his throat. "My lord, please leave this matter with me and set your mind at rest. I have been investigating not just Mr. Sedgemore's past, and as far as I can ascertain, you and he were the only children who could be identified as your father's offspring without question. Now, if it is at all possible, please leave this in my hands and enjoy the opening of your new play."

"Zounds, my play!" Richard groaned. "I forgot. What hour is it?"

"Only two, by the church bells," Elissa said, her confidence in Mr. Harding's knowledge reassuring her.

"Then I have not much time," he said with a sigh as he got to his feet. Still holding Elissa's hand, he went to the door, then glanced back at Mr. Harding. "Will we see you at the play?"

The lawyer shook his head. "There is the small matter of the body in my garden," he reminded Richard with a ruefulness that would have done credit to the playwright himself.

*   *   *

"Will, sit still or you are going to fall into the pit!" Elissa admonished as her son leaned precariously over the railing of their box in the gallery. "The play is about to begin."

Will reluctantly did as he was told. "It's smoky," he complained as the candles on the large chandelier were lit, along with the candles in pots lining the edge of the stage. He covered his hands with his ears. "And it's so noisy!"

The building was indeed crowded, noisy, and filled with smoke as well as the scent of many bodies pressed together, and not a little perfume. In addition to the throng in the pit below, there were several boxes along the upper gallery, each filled to capacity with well-dressed, constantly talking patrons.

"I think the smoke will clear in a little while and surely the audience will be quiet once the play begins."

"I wish there was going to be an explosion!"

"Richard explained that to you, dear."

"Weren't those ladies nice?"

"They certainly made a fuss over you," Elissa replied truthfully. And also in truth, the actresses were not at all the brazen hussies she had imagined. They had treated her with respect, and Will like a young lord.

She rather suspected Richard's sharp-eyed gaze explained their deference, just as his watchful eye prevented her from staring at the women and trying to decide which of them had found favor with her husband before he was her husband.

As he had escorted them to the box, she had gravely informed him that she was studying their hairstyles for future reference. He didn't believe it, and she didn't expect him to, and his expression had been priceless.

"How many people are here?" Will demanded.

"A great many. Richard is a very famous playwright."

"I would rather see him fight."

"He explained to you why he had to do that, and how unpleasant it was."

With downcast eyes, Will nodded.

Elissa looked about for something else to talk about, then nearly fell out of the box herself at the sight of Sir John and his family.

It was not so surprising they were there; it was Antonia whose appearance surprised her, for she was practically draped over a man who was young, but also unfortunately and unequivocally ugly, with a rather large wart on the end of his nose. On the other hand, Elissa realized, he was very well and richly dressed, which perhaps explained Antonia's attraction to him.

Suddenly there was a buzz of excitement in the crowded theater. "What is it?" Will demanded, his previous ill humor instantly forgotten.

"It is the king," Elissa answered as she, too,

rose and curtsied toward the center box in the gallery. "He has come to see Richard's play. Oh, Richard will be so pleased!"

"Which one is the king?"

"The man with the long dark wig and the mustache."

"Him?" Will cried, obviously disappointed.

"Is he not well dressed? And see how he greets the people."

"I thought he would be taller."

"A man's stature is no measure of the man himself," Elissa reminded her son.

Despite his initial disappointment, Will paid no heed at all to the play when it began, but kept his eyes firmly fastened on his sovereign. At the end of the performance, after the thunderous applause had died down, he watched the king wave again to the audience, then regally leave the box.

"I won't ask what you thought of the play, Will," Richard said with a wry grin as he joined them. "You never looked at the stage once."

Despite his jovial tone and smile, Elissa saw the shadow of sadness in his eyes. She wished there could have been another finish to his confrontation with Sedgemore.

She would do her best to make him forget that, and all the other painful memories that haunted him, as he helped her forget.

"How do you know I wasn't?" Will asked, flushing.

"I was watching from the wings. However, I fear I was just as bad, for I could not keep my eyes from this box," Richard said, running his hand slowly and seductively down Elissa's arm to take hold of her hand.

She lifted his to her lips and kissed him softly. Her reward was to see the veil of sadness lift a little, replaced by a smile.

"If you had looked at the audience, you might have seen some friends from Owston," she said. "Sir John and his family came."

"What, Antonia the Amazon was here?" he cried with mock horror, and she was pleased to see more of his usual wry manner. "I am happy I didn't know, or I might have been forced to flee in self-defense."

"An Amazon was here?" Will inquired with wide-eyed wonder.

Richard gave Elissa a contrite glance. "A woman of warriorlike spirit, I meant."

"They were with a well-dressed fellow," Elissa continued. "He, um, has a wart—"

"Ah, she has discovered Croesus Belmaris, the richest aristocrat in London. I wish her luck."

"Everyone seemed to enjoy your play," Elissa said, deciding it was time to change the subject, given Will's avid interest in anything Richard had to say, and probably not appreciating the sarcasm with which he said it. "The king laughed several times."

"Yes, he did," Will confirmed. "The lady beside him didn't, though. I expect that was because she lost something down her dress. The king was helping her find it."

"I think I should have paid more attention to the king myself," she whispered to Richard. "I had no idea—"

"That he doesn't keep his attention on the performance? Sadly, I fear this is often the case," Richard replied with feigned mournfulness. "It would seem he finds his paramour's bosom more entertaining than my writing."

The deep, familiar, regal chuckle sounded behind them.

"Odd's fish, say not so, Blythe!"

Blushing, they turned swiftly. Richard bowed to his sovereign and Elissa curtsied.

King Charles's eyes twinkled merrily as he entered the box. Outside in the corridor, they could see Lady Castlemaine and several courtiers waiting.

"Majesty, I meant no disrespect," Richard said.

"We know exactly what you meant," the king replied genially. "Such remarks are to be expected from such as you. We enjoyed your play immensely. Your talent has been much missed in London, and we are delighted you have returned, and with your lovely wife, too. It was only that Lady Castlemaine's necklace went astray."

"That's what I said," Will offered shyly from behind Elissa.

"Who speaks?"

"Your Majesty, this is my son, William Longbourne," Elissa said, guiding her son around to stand before the king. Will bowed and his action was so like Richard's, she had to smile.

"So, young Master Longbourne, how do you like the step-papa I chose for you?" Charles demanded.

"I like him very much, Your Majesty," Will replied. "But of course, he is not so fine as you."

"Odd's fish!" Charles declared, vastly pleased. "What a clever little man. He has the makings of a courtier already." He bent down so that his face was level with Will's and spoke in a conspiratorial tone. "Tell me, Master Longbourne, what did you think of the play?"

Will blushed. "I was looking at you, Your Majesty."

"High praise indeed!"

"Sometimes I watched the girls with the oranges," he confessed, his tone as secretive as the king's.

"Ah! Which one did you like the best?"

Will turned and pointed at the pretty girl Richard recognized as the one Foz had complained about.

"She is rather pretty." The king looked at Richard. "Who is she?"

"Nell Gwyn, sire."

"A name to remember," Charles replied. Then he turned his attention back to Will. "When you are a man, young Master Longbourne, will you come to our court and serve us?"

"If my mama will let me," Will answered gravely.

Chuckling, the king straightened. "Oh, we think she will, since she seems to have discovered that a king may indeed know what is best for his subjects." He glanced sharply at Richard. "Would you not agree, my lord?"

"Majesty, Solomon himself couldn't have made a better match."

"And like Solomon, we undertake legal decisions, too," the king replied, growing more grave. "We have heard some disturbing news about you and a certain Sedgemore."

"Majesty, I can explain—"

Charles waved his hand dismissively. "Have no fear, Blythe. What happened today will not cause you any further trouble. We understand what happened."

"Thank you, Majesty."

"We are determined that we shall not be deprived of your clever plays again. And we would not wish to deprive your very beautiful wife of her husband, or your child a father."

He smiled at Richard's surprised expression. "We know all about that, too, and we think if you should have a son, the least you could do would be to name him Charles."

"I would be delighted to, Majesty," Richard replied with another bow. Then his dark eyes got a mischievous gleam of their own. "If it should be a girl, what should we call her?"

The king smiled at Elissa in such a way that she could understand why women found him so attractive. "She should be named for her lovely mother, of course."

Richard moved closer to Elissa and she stifled a smile at what was undoubtedly a possessive gesture. The king wasn't blind to it, either, but he merely smiled more. "Are we to assume you intend to stay in London? Has the countryside lost its charm for you, after all?"

"No, Majesty," Richard answered, his hand finding Elissa's. "We are to return to Blythe Hall as soon as possible."

"But you will keep writing?"

"Yes, Majesty. I confess I cannot help it."

"Excellent!" Charles cried. He looked at the smiling couple before him, and the fine little boy with them. "We wish all our subjects could be as happy as you." His voice dropped to a confidential whisper as a wistful look came to his pleasant face. "Odd's fish, we wish *we* could be as happy as you. But"—his voice rose as he turned toward the lady and courtiers waiting for him outside the box—"we shall have to make do. Come, Lady Castlemaine, to Whitehall! I am famished."

With that declaration, the king sauntered

from the box. Will hurried after him and stared at the departing group.

Richard took advantage of Will's distraction to kiss Elissa. It was a brief—much too brief—kiss, yet her response enflamed him and reminded him of delights yet to come.

"What did he mean about a baby?" Will demanded when he turned back to face them. "Are we getting a baby?"

Elissa knelt in front of her son. She would have preferred to tell him in some place less public, but the king had forced her hand. "Will, you are going to have a little brother or sister in a few months' time."

"Why?"

"Because that is often what happens when a man and woman marry," Richard replied before Elissa could answer.

Will stared at his feet. "Oh."

Richard bent down and Will glanced up at him. "Of course, whether it proves to be a little girl or a little boy, a helpless, squealing infant is not very good company for a man like me. And a younger sibling will need the protection of an older brother. I will have to teach you how to wrestle, and shoot, too."

"Really?" Will cried, grinning with delight.

"As long as you both promise to be very, very careful," Elissa warned.

"My lady, I swear by yon—" Richard began.

"Just tell me you will be careful, and that

will be enough for me," Elissa interrupted Richard, smiling. "I trust you."

"I can think of no greater compliment," he said, sincerity shining in his dark eyes. "I promise not to disappoint you. In anything."

"I'm hungry!" Will declared.

"I agree it is time we dined," Richard remarked to his blushing wife as a smile of both joy and desire lit his features. "I do not want to retire late tonight."

"Neither do I," Elissa agreed.

Then she looked at the two men in her life, and sighed with happiness.

Dear Reader,

What a wonderful group of books are coming your way next month! First, fans of Sabrina Jeffries are going to be thrilled that *The Dangerous Lord*, her latest Regency-set, full-length historical romance, will be in bookstores the first week of March. Sabrina's known for sexy, sweeping love stories. Her heroes are unforgettable, and her heroines are ripe for love. You won't want to miss this exciting love story from one of historical romance's rising stars.

Rachel Gibson has tongues a-waggin'! She is quickly becoming known as one of the authors to watch in the new millennium, and with *It Must Be Love*, Rachel has once again proven she gets better and better with each book. Here, a ruggedly handsome undercover cop must prove to be his latest suspect's boyfriend—but when he begins to wish that this young woman really *was* his very own, complications ensue . . . and romance is in the air.

Suzanne Enoch's spritely dialogue and delicious romantic tension have captured her many fans and *Reforming a Rake*, the first in her "With This Ring" series, is sure to please anyone looking for a wonderful Regency-set romance.

And lovers of westerns will get all the adventure they crave with Kit Dee's powerfully emotional *Brit's Lady*.

Happy Reading!

Lucia Macro

Lucia Macro
Senior Editor

Avon Romantic Treasures

Unforgettable, enthralling love stories,
sparkling with passion and adventure
from Romance's bestselling authors